Another Country

ANOTHER COUNTRY

KATHARINE SWARTZ

THORNDIKE
CHIVERS

This Large Print edition is published by Thorndike Press, Waterville, Maine, USA and by BBC Audiobooks Ltd, Bath, England.
Thorndike Press, a part of Gale, Cengage Learning.

The text of this Large Print edition is unabridged.
Other aspects of the book may vary from the original edition.
Set in 16 pt. Plantin.
Printed on permanent paper.

LIBRARY OF CONGRESS CATALOGING-IN-PUBLICATION DATA

Swartz, Katharine.
Another country / by Katharine Swartz.
p. cm. — (Thorndike Press large print clean reads)
ISBN-13: 978-1-4104-0768-9 (hardcover : alk. paper)
ISBN-10: 1-4104-0768-3 (hardcover : alk. paper)
1. Widows — Fiction. 2. British — United States — Fiction. 3. Boston (Mass.) — Social life and customs — 19th century — Fiction. 4. United States — History — 1815–1861 — Fiction. 5. Large type books. I. Title.
PS3619.W368A8 2008
813'.6—dc22 2008010147

BRITISH LIBRARY CATALOGUING-IN-PUBLICATION DATA AVAILABLE

Published in 2008 in the U.S. by arrangement with Robert Hale Limited.
Published in 2008 in the U.K. by arrangement with Robert Hale Limited.

U.K. Hardcover: 978 1 405 64564 5 (Chivers Large Print)
U.K. Softcover: 978 1 405 64565 2 (Camden Large Print)

Printed in the United States of America
1 2 3 4 5 6 7 12 11 10 09 08

Dedicated to Hilary Lyall, a fantastic editor and wonderful friend. Thank you for all your work with this story as with so many others

Chapter One

'It's high time, Eleanor, that you made a decision about your future.'

Eleanor turned wearily from her position by the window, gazing out at the relentless rain that doused Glasgow in a deep, grey gloom. Her mother-in-law, Henrietta Mc-Cardell, stood by the fireplace, hands laced across her middle, her smile firmly in place, her eyes as hard as flint.

Eleanor sighed. 'You're right, of course, Mamma-in-law.' Even now she stumbled slightly over the title, meant to be an endearment allowed her as a sign of honour, yet even after nearly a year in the Mc-Cardell household, most of it with her husband John stationed in India, Eleanor did not feel part of the family.

She was afraid she never would.

'It's been three months since John died,' Henrietta continued, her voice trembling only slightly. 'Of course, we are all still grieving . . .'

'Yes,' Eleanor murmured. Was it grief, she wondered, or mere listlessness that kept her in this state of weary uncertainty?

She'd married John, a soldier she'd met when he'd stayed the summer with his aunt and uncle on Mull, two years ago. Of that time, they'd only spent six weeks together. He'd been called suddenly to India, leaving Eleanor alone, waiting for his summons which never came. At first, she'd stayed with her father, David Crombie, and his wife Jane.

But Eleanor had already felt like an intruder in that household for far too long. Jane made her more than welcome, of course, but ever since her brother Ian and sister Harriet had left, seeking their own fortunes, Eleanor had wondered when — and where — she would find her own destiny.

Then her father had passed on a year ago, and John's parents had extended an invitation to stay with them in Glasgow. Eleanor had been relieved to go. Her stepmother Jane had planned to retire to Inverness with her sister, and Eleanor had looked forward to life in the city, away from the small, stifling community on Mull.

If only she'd known then how much more

stifling Glasgow would be!

The McCardells lived a modest, pinching kind of life. They did not endorse any amusements beyond singing a hymn on Sunday evening; their society comprised middle-aged matrons and businessmen, with very few young people for Eleanor to meet or befriend. She spent her days helping Henrietta manage the household, or else accompanying her on her various charity works.

It had been bearable when John was alive, for she could nurture her dreams of sailing to India, being reunited with her husband — even if his countenance grew blurred and vague with time, the memory of his words, his smile, quite dim. Still, it was something different, an adventure she could call her own.

When John died of malaria only six months after his arrival in India, so had those frail hopes.

'You're welcome to stay with us, of course,' Henrietta McCardell continued, her lips curling into something halfway between a smile and a grimace. 'But as you know, our lives are quiet, and we are humble and modest.'

Eleanor resisted the impulse to ask her mother-in-law what kind of person she thought she was — a brazen woman? She'd spent the last year living as humbly and modestly as a church mouse, and before that her life on Mull had been one of a farm girl.

'No doubt you'd find it quite dull,' Henrietta continued in an accusatory tone. Eleanor did not bother to object. She already found it dull, and she knew Henrietta McCardell was trying to find a way to be rid of her. She'd heard her hushed conversation with her husband, James, last night in the front parlour.

Eleanor had gone to bed, and then returned downstairs to fetch a fresh candle. She overheard Henrietta's urgent whisper, and in shock, she'd remained rooted to the spot, listening.

'She can't stay here, James — really, the girl is too much! If there had been children, perhaps . . . but John barely knew the girl, and they were wed only six weeks! I'd always been expecting her to go to India with him, eventually, not remain with us. I'm not without Christian charity, but I can hardly consider her family.'

Eleanor had clenched her fists, wanting to throw open the door and shout that she didn't consider the McCardells family either, and didn't want to stay there anyway.

She and Henrietta had never got along well — the dour matron had always cast a critical eye over Eleanor. Either her dress was too worn, or her apron dirty, or her hair in disarray. Eleanor knew the woman didn't think her — a poor farm girl from Mull — a good enough bride for her son.

And perhaps she wasn't, Eleanor thought now, since she was finding it hard to nurture her grief. Sometimes she could barely remember John's face, yet she'd married him! She'd loved him.

Their courtship had been short but sweet, and Eleanor had revelled in John's simple affections, the attentions he was happy to lavish upon her. For too long she'd lived a half-life in shadows, first under the spectre of uncertainty when her family farm, Achlic, was lost, and then later in her father's new household; still — always — a stranger.

Eleanor thought of Jane, her father's wife since she was thirteen, now in Inverness. Her own mother had died at her birth. Their home had been a happy one, and Eleanor still felt a flicker of uneasy guilt when she thought of how ungrateful she'd been to flee such happy confines.

Perhaps if Ian hadn't run away to sea, or Harriet married and gone to Canada, she wouldn't have felt so left behind, so alone.

Yet she had, and so when John asked her to marry him, promising a new life, the life of an army wife which would certainly bring with it adventure and change, Eleanor had accepted. Then it had been her turn to leave, to find her own calling.

Except she hadn't. Not yet.

Henrietta made a tsking sound with her tongue, and Eleanor knew she'd let her thoughts wander away once more. 'She's half daft, that one,' she'd heard Henrietta say more than once. If only she didn't feel this lassitude, this terrible weariness all the time! It was as if John's death had paralysed her, left her unable to imagine any kind of future at all.

Eleanor forced herself to smile at her mother-in-law. 'That's very kind, mamma-in-law, to think of me so carefully. But I assure you I wouldn't find your life dull in the least. The months I've passed here have been very pleasant.' It was a lie, but Eleanor felt indebted to say it.

'Indeed.' Henrietta spoke through her teeth. 'Then of course, my dear, you must stay as long as you wish. I thought perhaps your stepmother might want to visit with you. . . .'

When Eleanor's father had died, Jane had sold the farm to live with her sister in Inverness. Eleanor had briefly imagined residing alone with Jane, working the farm together, until John returned or called for her. But it was not to be. That, like so many other avenues, had been closed to her.

'Perhaps,' Eleanor replied to Henrietta, though in her heart she knew a visit with Jane and her sister was a remote possibility. While the older woman would welcome her, the small house in Inverness would be crowded, and the cost of Eleanor's keep dear.

'You wish to write to her?' Henrietta prompted, and Eleanor almost smiled. Goodness, the woman wanted her gone! She didn't blame her, even though last night she'd shed tears of bitterness and humiliation. They'd been thrown together, virtual strangers, the ties of kin tenuous at best.

'I've written to my brother,' Eleanor said. She felt a tingle of satisfaction at the look of Henrietta's surprise. She'd rarely spoken of Ian, who had run away to sea a decade ago and ended up in Boston, living with the wealthy Moore family. Fortune had favoured him, and Eleanor hoped it would favour her as well.

'Your brother?' Henrietta asked now, as Eleanor had stopped speaking, lost in thought as she was over the possibilities Ian and his life presented to her. 'What are his circumstances?'

'He's a doctor in Boston. In America,' Eleanor clarified, heartened once again by Henrietta's widened eyes. 'I'm hoping to hear word from him shortly, when the next ship comes in.' Eleanor glanced out the window, as if she could see all the way to the docks. The *Julia Rose* was due any day now from Boston, and Eleanor hoped fervently that it would carry on it a letter from Ian.

'You'll stay with him?' Henrietta could not seem to get her head around the idea, novel and unexpected as it was. 'Is he a bachelor?'

'Yes, but it is surely respectable for a sister and brother to reside together?' Eleanor smiled sweetly. 'He will need someone to keep house.' Not that she had any intention of mouldering away as her brother's cook and housekeeper. Although what aspirations she *did* have, Eleanor could not yet say.

She just wanted to do something. She wanted to live.

'Indeed,' Henrietta replied after a moment. 'But how will you get there? Your brother surely isn't going to fetch you, and a woman your age unchaperoned on a ship! I dread to think of it.'

No doubt you do, Eleanor thought with a

fleeting, grim smile. 'I should think a widow may travel alone without too many questions raised,' Eleanor said mildly. 'There will be other women on the ship, joining their husbands and brothers.'

'Will there?' Henrietta looked sceptical, and Eleanor forced herself to offer a bland smile. In truth, she did not know what kind of vessel — much less with what sort of passengers — she could afford to travel to America in, but she did not wish to inform her mother-in-law of this fact, who knew as well as she did that John had died a penniless soldier. 'Tell me,' Henrietta said after a moment, her eyes narrowed, her expression both shrewd and strangely satisfied, 'will your brother welcome your visit? I have not heard mention of him in all the time you've been with us in Glasgow.'

Eleanor swallowed.

She had not seen Ian since he'd run away at the age of sixteen, after having lost the family farm, Achlic, in a reckless business deal. He'd written, of course, telling her his news, and Eleanor knew she'd cause to be proud of him.

But would he be glad to hear from her? Did he have the means to offer her an escape from this dreariness? Eleanor didn't know the answers to those questions. Her only hope lay in the arrival of the *Julia Rose.*

'Of course he will,' she told Henrietta firmly, for the alternative was too grim to bear. 'He's my brother.'

'Your uncle is expected for tea, miss. A messenger just came from Tobermory, and the master will be here shortly. He asked particularly that you wear your rose silk, and put your hair up.'

'Did he, Simmons? Oh, how lovely!' Caroline Campbell spun from the drawing room window in delighted anticipation of her uncle's visit. 'And I was so afraid the afternoon was going to be deadly dull. I'll go and change right away. Is he bringing guests, do you think?'

'He didn't say, miss.' Simmons, the butler, did not change his expression as Caroline skipped gaily to the door.

'Well, he must be, mustn't he?' she cried. 'Uncle Edward would hardly mind what frock I wore, or if my hair was up or down.' Humming under her breath, Caroline hurried down the corridor. Her uncle rarely came to Lanymoor House any more, spending most of his time at his estate in Berwick, and more recently, in America.

He'd travelled the Atlantic Ocean across and back six times by her last count, though he never stayed for long on his business trips. Caroline had never asked what new enterprises were to be found on those distant shores. America held little interest for her; though it had gained its independence over fifty years earlier, it still struck her as a land full of colonials and savages.

Still, she sometimes wondered why her uncle did not visit Lanymoor House, when he used to spend so much of his time here. Caroline had heard vague rumours that her uncle was disliked in these parts, due to the mass clearances that had been going on, crofters evicted from their land to make way for sheep.

She dismissed this train of thought with a toss of her head. What did it matter what farm people thought, after all? Her uncle was coming to visit today, and he always brought her a present or treat. Perhaps this time he had something even better . . . news, or hopefully even guests. Anything that would make life at Lanymoor House more interesting, more bearable.

Life at Lanymoor House was, at best, mildly interesting, Caroline thought. The village happenings were scarcely amusing, and there were few people of her own age and social standing. The few country dances and card parties the pitiful season presented were hardly encouraging to Caroline, who dreamed of more elegant surroundings and people.

Indeed, she had been pleading with Uncle Edward for over a year to take her to London for her season. She was eighteen years old, after all. She should have had her coming-out ages ago, but Uncle Edward had been away in America on business too much to pay any notice to her age. Caroline had pouted for several weeks over the disappointment, much good it did her.

Even she was honest enough to acknowledge that her uncle might enjoy her company when he saw her on his infrequent visits, but for the rest of the time he put her quite completely out of his mind. Perhaps this time, Caroline thought with a sudden burst of hope, it would be different.

'Mrs Stimms, I need you upstairs,' she announced breathlessly from the kitchen doorway. It still put her out that she had to use the housekeeper as her lady's maid, when only a few months ago she'd had her own maid, Millie, at her constant disposal.

Then a rather terse letter had arrived from Uncle Edward, dismissing Millie with the explanation that a household of one needed only the most basic of staff, of which Mrs Stimms was included.

Now Mrs Stimms followed Caroline with a grim expression. Caroline knew the housekeeper disliked being taken away from her usual domain, and what was worse, her hairdressing skills were barely passable.

'I wonder what guests Uncle Edward is bringing,' Caroline said as she nearly flew up the stairs to her bedroom. 'Have you made anything fresh for tea, Mrs Stimms?'

Mrs Stimms pursed her lips. 'There's half a jam sponge from yesterday. If I'd known he was to arrive today . . .'

'Oh, you know how Uncle Edward is,' Caroline replied as she took out her rose silk and spread it on the counterpane, inspecting it for rents or tears. 'He's always coming or going, it seems.' She paused to give a pretty pout. 'Although he hasn't been to visit me since Hogmanay!'

Her dress was a bit worn along the shoulders, the material too shiny, but it couldn't be helped. The dress allowance Uncle Edward provided her had never been exceedingly generous, and this year it had been sparing indeed.

Mrs Stimms stepped forward to help Caroline with her dress. 'I'll make a fresh batch of scones, after this,' she said in a warning tone. 'So you'd best get ready quick, miss.'

With a sunny smile Caroline sat down at her dressing table and handed her housekeeper the heavy silver brush. 'Oh, I'll be as quick as a wink, Mrs Stimms,' she promised in a tone she'd practised and knew to be charming.

A quarter of an hour later, Caroline was seated in the drawing room, awaiting her uncle's arrival, while Mrs Stimms had returned to the kitchen to make hurried preparations for the afternoon tea.

Outside the rain beat steadily on the gardens, the trees with their barely opening buds just visible in the thick gloom. Caroline sighed. How she longed to be away from here! It seemed as if she'd spent her whole life waiting for something truly exciting to begin.

As a child, she'd enjoyed the run of Lanymoor House, and her brother James as well as her uncle had been in attendance. Then James had left in disgrace, after his fiasco of a betrothal to Harriet Crombie, her pianoforte tutor. Caroline had been only eight years old at the time, but she still remembered the letters James had hidden in his room, and how she'd been the one to alert Harriet to them.

A flicker of regret passed over her like a shadow. If she hadn't told Harriet about the letters from her first betrothed, Allan MacDougall, that James had hidden, Harriet would have stayed and married James. Instead she'd disappeared from their lives as quickly as a ghost, and both James and Uncle Edward tried to act as if she'd never existed.

How different life might've been then, Caroline thought. With James and Harriet in residence, Lanymoor House would've been alive and happy, with children and servants and not this mouldering, ghostly air.

Caroline ran her fingers lightly over the pianoforte keys, wincing as the notes were badly out of tune. She couldn't regret telling Harriet about the letters. If anything, she was a romantic, and in her heart Caroline knew Harriet had not loved James. If she'd stayed, Lanymoor House wouldn't have been full of love and laughter, for its mistress would've been terribly unhappy. Caroline was glad she'd spared Harriet Crombie that fate.

With an impatient sigh she whirled away from the pianoforte. When would Uncle Edward arrive? She felt instinctively that this visit was going to be important; it had to be. She was tired of watching as life passed her by . . . waiting for her own to begin.

If Uncle Edward was in a receptive mood, perhaps she could convince him to take her to London for the season. It was due to start in just over a month, but perhaps if she found a suitable dressmaker, she could be ready in time.

She imagined the gowns she'd have fashioned, with the full *gigot* sleeves and V-shaped bodice, *à la* Marie Stuart. She'd have a full skirt — the dresses she owned now could only be worn with four petticoats, and everyone knew you needed at least six to have any sense of fashion at all.

The sound of crunching gravel outside had Caroline rushing to the window. Her uncle's carriage had arrived, and she watched as he stepped out, followed by a tall gentleman. Her heart pounded. Uncle Edward had brought a guest! A male guest, and though she couldn't see his features, shaded as they were by an impressively tall silk hat, she was sure he was dark and handsome. What could be the meaning of this?

'Your uncle, miss.' Simmons closed the door behind Edward and his visitor.

Caroline curtseyed more deeply than usual to her uncle, gazing up at him from under her lashes. 'Good day to you, Uncle.'

Lately her uncle had been rather grim and preoccupied when he'd visited her, but now he was all joviality, albeit a bit forced. 'Isn't she charming, Dearborn?'

'Charming, indeed.' The gentleman spoke with a strange, flat accent.

Caroline glanced at the visitor, and felt a stab of disappointment. Close up and without his hat, he was tall and slightly stooped. He had to be as old as her uncle, with thinning grey hair compensated by immense, bushy eyebrows.

He gave her a thin-lipped smile, his grey eyes narrowed, and Caroline forced herself to smile back with all the charm she could muster.

The man Dearborn's lips curled into a coldly knowing smile, as if he suspected she was only practising her charms on him, which was indeed the case.

Caroline found herself blushing, even as a vague unease stole over her. With a toss of her head, she turned away. There'd be no entertainment from that quarter, although she could still plead her case for London.

Mrs Stimms brought the tea tray in and, as was her custom, began to pour. A flicker of irritation crossed Edward's face.

'Leave the tray, Mrs Stimms. Caroline may act as hostess for us. She is mistress of this household, is she not? It is high time she took on the responsibilities of her station.'

Caroline was torn between humiliation and pride. She was glad Uncle Edward saw her as a young woman, yet at the same time he managed to make her feel like a gauche girl. Flustered, she lifted her chin and took the tray from the housekeeper. 'Thank you, Mrs Stimms. That will be all.'

Mrs Stimms glowered, and Caroline knew she resented this interference. She sighed inwardly. After Uncle Edward left, there would be the fallout to deal with . . . but perhaps she wouldn't be here! Perhaps she would be in a carriage, halfway to London. . . .

'I've been remiss in my visits here, I see,' Edward said as Caroline served the tea. 'It's high time I took you in hand, Caroline. You must be . . . seventeen?'

'Eighteen, Uncle,' Caroline replied demurely.

'A lovely age,' the visitor, Dearborn, murmured. His eyes, underneath those eyebrows, were flinty grey and all too shrewd.

Caroline handed him a cup, and as he took it his hand touched hers. His skin was as cold as a fish, Caroline thought with a jolt, and slimy as well. She pulled her hand away too quickly.

Tea sloshed on the saucer, and Uncle Edward grimaced again. 'Careful, girl! You're not fit to be in company, as far as I can see.'

Caroline bit her lip, flushing, but Dearborn merely chuckled. It was a dry raspy sound. 'We've taken her by surprise, Rydell. Give her some time.' He smiled at Caroline, and she saw that his teeth were quite yellow. 'I find her entirely charming, as you promised her to be.'

Caroline gave her uncle an uneasy look. Why was Dearborn here exactly? she wondered. Surely such a man had nothing to do with her.

'Keep pouring,' Rydell barked, drumming his fingers on the arm of his chair, and Caroline resumed her serving.

Lord Edward Rydell was not one for small talk, and he soon came to the reason for his visit. 'I've news you should be pleased about, Niece,' he told Caroline. 'As I said, it is high time I took you in hand. I have to travel to Boston for certain business, and I want you to accompany me.'

'Boston?' Caroline repeated, shocked. She'd been hoping for London . . . but all the way to America? She couldn't help blurting, 'But I've heard the colonials are terribly ill-mannered . . . some say even barbaric!'

Dearborn chuckled, the sound like the rustling of paper, or dead leaves. Edward levelled his niece with a single look. 'Perhaps a trip to the States will correct your erroneous impression,' he said coolly.

'I certainly hope so,' Dearborn agreed, and too late Caroline realized that the stranger's flat accent must be American.

She flushed in embarrassment, murmuring, 'I certainly hope so, Uncle.' There was a moment's pause, while her uncle sipped his tea with a tense, preoccupied air, and Dearborn lounged back in his chair, entirely at ease, a smug smile on his craggy features.

Caroline couldn't resist asking, 'Will I have a season there? In Boston?'

'A season?' Rydell's eyebrows rose to his hairline, and he darted a rather anxious look at Dearborn, who gave an infinitesimal nod. 'Yes, I suppose so. From what I hear, the entertainments to be had in Boston quite rival London or Edinburgh.'

Caroline smiled in pleasure, although she privately doubted whether Boston could rival London. She wondered briefly at the relationship between her uncle and his guest; the way he kept darting looks at

Dearborn, as if seeking his permission, was indeed strange. As she did with most things that bored or confused her, Caroline dismissed both her uncle and Dearborn from her mind and focused instead on the prospect of a season in Boston.

A season meant new gowns and cloaks, boots and shawls, reticules and gloves . . . her uncle would baulk at the expense, but Caroline was confident she could make him see it was all an investment. An investment in her, and the rich, handsome young husband she fully intended to ensnare.

Her lips curled into an almost predatory smile, and Dearborn leaned forward, his eyes suddenly blazing with a feral light. 'My dear, what thoughts are in your pretty head to make you smile like that?'

Caroline turned, startled, and the sight of Dearborn's strangely heated look made her barely suppress a shudder.

'I'm simply looking forward to Boston,' she said after a moment, and he smiled in satisfaction.

'I am well pleased to hear it.'

The rest of the visit passed in a blur of meaningless pleasantries, and all too soon her uncle was taking his leave.

'But aren't you staying at Lanymoor?' Caroline asked in bewilderment. 'I'm sure

Mrs Stimms has made up your room.'

'I must travel to London immediately,' Edward informed her brusquely. 'And I'll be going on to Boston from there.'

'From London!' At last, Caroline thought. 'Shall I meet you there?'

Edward looked startled, and Dearborn smiled slightly, almost indulgently. Once again Caroline felt as if she'd said entirely the wrong thing, and she wanted to stamp her foot in both frustration and embarrassment.

'No, of course not,' Edward said, his tone irritable. 'You shall travel from Tobermory to Glasgow, and take a ship there in a month's time. I've arranged for a chaperone for you for the journey.'

He spoke as if she should have already known this, and Caroline was tempted to be querulous, but she knew no good would come from it. In the last few months, her uncle had become more distant, and at times seemed to be so cross as to actually dislike her.

In a rare bout of timidity, Caroline didn't want to cross him. The prospect of bidding Dearborn adieu rather than having him stay at Lanymoor also vaguely relieved her, so she smiled and bobbed a curtsey. 'Very good, Uncle.'

They left soon after that, and conscious of wanting to seem a good hostess, Caroline saw them to the door.

'Godspeed on your journey, Uncle. Mr Dearborn.'

Dearborn took her hand in his, lifting it to his lips. His lips were cold and wet and Caroline had to struggle not to yank her hand away.

'Charmed to make your acquaintance, my dear. I look forward to entertaining you in Boston.'

Caroline withdrew her hand as politely as she could, murmuring her thanks. Although she'd no notion of what Boston might be like, she trusted she would be able to find better entertainments than men such as Dearborn.

Still, she smiled prettily, for she liked to be admired, and gave another quick curtsy as they left.

She watched her uncle and his visitor climb into the carriage, the rain like a heavy curtain that hid the vehicle from view as it went down the lane.

Caroline sighed, feeling a strange mixture of elation and disappointment. She was finally leaving Lanymoor House, and her life would surely begin at last! Yet still there were many unanswered questions.

What kind of season could she have in Boston? Despite her uncle's words, Caroline wasn't convinced such a new city would truly have a social season for quality.

And Uncle Edward had not been forthcoming about his purpose in Boston . . . or hers. A small seed of doubt unfurled inside her. Really, why did Uncle Edward want to take her to Boston at all? He rarely did things without some purpose of his own.

'He's gone, then?' Mrs Stimms asked dourly as she came in to collect the tea things.

'Yes . . .' Caroline smiled suddenly, banishing her earlier qualms. 'And I will be as well, in a month's time . . . to Boston, to find a husband!'

Mrs Stimms sniffed, clearly unimpressed. 'Is that what he said?'

'Yes,' Caroline replied firmly; she could just about believe that was what her uncle had told her.

Mrs Stimms clattered cups on to the tray. 'I suppose he's got that older gentleman in mind for you?'

Caroline gaped for a moment, before giving a sharp laugh. 'Dearborn? How utterly absurd. He's a cold fish, and certainly not a husband I'd choose.'

Mrs Stimms looked at her shrewdly. 'Oh,

aye? Will you be doing the choosing then, miss?'

Caroline eyed her with cold dislike. 'Of course I will, Mrs Stimms. Now why don't you be careful with those tea things? Those cups are Crown Derby, and my dear uncle hardly wants them broken by your big, clumsy hands.' With a cool little smile she flounced away, as Mrs Stimms' words echoed remorselessly in her mind.

Chapter Two

Harriet Crombie MacDougall knelt in front of the plain wooden cross. With her fingers she lovingly smoothed the patch of early grass in front of her brother-in-law's grave. It had been eleven years since Archie MacDougall had died, drowned when the mail packet to Prince Edward Island had foundered in a late spring storm.

Archie's mother, Betty, had tended the grave till she'd grown too frail. Now Harriet, by unspoken agreement, had taken over the chore. She leaned back on her heels and sighed. The last ten years had been, in many ways, joyous ones for her and Allan.

They'd built up their farm on a neighbouring lot to Allan's father, Sandy, and it was now one of the more prosperous settlements on the river, if not the whole island.

The island was changing too . . . Charlottetown was now a bustling town, with schools and shops. The ferry to the mainland ran more regularly, and the wilderness was slowly but surely being tamed.

'Mamma!'

Harriet turned and, smiling, saw her eldest daughter, Maggie, making her way from the homestead to this little copse. Maggie was nine years old, and a great blessing to Harriet with the little ones. Her gaze instinctively slid to the second, smaller cross next to Archie's. It would be five years ago this autumn that the scarlet fever had taken her eldest son, Andrew, when he was not even six years old.

Harriet's smile was bittersweet as she remembered her curly haired boy. These years with Allan had been happy ones, but they'd not been without their share of trials and sorrows.

'Mamma?' Maggie's voice held a questioning lilt. Even at nine years old she knew her mother liked to have a quiet moment at her son's graveside.

'Yes, Maggie?'

'Papa's home!'

'Is he now?' Harriet smiled as she stood up and brushed the dirt from her apron. Allan had gone to the town market to fetch supplies. Now that the long winter was finally over, it was time to clear the fields once more and plant their harvest.

'George saw him coming up the river,' Maggie continued in excitement. 'Do you think he's bought us a treat?'

'We'll just have to go and find out.'

Although the island roads were improving, they were still rutted and hopelessly muddy this time of year. Often it was easier to take a canoe up the river to the market instead of hitching the wagon.

Allan had left yesterday, and Harriet had been worried, for the river was cold in early spring, with ice floes still breaking up.

She'd heard many times the story of how Archie and Allan had taken an iceboat across to the mainland, and been trapped by the floes. It was only because of Archie's courage in finding help that they'd survived the experience.

Maggie slipped her hand in her mother's, and they left the secluded little spot in the birch grove to walk back to the homestead.

The MacDougall farm was nestled in a bend of the river, with the fields of rich soil and verdant grass spreading out from the water in a patchwork of red and green.

From the porch of their home Harriet could see Allan securing the canoe to the dock, its frame weighed down with boxes and crates.

'May we go see him, Mamma?' Maggie

asked. George, her younger brother by three years, was bouncing up and down with excitement.

'Please, please?' he begged.

Harriet nodded, and the two children needed no further encouragement. They raced down to the water like two puppies, eager to see their father and the things he'd bought.

'Mind the water!' Harriet called after them. 'I don't want you falling in, not this time of year.' She shivered slightly; living so close to the river, the fear of drowning was always present.

She could hear the children's gleeful cries, and Allan's responding laughter. With a smile, Harriet went inside. The scent of fresh baking filled the air, and she saw that the baby, Anna, was still sleeping peacefully in her basket, one fist loosely curled upwards on the blanket. She glanced around her neat home with pride, glad Allan would have a welcoming sight to greet him.

'Mamma!' George's shriek had her hurrying outside again. 'Papa got us a puppy!' In his arm, squirming to get free, was a little black silky-eared puppy. George had a worshipful look on his face, and Allan strode behind him, grinning widely.

'He'll be good for the sheep.' He caught

Harriet up in a hug, kissing her soundly. 'You're a sight for sore eyes.'

'As are you,' Harriet returned. 'It's near twilight, I was getting worried.'

'I thought of stopping by at the Campbells,' Allan told her. 'I didn't want to paddle in the darkness, but I knew I'd worry you if I didn't get home by nightfall.'

'As long as you're safe,' Harriet murmured, and he kissed her again.

'Papa bought two geese!' Maggie said as she came hurrying up from the river landing. 'They're hissing and spitting like mad!' She threw her arms around her father with obvious affection. 'And he got me a hair ribbon!'

The silky length of scarlet was duly admired, and George, in a familiar game, tackled his father to find the bag of barley sugar he always bought when he went to market.

Night was falling fast, a dark, icy cloak, and Harriet ushered her family inside for supper.

'Can the puppy come inside as well?' George begged. 'I've named him Patches.'

'He hasn't got any patches,' Maggie said indignantly, and George stuck out his lower lip in mutinous denial.

'Very well, he can come in,' Harriet relented. 'But only for tonight.' As the puppy scampered joyfully by her heels, she had a feeling he would be curled by the fire for more than the one night.

Anna soon awoke, and Allan bounced her on his knee as Harriet served up the meal.

'Didn't you get Mamma anything?' Maggie asked as they ate fried pork and griddle cakes.

Allan chuckled. 'Took you a while to notice that,' he told his daughter, and Maggie grinned.

'You always get something special for Mamma.'

Harriet shook her head. 'There's no need . . .'

'Now, now.' Allan held a finger to his lips to laughingly shush her. 'What about your egg money?' It was custom for the money they received from selling eggs to be spent at Harriet's discretion.

'Don't trick me with that nonsense, Allan MacDougall. The hens haven't laid eggs all winter!'

Allan's eyes twinkled with mischief. 'Well, let's just say they had . . .' With a teasing smile, he withdrew a length of green calico from one of the crates.

'Oh, isn't it beautiful!' Maggie cried.

George shrugged in disdain. 'It's just cloth.'

'There's enough for new dresses for both my girls,' Allan said, and Maggie clapped her hands in delight.

'You shouldn't have,' Harriet said in reproof, but her eyes were warm with love and she couldn't resist smoothing one hand over the material. 'Thank you, Allan.'

After the children were in bed, it was Harriet and Allan's custom to share a cup of coffee by the fire. Normally it was bitter stuff made from chicory or dandelion, but after a trip to town they were able to enjoy some of the precious ground beans.

'I stopped by Mother and Father's,' Allan said quietly. Even though their farm was adjacent to the older MacDougalls, in winter they barely saw them at all, due to the heavy snows and fierce storms.

'Are they well?' Harriet asked, and Allan nodded thoughtfully.

'Mother looks as if she's gained some of her strength back. Father insisted she rest most of the winter, thankfully.'

'And Rupert?' Rupert was Allan's younger brother. He'd been living at Mingarry Farm since he travelled over with Harriet ten years ago.

'A bit restless, I'd say,' Allan said slowly.

'It is that time of year. A boy like Rupert can hardly stand to be cooped up indoors for months on end!'

'He's twenty-three years old, hardly a boy.'

'Too true,' Harriet agreed. 'The time does slip by, doesn't it?'

'It does, although it's going slowly for Rupert, I warrant. He won't stay at Mingarry for ever, I shouldn't think.'

'But your father needs him!' Harriet protested, shocked. 'Why, you know how he relies on him. Even after he's hired a man, there's too much to do. And he's getting older . . .' she trailed off, thinking of her father-in-law Sandy, proud and white haired, with affection.

'He is.' Allan gazed into the fire. 'But he can't tie Rupert to the land, no more than he could tie me.'

'But you came back,' Harriet reminded him softly. 'This land is in your heart, Allan. Why, sometimes I think the very soil is a part of you!'

'Aye, it is. But perhaps it's not so for Rupert.'

Harriet was silent. Admittedly Rupert was different to Allan. Allan had always been quiet, a thinker. Rupert was more impulsive, full of energy that could never quite be suppressed . . . or perhaps, satisfied.

'What would he do?' Harriet asked after a long moment when the only sound was the crackling of the fire. 'Leave the island, as you did? Become a fur trader?'

Allan shrugged and stretched his legs. 'He'll have to discover that for himself. But the fur trade has moved farther and farther away . . . even in just the last ten years the game's become terribly scarce. And I don't know if that sort of solitary life is for Rupert. Truth be told, it wasn't for me after the first few months. If I hadn't found you . . .' Allan smiled at his wife with deep affection. He remembered well the moment in a broken-down shack on the prairies near Red River, when Harriet had gazed at him down the barrel of a shotgun. With his bushy beard and fur cap, she hadn't recognized him, and it had been a tense moment before their joyful reunion.

'Perhaps you could invite Rupert to stay with us for a spell, once the planting's over,' Harriet suggested. 'A change of scene, however small, might do him good, and I know he enjoys the children.'

'A fine idea,' Allan agreed. 'Perhaps it will help him sort out what he wants to do with his life. It's not easy, making that sort of decision.'

'I hope, for your father's sake, he stays on

at Mingarry. But for his own sake . . .' Harriet sighed. 'Why must it be so difficult to discover what makes us happy?'

'For some, it isn't. And I'm grateful every day that I've found my happiness.' Gently Allan touched Harriet's cheek before blowing out the lantern.

Smiling, Harriet slipped her hand in his. Yes, she'd found her happiness, and she dearly hoped the same for Rupert. What more joy could there be than this, for anyone?

'Thank you kindly, Mr Crombie.'

Ian smiled as the young man nodded his thanks before leaving the examination room, the paper cone of stomach powder clutched in his hand. In this case, the man's stomach ailment was easily cured. It was nothing more than a mild digestive complaint, and the cases Ian normally saw were so much more severe . . . and hopeless.

People stumbled into the clinic when it was their last hope, their last chance. They gazed at Ian with wide, despairing eyes, for it was often too late to do anything, or else what needed to be done was impossible.

How many times had he advised rest and wholesome food, only to be stared at incredulously? No one could afford to miss a day of work, for they'd be sacked, and despite the growing economy, jobs were precious. The Irish had started their steady trickle into the city, and were lined up at the mill and factory gates, ready to take any person's job for lower wages.

As for wholesome food . . . in a city, you took what you could get, often rotten vegetables off the back of the wagon, pottage that was more water than potato or meat.

Ian leaned back in his chair and sighed, running a hand through his unruly auburn hair. He'd been working at the Massachusetts General Hospital for nearly eight years, ever since he'd finished Harvard Medical School. The hospital was newly established, meant to be for those too sick and too poor to afford private care in their homes.

Too often, however, it was simply a place to die.

'Are you finished with your clinic, Crombie?' Another doctor and friend, David Blackburn, stuck his head in the doorway. 'I'm off as well, if you care to join me in a pint of ale at the Plough and Stars?'

Ian shook his head regretfully. 'I'm expected for dinner at the Moores,' he said.

'Ah,' Blackburn said with a knowing wink. 'Society beckons.'

Ian grimaced even as he acknowledged the dig. The Moores were part of Boston's elite, a segment of society he'd become familiar with, even if at heart he was ever a stranger to it. 'Yes,' he replied, 'and I must heed its call.'

Taking his hat and top coat, Ian left his cramped quarters at the hospital.

Dusk was falling as he walked the short distance to the Moores' residence on Beacon Street, cutting across the Boston common, enjoying as always the quiet peacefulness of the meadowland. There was talk, he knew, of creating a public garden here, although only recently the city had banned cattle grazing on the fine green meadows.

Ian smiled to himself. Boston, like all of America, was a strapping adolescent, his body growing and changing, and still learning to accommodate those changes.

Perhaps that was why he loved America, he thought, so different from his homeland of Scotland, the tiny island of Mull, where he had spent his childhood. Mull had been narrow, restrictive. A man there was born into his trade, and he rarely left it.

America, however, was a place where a man could choose what he wanted to do, to be. The country expanded to allow everyone freedom and comfort, if they were prepared to work hard for it. And Ian was.

Arabella Moore met Ian in the foyer of her gracious home, after the butler had taken his top coat and hat.

'Ian, my dear, it's so lovely to see you. Isobel is in the music room — she has a piece she's been hoping to play for you. A Mozart.' Arabella's smile was sweetly expectant, and Ian felt a twinge of unease. It wasn't the first time he'd felt such a twinge when Isobel was mentioned. He cast it aside, however, for the moment. He enjoyed the Moores' company too much to worry about possible expectations. There would be time for that later.

He moved into the music room, a dark panelled room with a piano in one corner. Isobel was seated at the instrument, in a modest white dress, her dark hair dressed up.

She turned to Ian with a radiant smile, stretching her hand out to clasp his, 'Ian! It's so good to see you.'

'As always, dear Isobel.' Ian had known Isobel for over ten years, since he started boarding with the Moores. Her thoughtful words had helped him in many respects to put the past behind him and begin anew at the medical school. Since that time, he'd come to depend on her calming presence, her listening ear. There was something innately comforting about Isobel's unobtrusiveness, her lack of demand, and Ian knew it was selfish of him to expect her to revolve around his own world. The fact that Isobel seemed content to do so was no balm, especially as of late he'd begun to wonder what she hoped might develop from their simple friendship.

Now, however, she smiled sweetly and began to play. Ian stood by the instrument, allowing the music to wash over him.

'You look so tired.'

Ian looked down, startled, and saw Isobel smiling up at him with gentle uncertainty, her hands resting lightly on the keys. The music, he realized, had stopped.

'I'm sorry, my dear,' he said with an apologetic grimace. 'It's been a long day, and my mind wandered, lulled as it was by your soothing music.'

Isobel smiled wryly. 'You have a way with words, Ian Crombie. I know I'm not that good.'

'But you are,' he said, somewhat in surprise, for Isobel was really quite skilled at the pianoforte.

Isobel stood up, shrugging lightly as she moved away from the instrument. 'There are better uses of my time, I suppose. I'm twenty-two, you know.' She didn't look at him as she added, 'most women my age are married, and have put such childish pursuits aside.'

Ian saw that a faint blush was stealing across her cheeks, tinting her porcelain complexion a lovely rose. He swallowed, shoving his hands in the pockets of his trousers. 'Time passes so quickly,' he said after a moment, for he was unable to think of an adequate reply.

Isobel's dark eyes briefly lifted knowingly to his. 'Yes,' she replied quietly, 'it does.'

Dinner was excellent, as always, and Ian enjoyed chatting about hospital business with Stephen and Arabella. Isobel, he noticed, spoke little, and when his gaze rested on her, she quickly looked away.

Again Ian felt a deepening twinge of unease, thinking of her words in the music room. Could she really be twenty-two? Ian could hardly credit it. He had meant it when he said time passed quickly, and he wondered why Isobel had not married. Could it be possible that she was waiting for him? He was twenty-eight, and he had every intention of marrying one day. But to Isobel? He paused, a glass of wine at his lips, as this idea took hold of him. He had not truly considered it before because he'd always assumed Isobel would marry within her social sphere. No matter how much the Moores welcomed him, or contrived to have his name on the invitation lists for Boston's many balls, dances and suppers, he was not of their class and never would be.

He was, Ian thought with only a trace of bitterness, a farm boy from Mull, wet behind the ears, who had made a foolish mistake and run away to sea. In the last ten years he'd been blessed by other people's kindness to him, but it didn't change who he was, or what he was.

'Ian?' Arabella spoke with a slight sharpness, and with a start he realized he'd once again lost the thread of conversation.

'Ian's worn out, Mother,' Isobel said with a soft smile meant only for him. 'You know how hard he works.'

'Indeed I do.'

'I apologize,' Ian said hastily. 'You were saying . . . ?'

'You've done well for yourself, certainly,' Stephen told him after the women had retired to the drawing room, and he'd taken Ian into his own private enclave, the library, for port and cigars. 'Very well indeed.'

Ian murmured his thanks. 'I love my work,' he said simply. 'And I am profoundly thankful that your son saw a flicker of ability in me that I'd been unable to see myself.'

Stephen nodded thoughtfully. 'Yes, Henry was always clever that way. He took risks, still does, and it's helped him. Instead of one ship now, he owns what . . . four? Five?'

'Six, I believe,' Ian said with a smile. It amused him to think that Stephen Moore didn't even know how many ships his son owned in Boston's harbour. Of course, Stephen didn't depend on enterprise for his keep. Neither did Henry, for that matter, but he loved ships and business.

'Six . . .' Stephen mused. 'Yes, he's done well for himself. Tell me, how is Margaret?'

Henry had married Ian's relative, Margaret MacDougall, nearly ten years ago. They resided not far away in the newer South End, although Henry was still gone most of the year on ship business.

'She's well,' Ian replied. 'I don't see her or Henry as much as I'd like, of course.'

'Yes, I'm sure the hospital keeps you busy. She's reforming the city as usual?'

Ian nodded, chuckling. 'Of course. I believe she is tackling the schools now. You know how she is.'

'It's a pity they never had children.'

'Yes, it is,' Ian agreed quietly. He knew the lack troubled Margaret, although she'd managed to put it behind her some years ago.

'Of course, there might be help from another quarter.' Stephen's tone was surprisingly jocular. 'You must be nearing thirty, Ian.'

Ian swallowed. He'd been expecting this, and yet it still left him alert and uneasy, afraid that one word might misdirect both him and Stephen. 'I'm twenty-eight.'

'High time to find a wife.' Stephen nodded, rubbing his chin. 'Don't you think?'

'I haven't . . .' Ian shrugged helplessly. 'The hospital work keeps me so busy, I have very few social concerns, as you well know.'

'Of course. But a man can't be a bachelor all his days, surely. I speak in such a forthright manner only because you are like a son to me.'

'And you, a father.' Ian was silent, remembering how the Moores had made him welcome when he'd arrived with Henry, a mere ship's boy, sulky and defiant. Henry had given him the job as surgeon's mate, and then suggested he go to medical school. The Moores had gladly offered to house Ian during his schooling, and even paid for his lecture tickets. The bond they'd formed was strong, and Ian felt they were as much his family as the Crombies he'd left back in

Scotland.

'Speaking of family,' Ian said, wishing to change the subject but not entirely sure why. 'I've heard from my sister, Eleanor. She's been widowed and is hoping to start a new life, possibly in America.'

Stephen raised his eyebrows in surprise. 'Do you mean here?'

'I've sent her passage here, on one of Henry's ships,' Ian confirmed. 'God willing, she'll arrive in the beginning of June.'

Stephen frowned. 'And what shall she do? A widowed woman may not need to be as closely chaperoned as a maiden, but it would surely be unseemly for her to live alone, a stranger in this city.'

'She'll live with me, for the meantime at least. She hopes eventually to visit our sister, Harriet, in Canada.' Ian smiled as he thought of it. He hadn't seen Eleanor for eleven years. When he'd run away from their family farm, Achlic, after losing most of the property to Edward Rydell in a foolish business venture, Ian had been too ashamed to keep in contact with those he loved. He'd vowed to win back Achlic, and it was a dream that still haunted him, despite his successful life in the new world. Well, he thought, he may not have won Achlic Farm back, but at least he could shelter his sister when she needed him. It was something.

'Have you told Isobel this news?' Stephen asked, and Ian shook his head.

'No . . . the occasion has not arisen.'

'Perhaps it should,' Stephen replied, his voice pleasant yet firm with implied meaning. 'You are quite close to her, are you not? I daresay you realize society has noticed such an alliance.'

'Of course,' Ian murmured uncomfortably. Stephen seemed to imply that Isobel would be shamed if Ian didn't ask her to marry him. Had they been seen together that many times? He knew the gossip of Boston society was rampant, and he tugged at his collar just thinking of Isobel as the target of so many sharp tongues. Still, he was surprised. He was sure he'd not acted inappropriately towards Isobel. She was like a sister to him.

Perhaps he was the only one who saw it like that.

'Isobel has an attachment to you,' Stephen said quietly. 'She always has. No matter what Arabella or I may think of it, we cannot deny her anything she so ardently desires. I daresay we spoil her.'

'Sir . . . ?' Ian could feel a flush creeping up his neck. Stephen Moore seemed to be saying that Isobel wanted him. Would he really speak so forthrightly? Ian wondered.

'Come,' Stephen said. 'Isobel and Arabella are waiting in the drawing room. I know Isobel would like to play for you.'

Ian let the tinkling pianoforte music wash over him as he sat in the drawing room, his thoughts still racing. If the Moores expected a proposal from him, what could he do? The last thing he wanted was to jeopardize his relationship with them, or lose their respect.

He glanced at Isobel, dark haired and rosy cheeked, her face animated as she played. When Ian had lived with the Moores, he'd spent a great deal of time with Isobel, playing whist and draughts in the evening, sharing a camaraderie like that of siblings.

Since then, it had seemed natural for Ian to accompany her to the occasional musicale or supper, and yet now he saw how those pleasant evenings together could be misconstrued.

Isobel caught his gaze and smiled at him, her own eyes seeming to shimmer with some kind of hope . . . and promise. She was a lovely girl, Ian thought. Perhaps he could grow to love her. Surely it was not impossible.

He glanced at Stephen, and saw him nodding approvingly at his wife. Whatever else, Ian knew, he would have to make his intentions clear quite soon. Only first, he needed to decide what they were.

Chapter Three

'This ship is dreadful!'

Eleanor listened to the complaining squeal of her companion on board ship and grimaced. She'd not exchanged more than a few words with Miss Caroline Campbell in these first six days of their voyage, but she could already tell the girl was thoroughly spoiled.

Their cabins were adjacent, and she could clearly hear the little madam complaining about everything in sight: the food, the linens, the company.

Her chaperone, Florence Cabot, was a rather vague woman in her fifties, seemingly more attached to her smelling salts than to people. She never took the girl to task, as Eleanor ached to do. Instead she murmured placatory remarks, which made Miss Campbell only more disagreeable.

Eleanor rose from her bed, where she'd been reading. Her cabin was small but comfortable, and yet for Eleanor it felt like paradise. Ian's letter had come a fortnight ago, together with passage on Henry Moore's ship, *The Endeavour.* It felt like a lifeline had been thrown to her, rescuing her from drowning in the gloomy boredom of Glasgow.

The McCardells had been nonplussed by Eleanor's abrupt plans to depart not only their home, but the entire country.

'Really, I don't think you should travel across the ocean by yourself,' Henrietta had said in tones stiff with disapproval. 'I accept I have little control over your actions, but I hope you are able to remember your position as my son's widow.'

'Of course, Mamma-in-law,' Eleanor replied soothingly. She was almost free, she could afford to placate the older woman. 'I assure you, I will conduct myself accordingly. And, as you know, the ship is owned by a relative of mine, so really it is all in perfect order.' This was stretching the truth a bit, as Henry Moore would not actually be on the ship, but Eleanor didn't care. She only longed to leave the stuffy confines of the McCardell home, and begin anew.

The ship lurched uncomfortably, and Eleanor grabbed the door frame. The captain had warned them of the weather turning rough, and it appeared to be doing so.

She heard another squeal of dismay from her neighbour, and closed her eyes. Her stomach turned over with queasy indignation.

The weather worsened over the next few hours, so by the time Eleanor prepared for dinner, she was barely able to perform the necessary functions without stumbling or falling. She opened her cabin door, grateful for what little fresh air the space provided.

There were only five passengers on board *The Endeavour,* Eleanor, Caroline and her chaperone, and an elderly widow with her middle-aged spinster daughter, both rather sullen and silent.

At the table this evening, however, Eleanor saw there was only Caroline and herself. She sighed inwardly. Caroline was closest in age to her, and by all accounts they should have become friends. Yet Eleanor could not think of a less likely companion.

'You ladies seem to be the only ones free from the seasickness,' Captain James Barker remarked as they sat down to their meal.

'Hopefully this storm will abate soon?' Eleanor asked questioningly, but Captain Barker shook his head.

'I'm afraid it's only likely to get worse. I hope the other ladies are not too put out.'

Caroline made a pretend pout. 'How terribly dull, to be in such good health,' she said with a pretty laugh. 'I'd much rather be confined to my bed, with someone to administer cloths to my forehead and hold my hand.' Another tinkling laugh, and Eleanor barely refrained from rolling her eyes.

'What nonsense,' she replied briskly. 'If you had the seasickness, you'd be spilling your guts into a bucket, not swooning on a bed, longing to be mollycoddled.'

Caroline's eyes narrowed in anger, and Captain Barker chuckled drily. 'Mrs McCardell has the right of it, I'm afraid. I'd be obliged if you ladies would look in on your fellow passengers. Seasickness can take some people terribly, you know.'

'A sound idea,' Eleanor said, but Caroline merely pursed her lips and looked away.

Eleanor longed to shake some sense into her. When she considered her own life, she was sure she'd never acted as thoroughly spoiled and vain as the young miss across the table. She wondered what Caroline Campbell was travelling to in Boston . . . fancy frocks and a season?

The tiny twinge of envy made Eleanor bite her lip and look away. She was too old for those things, and she'd never wanted them anyway.

She simply wanted freedom.

Sure enough, the weather worsened, and the captain had to excuse himself to look after the ship.

'We might as well check on the others,' Eleanor told Caroline. 'Has Miss Cabot been very ill?'

Caroline shrugged. 'She was sleeping when I left. I wouldn't know.'

'You didn't bother to ask, I suppose?' Eleanor returned. 'You really are the most selfish creature.'

Caroline's eyes flashed. 'I'll thank you to keep your opinions to yourself,' she replied with cold haughtiness.

'Very well, but the others might be gravely ill.'

'It can't be as bad as all that, surely.' Caroline waved a hand in dismissal. 'Miss Cabot was fine when I departed for supper, I'm quite sure.'

'You are, now?' Eleanor said sarcastically. 'We should check on her, and the others, just the same.'

The ship was pitching and rolling so badly by that time, the two women were practically thrown into each other's arms as they made their way down the narrow corridor.

The smell in the confined space was rank with illness, and even Eleanor shuddered.

She had a feeling it really was as bad as all that, and worse.

She knocked once on Caroline's cabin door. 'Miss Cabot, are you in there? Can you hear me?'

The only answer was a feeble groaning. Eleanor opened the door, and Caroline hurried into the small cabin with her, gasping at the wretched sight of her chaperone.

The older woman lay in bed, moaning faintly, a puddle of vomit drying beside her berth. Caroline drew back, fumbling for a handkerchief.

'You stay here with Miss Cabot,' Eleanor ordered. 'I'll check on the others.'

'I cannot!' Caroline cried. 'The stench alone . . .'

'You'd better be good for something,' Eleanor snapped. 'I can't manage everyone on my own. There's water in the bucket on the hook, if it hasn't sloshed all over the floor. Dampen your precious handkerchief and clean poor Miss Cabot's face. I won't ask you to clean up the sick. I know you wouldn't do it.'

'No, I wouldn't,' Caroline retorted. Still, Eleanor watched with grim satisfaction as she went to the water pail and cautiously dipped her handkerchief in.

When Eleanor entered the other cabin,

she found Mrs and Miss Standish lying pitifully in their beds, just as badly off. She groaned herself, all thoughts of a pleasant crossing flown from her head. The sick needed tending to, and it would be a difficult task indeed.

'Oh, not them too!' Caroline wailed, skidding to a stop in the cabin doorway.

'Why have you left Miss Cabot?' Eleanor asked sharply. 'She's hardly in a state to be left alone.'

'I didn't know what to do!' Caroline's voice rose in a helpless wail, and she looked at Eleanor pleadingly, all traces of the haughty princess wiped away. 'I washed her face a bit. But it was so . . .'

'I know what it was. But the fact of the matter is, we're the only ones not cast down by seasickness. It's up to us to take care of the others, Caroline Campbell.'

Caroline shook her head, her face leached of colour. 'I can't . . .'

'You can,' Eleanor said firmly. 'And so can I. It won't be easy, I warrant, but we'll have to work together.' The very idea made her sceptical, for Caroline Campbell was surely the last person she would have chosen as a helpmate. Still, there was no other choice, and so, with a grim sigh, Eleanor began to roll up the sleeves of her dinner gown.

'You'd best do the same,' she warned Caroline. 'Unless you want your gown sullied beyond all cleaning.'

'This is my second best one!' Caroline fairly yelped, and Eleanor spared her a wry smile.

'Then you ought to change.' She couldn't blame Caroline for who she was; the girl had obviously been sheltered her whole life. Still, Eleanor felt a blaze of satisfaction that just like her, Caroline Campbell was going to have to get her hands dirty.

Several hours later, bent over a foul-smelling sick pail, Eleanor realized they were getting far more dirty than just their hands. Mrs Standish had vomited three times, twice on Eleanor. She was exhausted, sweaty, and worst of all, she stank.

She'd given Caroline the charge of watching Miss Cabot, since she knew her, although also in part because the chaperone seemed the least ill, and Eleanor thought Caroline had the best chance of coping with her.

Eleanor moved the pail to the door, glad to notice that the rough movements of the ship had slowed, and the pail's contents did not slosh on to the floor. A glimpse out the porthole showed a livid sky, but the ocean beneath had begun to calm its restless, angry surging.

As she sponged down Mrs Standish's face once again, Caroline appeared in the doorway of the cabin, wringing her hands. 'I can't do it,' she said shrilly. 'I can't. I won't. I hate the smell, the sickness, I won't do it!' Her voice rose to a shriek before she dissolved into inelegant, noisy sobs.

Eleanor watched her for a moment before walking over and calmly slapping her on the face.

Caroline's sobs cut off mid-gulp and she gaped in surprise. Eleanor wondered if anyone had ever raised a hand to her before.

'You were hysterical,' she said. 'Or nearly, and we haven't time to indulge in such senseless wailing. Miss Cabot and the others depend on you, as well as me, to make it safely across this accursed ocean, so you'd best be on hand!'

There was a moment of silence, tense and heavy, and Eleanor wondered if Caroline would rebuke her, dissolve into more wails, or preferably, stiffen her spine.

Caroline, to her credit, chose the latter, and nodded in mute acceptance.

'Go and see to Miss Cabot,' Eleanor said gently. 'If she's comfortable, you might as well get some sleep.'

Caroline looked again as if she longed to

protest, bitterly, but she simply nodded again and left the room.

From the bed, Mrs Standish let out a feeble moan. 'Water . . .'

It took three more days of nearly constant nursing before the ailing women had finally found their sea legs, and Eleanor and Caroline could find some rest.

Even after a sponge bath, her dresses stiff and salty from being washed in ocean water, Eleanor felt unclean. This was hardly the way she'd intended to begin her new life in America, but there was little she could do about it.

They were a day's journey off Boston harbour as she sat in her cabin, attempting to mend the worst of the rents in her dresses.

A hesitant knock sounded at the door, and when Eleanor bid enter, Caroline peeked her head around the oak frame. 'The captain said we should see land tomorrow,' she said breathlessly. 'It's been a fearful journey, hasn't it?'

'Indeed it has.' Biting her lip in concentration, for she'd never been an accomplished seamstress, Eleanor threaded her needle once again.

'I'm so glad I brought as many frocks as I did!' Caroline confided. She peered in the cracked mirror above the washing pitcher and bowl, smoothing one hand over her glossy ringlets. 'I should hate to arrive in Boston in something dirty and stained. My uncle expects me to be well turned out at all times.'

'Does he?' Eleanor hadn't had much opportunity to learn of Caroline's circumstances. 'Is he giving you a season, then?'

Caroline whirled around, her reflection momentarily forgotten. 'Oh, yes! He quite assures me that a Boston season is just as well as a London one, and I am hoping it's true. I shall find a husband, of course, but not before I enjoy myself immensely!'

'I'm sure the delights of the Boston season are manifold,' Eleanor said. She imagined the offerings briefly . . . balls and midnight suppers, musicales and masquerades. She smiled. It was the stuff of the romantic novels Jane McCready had sometimes read on the sly. Eleanor had never bothered with it, and she couldn't imagine herself in such surroundings now.

'Why are you going to Boston, Eleanor?' Caroline asked, almost timidly, as if she realized she perhaps should already know.

'My brother is a doctor there. I'm going to live with him.'

'Just the two of you? Is that . . . well . . . don't you need a chaperone?'

'I hardly think so,' Eleanor replied, stabbing her needle in the cloth once more. 'America is different, and I'm a widow as it is. I should think it is completely respectable.'

'A widow!' Caroline's eyes widened. 'Oh, but I'm sorry! Did you love him very much?'

Eleanor thought briefly of John's face, the shock of brown hair, the warm eyes, the ready smile. All were slightly blurred, nameless features arranged in a pleasing pattern. Had he really looked like that, or was it just what she liked to remember? 'I did love him,' she said after a moment, 'but we only had six weeks together before he went to India. Sometimes it's hard to remember.'

Caroline was silent, and the only sound was the creaking of the ship and the gentle lapping of the sea against its broad sides.

'I can lend you a dress,' Caroline said quietly, 'if you like.'

'Catch me, Uncle Rupert, catch me!'

Harriet gazed from the doorway of the cabin, baby Anna in her arms. Rupert was playing a game of tag with Maggie and George, while Patches, now half grown, frisking at their heels.

Rupert had arrived two weeks ago, and he'd been a blessing to their family, filling the house with laughter and delighting the children with his games. His company was a special boon this summer, when the days had been cold and wet.

'Careful, now,' she warned as her children made towards the house. 'Your boots are caked with mud and Margaret Jane, look at the state of your apron.' The scold was light-hearted, and, all offending boots removed, Harriet ushered them into the house.

There were honey and oatcakes on the table, along with a fresh pot of tea, and the children eagerly helped themselves. Harriet laid Anna in a fleece-lined basket and poured the tea into thick mugs.

'Little savages.' Rupert ruffled George's hair as he took two oatcakes himself. 'When did you get this marvellous honey?'

'Papa found a honey tree,' Maggie said between mouthfuls of oatcake. 'A great big hollowed-out one, simply buzzing with bees!'

'Lucky for him.'

'We took most of it to market this past spring,' Harriet said. 'It paid for Patches, and the two fat geese that will be our Christmas dinner and then some.'

'Maggie was sad about the bees,' George said scornfully, 'because they wouldn't have any food!' He shrugged, taking a large bite of honey-smeared oatcake. 'I'd rather have honey. May I take another, Mamma?'

Rupert chucked Maggie under the chin. 'You think of everyone, don't you? I'm sure your pa left enough honey for the bees.'

'He certainly did,' Harriet said with a smile. 'And God willing, we'll have more honey this fall as well.'

This was greeted with a chorus of delight from the children, and Harriet laughed. 'Away with you, and finish your oatcakes. Don't be greedy, George. Honey is still a precious treat — we want it to last the summer.'

Rupert leaned against the fireplace mantel, his expression thoughtful. 'You've certainly made a good life for yourself, with this holding.'

'You could do the same, if you'd the mind,' Harriet said lightly, but Rupert was not fooled and he burst out laughing.

'I know how you want to see me settled, Harriet. On a holding across from yours, with a wife, and half a dozen children!'

Harriet smiled in acknowledgement. 'At least that many, I'm sure.'

Rupert pushed away from the mantel, shaking his head. 'I don't yet reckon if that's the life for me.'

'Of course, you must make your own way,'

Harriet allowed. 'Allan did the same. But I wouldn't be honest if I denied that I hope the path leads you back to your own hearth, here on the island, however far you may go.'

George perked up at this. 'You aren't leaving us, are you, Uncle Rupert?'

'Not yet, scamp.'

'Not yet?' Harriet raised her eyebrows. 'You sound as if you've plans.'

'A few, but young ones yet. Nothing is settled, to be sure.'

Anna began to fuss, and Harriet scooped her into her arms, kissing her downy head. She was inordinately curious about Rupert's plans, whatever they were, but she knew better than to push for information. 'You must tell us,' she said lightly, 'when they've settled.'

Rupert smiled, the cheeky grin of his youth. 'You'll be the first to know.'

The front door opened and Allan came in, muddy, wet, with an equally dirty dog at his heels.

'Allan MacDougall, get that dog out of the house!' Harriet ordered, and Allan grinned shamefacedly.

'Sorry, my love.'

Patches whined in protest, and Allan grabbed him by the scruff of his neck. 'Come on, beast. We're both unwanted at the moment!' He waggled the papers he held in his hand at Harriet. 'Although you'll be wanting these, I warrant!'

Harriet gasped and stood still. 'Are those letters?'

'From Eleanor.'

'Give them to me, Allan!'

Allan grinned. 'I've got to take my boots off first.'

'Never mind your boots,' Harriet cried, and snatched the letters from him.

Laughing, Allan went outside.

'How does Eleanor fare?' Rupert asked with mild curiosity, and Harriet spread her hands.

'I haven't heard from her since before the first snow. Her husband was posted to India, I know, and she'd removed to Glasgow to live with her in-laws.'

'I didn't realize she was married.'

'Two years ago,' Harriet confirmed. 'Surely we told you, Rupert. If we'd heard in time, I'd hopes of travelling back for the wedding. But it can take a year or more to receive a letter, and by the time the news reached us, the vows had already been spoken.' Harriet paused, sadness clouding her eyes briefly. 'I haven't seen my sister in ten years.'

'You'd better read the letter, then,' Rupert

said with a chuckle, and Harriet smiled in response.

'Yes, indeed.' She thrust the baby at Rupert, who took the bundle with awkward surprise.

'I'm not used to these,' he blustered and she shot him a pert, knowing look.

'Perhaps you should become accustomed.' Harriet broke open the seal and scanned the paper.

'Well?' Allan asked as he entered the house in just his socks.

'John has died,' Harriet said quietly.

'John?' Rupert asked.

'Her husband. She's written to Ian in Boston . . . why, she hopes to sail for Boston and stay with him! But of course she must stay with us!' Harriet looked up in dismay.

'She must do as she pleases, Harriet,' Allan reminded her gently. 'She is not the girl of thirteen you left so long ago. She's a woman grown, as well as a widow.'

'Of course. I only thought . . . surely it is fitting and proper for my own sister to live with us, now she is widowed. Alone in Boston! It's quite a big city, isn't it? I can't imagine what she is thinking of.'

'Listen to you!' Rupert laughed. 'You sound positively priggish. She'll be with your brother, after all. I'm sure Ian will take good care of her.'

'Still, he is a bachelor living alone,' Harriet protested, then sighed. 'I see the right of it, of course. She's likely to meet more people and have a livelier time in a place like Boston, but . . .'

'Why don't you read the second letter? They came on separate ships, apparently. She's likely to give us further news,' said Allan.

Harriet opened the second letter and gasped in surprise. Rupert and Allan exchanged looks filled with exasperated humour.

'But she's already sailed!' Harriet cried. 'On *The Endeavour,* one of Henry's ships. And it was likely to dock in early June, so that means . . .'

'She'll arrive any day, if she hasn't already,' Rupert finished. 'The decision has been made, I'd say.'

'She would like to visit us, after she's been with Ian,' Harriet continued. 'Although I doubt she has any idea what kind of journey she'd be undertaking!'

'This from the woman who travelled alone to Red River,' Allan said mildly. 'Untamed country, far from a gentle city such as Boston.'

'I was chaperoned,' Harriet retorted. 'And

it was all quite proper.'

'I hardly think propriety need be her first concern,' Rupert interjected. 'As you say, she's a widow and certainly has more license. And this is the new world, not some stuffy Scottish parlour. Men *and* women go freely.'

Allan raised his eyebrows. 'So speaks the libertarian!'

Rupert shrugged. 'I can hardly see what there is to fuss over.'

Harriet put the two letters on the mantelpiece and took Anna from Rupert. 'You're right, of course. I suppose I'm just a bit hurt that she didn't come here first.' She bit her lip. 'Of course she must do as she pleases. As you said, Allan, she's not a girl of thirteen. I can hardly tell her what to do. But still, I don't like her travelling alone. Even I had Katherine with me.'

'Perhaps Ian will come with her,' Allan suggested. 'It's high time he paid a visit.'

Harriet's expression lightened. 'That would be a gift indeed. But if he doesn't . . .' she looked thoughtfully at Rupert.

Rupert chuckled. 'You want me to fetch her? I hardly think I'm a suitable chaperone. We're not related, after all.'

'Nonsense,' Harriet said briskly. 'You shared the same home in Achlic, and you've grown up together. It would be perfectly proper.'

Allan laughed aloud. 'You have a funny idea of what is proper and what is not, Harriet, depending on what suits you!'

Harriet blushed. 'Perhaps, but it's still an idea.'

Rupert nodded thoughtfully. 'Aye, that it is.'

Chapter Four

The Endeavour sailed into Boston harbour on a clear, sunny day in early June. Eleanor stood at the railing, grateful for the fresh breeze that cleansed the smell and pallor of sickness which had surrounded her and the entire ship over the last few weeks.

It had not been an easy time. The days became a blur of holding buckets and wiping foreheads, falling into her narrow bed in filthy exhaustion.

'Look, there it is!' Caroline, still in the process of tying her silk bonnet strings, hurried to join Eleanor at the ship's railing.

Land had been sighted early that morning, and *The Endeavour* had been sailing between islands in the deep part of the harbour for a good part of the day. Finally, they were nearing the bay and the city itself beyond.

From the railing they could see the busy port with its many wharves, the tall sailing ships and squat steam boats moored close by.

Above the port was the city itself, a mass of buildings, brick and wood, some several storeys high, all of it bigger than Eleanor had originally thought.

'It looks more civilized than I expected,' Caroline said with a little sniff, and Eleanor laughed.

'Let's have none of your haughty ways,' she said. 'I'm sure there'll be plenty of society for your tastes in Boston.'

'I'm not haughty,' Caroline snapped, then relented. 'Very well, I don't mean to be snobbish. You know I don't. I suppose I'm still disappointed that I shan't have a season in London.'

'Think of it as an adventure,' Eleanor suggested. 'It's not many young women who are launched in a new city. And these colonials . . .' Eleanor said the word laughingly, even though Caroline was all sobriety, 'will admire your polish and nice ways. No doubt you'll be the toast of the town within minutes of your arrival!'

Caroline's eyes lit up and Eleanor could tell she'd not considered this particular angle before. 'But who knows what eligible bachelors reside here,' she said doubtfully. 'All ill-mannered colonials, I'm sure.' She thought of Dearborn, and shivered.

'Nay, that time is far past,' Eleanor said firmly. 'America is a country unto itself, with its own society. Ian wrote of it in his letters. Besides, Boston is a prosperous place, with many who are well-to-do. You will not be lacking in company.'

'And what of you?' Caroline looked at her curiously, and Eleanor knew she was wondering what sort of life she hoped to lead in the new world. The truth be told, she didn't yet know.

'I've told you, I'll lodge with my brother.'

'But surely you won't keep house for him for ever?' Caroline looked appalled. 'Why, won't you want a home of your own, and a husband?'

A home of her own. Eleanor sighed. She'd never had that, not since she was a child. Lodging with Ian was the closest thing to her own hearth and home that she could hope for, at least for now. 'I scarcely need to think about for ever,' she told Caroline briskly. 'It's the present that needs my care.' With that, she turned back to the railing and the view of the harbour, pinning her hopes firmly on that unknown city.

The wharf was seething with a motley crew of sailors, merchants and immigrants when Caroline and Eleanor disembarked, the captain having enquired solicitously as to their comfort.

'My brother is meeting me,' Eleanor told him. 'I'm well provided for, I assure you.'

'My uncle no doubt will send his carriage,' Caroline said, although an uncertainty flashed in her eyes, and Eleanor wondered again at her situation. She'd still not managed to learn much of Caroline in their time on the ship, occupied as they had been with caring for the sick. She supposed, judging from her accent, Caroline was from the same part of Scotland as she was, yet the younger woman had been surprisingly reticent in offering information about her former life. Eleanor felt the same; it was the future they cared about now.

Eleanor felt a sudden pang of guilt for having dismissed the younger girl as shallow and vain, stupid even. To her credit, Caroline had risen above such judgements and proven herself to be made of sterner stuff. 'I'm sure your uncle will send a carriage,' she said now, in an attempt to bolster the girl's spirits. 'No doubt a fine one, too.'

Caroline managed a trembling smile back. 'Yes, of course he will. He knows what ship I came on; he arranged the passage himself.'

'There you are, then.'

For a moment, on the wharf, with the indifferent mob surrounding her, Eleanor felt her spirits falter. She couldn't see Ian and everything seemed so strange, so new, so . . . raw.

In the next moment, she was swept up in a near bone-crushing embrace, and she shrieked in surprise. 'Ian! You nearly scared the life out of me!'

Ian laughed and set her down. 'I'm glad to see you, is all. It's been eleven years since I've looked on my own kin, Eleanor.'

Eleanor searched his face, all boyishness gone from the lean planes of his cheeks and angular jaw. His hair was still thick and auburn, his eyes as sparkling as the sea that lapped at their feet. He wore the dress of a prosperous businessman, a fine overcoat and fawn-coloured breeches.

'You look well,' she said with a shaky laugh.

'As do you.' Ian surveyed her in silent appreciation. 'You've grown into a woman. I scarcely recognized you!'

'Well enough to sweep me into an embrace,' Eleanor retorted. 'What if you'd been mistaken?'

'But I wasn't.' Ian grinned and then paused as he noticed Caroline hovering at Eleanor's elbow. 'But who's this?' He sketched a bow. 'Ian Crombie, madam, at your service.'

Caroline blushed prettily and curtseyed.

'This is Caroline Campbell.' Eleanor made the introductions. She saw Caroline glance furtively around for her uncle's carriage, clearly absent. 'We'd be happy to take you to your residence, Caroline,' she said, 'in Ian's carriage. That is . . .' She darted a look at her brother. 'If he has a carriage! There is much I do not yet know about your life, Ian.'

'I'm afraid I don't have my own — yet — but I've hired one for this glad errand. And of course I'd be more than happy to escort Miss Campbell to her destination.'

Eleanor smiled inwardly at this gallant speech, for she could see interest and appreciation shining in Ian's hazel eyes as he took in Caroline's trim figure, her neat coil of dark blonde hair, and the fetching dimples in her porcelain-pale cheeks. Clearly he was not immune to Caroline's charms.

Caroline looked vulnerable and as lost as a little girl for a moment, then she lifted her chin and gave a quick, brisk nod. 'That would be very kind of you indeed. I'm afraid my uncle must have had more pressing matters to attend to.'

More pressing than fetching his own niece? Eleanor wondered silently. She did not envy Caroline that relationship, at any rate.

Within a few minutes Ian had negotiated their trunks on to the carriage, and they were safely inside, away from the jostling crowds of the city's dockside.

'There's Quincy Market . . . you can see the State House on the hill if you look.' Ian pointed out some of the city's landmarks as they travelled.

'It's all so new,' Caroline exclaimed. Ian smiled indulgently.

'America is a new country,' he answered with a touch of pride. 'And a growing one.'

'I've heard all the men carry rifles,' Caroline said. 'Are you much afraid, to walk alone?'

Eleanor watched as she lay one gloved hand on Ian's arm.

'No, of course not. Not in the better places, anyway. Besides, carrying firearms is often a necessity in this wild country, though perhaps not in Boston as much.'

'You sound positively American!'

Ian chuckled. 'Perhaps I am. It's home to me now.'

Caroline had her uncle's address, and in a short time they'd reached an elegant brick house on Beacon Hill.

'Shall we see you in?' Ian asked as a matter of form, although he'd already started to alight from the carriage.

'No . . . no.' Caroline managed to exit the carriage with both grace and speed. 'My uncle is a very busy man . . . it is better for me to see him alone.'

Eleanor wasn't sure how these two statements related, but she could see plainly that Caroline was a mass of nerves when it came to her guardian.

A butler had emerged from the house, a long scar running down one cheek, and had already directed someone from the stables to take care of Caroline's trunk. 'Mistress Campbell,' he said politely. 'Your uncle awaits.'

'Are you sure we should not go in?' Ian asked dubiously. 'Your uncle no doubt will want to know who brought you here. He might think us all sorts of ruffians.'

Caroline laughed and pressed her hand to Ian's. 'Surely not! Besides, I am determined to extend an invitation to you when we are all settled properly. You must let me know your address. My uncle will certainly want to thank you in person.'

'Very well.' Ian took his leave of Caroline with obvious reluctance, and Eleanor was forced to curb her own impatience. She was dusty, tired and hot, as well as eager to know her own accommodations.

Finally the carriage rumbled on. Ian gazed pensively out the window at Caroline's slight form retreating into the grand house. 'It seems a bit awkward, her uncle not even coming out to greet her, don't you think?'

Eleanor shrugged. 'She told me more than once what a busy man he is, and he must be to have a house like that!'

Ian pulled a face. 'I'm afraid my own accommodations are meagre in comparison. Do you mind terribly, Eleanor? I've been living in a set of rooms, but in expectation of your arrival I've rented a small house in the South End. It's respectable, but nothing like this. If you wanted something more comfortable, you could stay with Margaret and Henry. They've offered, and their house is certainly far grander than mine.'

Eleanor shook her head. 'I've been the third wheel in too many homes as it is. I want nothing more than to live in a place I can at least half-heartedly call my own.'

'You may certainly do that! I haven't even employed a housekeeper yet.'

'Then don't,' Eleanor said firmly. 'I shall see to all the mundane details you needn't trouble yourself with.' She liked the idea of taking over the housekeeping. She'd once dreamed of her own home, filled with her own family. Now that John was dead, such a prospect seemed unlikely. This would have to do for now, and as she leaned her head against the carriage cushions, Eleanor decided it was more than enough.

The sun broke from behind the clouds and Harriet lifted her face gratefully to the warmth. It was August, and the wet days had finally given way to sunshine.

The MacDougalls were gathering together at Mingarry Farm to help bring in the wheat, an effort that included nearly every member of the family, as well as some neighbours.

George brought water to the men as they cut the wheat with sharp scythes, and Maggie helped Harriet and Betty tie the stalks of grain into sheaves. Others had come to help as well, and that evening when everything was safely packed in the barn, there would be food and dancing in the swept barnyard.

'It's a good thing you've already got your crop in,' Betty said as she and Harriet tied the bundles of grain together. 'What, with Rupert's help.'

'He's been a wonderful help to us.' Harriet smiled. 'Although the rain has made the wheat crop modest, at best.' Still, she'd enjoyed the summer, with Rupert's fun-loving company. A letter had come for him from Henry Moore, his sister Margaret's husband, and Harriet had been burning with curiosity as to its contents. Rupert was clearly planning something . . . but what?

Stars studded the sky by the time the wheat was finally in. Rupert and Allan had brought out long tables now laid with sliced meats and summer pies, all from neighbours' homes, as well as a fair sampling from Harriet and Betty's own kitchens.

'Care to dance, Mrs MacDougall?' Allan put his arm around Harriet's shoulders as she sipped some cold lemonade.

'Oh, aye, I'm always ready to kick up my feet! I've barely seen you all day, with the work being done. Is Father pleased with the crop?'

'As pleased as any of us are. It's been a poor summer, but we'll manage.' Besides bringing in their own wheat, Allan and Rupert had helped Sandy with his. It was the way of island families, especially in the strong Scots' community.

Allan frowned. 'I didn't like the sound of his cough. I know he was a bit poorly this winter, but surely it should have gone by now.'

Harriet glanced at Sandy, sitting with Betty on an upturned bale of hay. He looked as strong as ever, although his hair was whiter and the lines scoring his cheeks deeper. 'Like you said, it's been a wet summer,' she said. 'Surely his cough will disappear now that we have a bit of sunshine.'

'Just in time for winter again.' Allan took her in his arms as the fiddle struck up another tune. 'It's hard to believe on a balmy evening like this, but the first frost is no more than a month away.'

Harriet laid her head on Allan's shoulder. She could hear the crickets calling by the river, and the moon cut a silver swath through the inky black waters. She didn't want to think about the long, frozen months ahead, or the hardship. Right now she was just happy to rest in Allan's arms, with the warm night air like a cloak around her.

'I wonder if Rupert will be with us at the frost,' she murmured. 'He seems to have a head full of plans.'

'Indeed he does,' Allan chuckled wryly. 'I'm sure he'll tell us, in time.'

In time turned out to be the very next day. Rupert laid a letter on the breakfast table, next to his tin cup of coffee. 'From Henry Moore,' he said in a voice radiating pride. 'I didn't want to tell any of you, until I was sure.'

Allan raised his eyebrows, bemused. 'Sure of what?'

'He's offered me a position, as clerk, in his shipping office. In Boston.'

'What?' The spoon Harriet had been stirring the pot of porridge with fell on the floor with a clatter. 'Rupert, you can't be serious!'

'Why not? I've always had a head for figures, and those years being tutored in Fort William shouldn't go to waste.'

'But this is your life here,' Harriet protested.

Rupert shook his head. 'No, it's not, Harriet. It's yours.'

'Clerk? Hmm.' Allan sipped his coffee thoughtfully. 'I suppose it's a start.'

'It is that. I won't be satisfied as a lowly clerk for too long, I can assure you, but I'm grateful to Henry for giving me the offer. For all that we're kin, we're still strangers to each other.'

'When do you leave?'

'There's a ship leaving Pictou for Boston in two days.' Rupert glanced apologetically at Harriet. 'I'm sorry to leave so quickly, but Henry wants me to start as soon as possible.'

Harriet nodded in understanding, although she'd a feeling it was Rupert who wanted to start in haste, not Henry. His life, she realized with a pang, was about to begin, and in a place far from here.

'You must look after Eleanor, then,' she said. 'My suggestion wasn't as far-fetched as it seemed!'

'No, indeed.' Allan nodded at Rupert. 'Perhaps you will fetch her back for us in a few months' time. I'm sure Father and Mam will want word of you, by then.'

Rupert nodded. 'When the time comes, I'll be happy to bring Eleanor back. It's high time this family saw one another! As for me . . .' he rose from the table. 'I'll start to pack.'

Eleanor clutched the embossed stationery with Caroline's address in one gloved hand. She'd walked from Ian's lodgings in the South End to this Beacon Hill mansion, enjoying the sights and sounds of a new city.

Caroline, in a decidedly imperious fashion, had summoned her to tea at her residence that afternoon. Eleanor was in the mood neither to complain nor decline. Although only a week in Boston, she longed for companionship. It was invigorating to set Ian's house in order, but the maid who came twice weekly to do the heavy work was virtually the only other woman she'd spoken to since her arrival. She was also curious about how Caroline had fared since she'd left their carriage. Had her uncle been pleased to see her?

Eleanor was taken aback when Caroline herself answered the door, her cheeks flushed and her hair not yet arranged. 'I needn't stand on ceremony with you, I know,' she said. She made a face as she touched her rumpled hair. 'I haven't yet had the time to engage a lady's maid, and I'm hopeless at dressing hair. I've begged the cook to arrange it for tonight . . . I'm going to a musicale and you must come with me!'

Eleanor smiled inwardly. 'Why don't you let me dress your hair?'

Caroline looked at her hopefully. 'Are you skilled?'

'Not overly, but I've been putting my own hair up since I was seventeen.'

Over tea and cake, Caroline regaled Eleanor with her already vibrant social life in Boston. 'I had no idea there was such pleasant society to be had! Of course, some people are hopelessly rusticated, but I have been happily surprised.'

'Indeed.' Eleanor's lips twitched and she

took a sip of tea.

'Oh, yes,' Caroline continued firmly. 'My uncle is most determined to give me a proper season, since his business prevented him from doing so in London.'

Eleanor glanced again at Caroline's flushed cheeks, her strident tone. What was the real story? She wondered.

There could be no question that Caroline was accustomed to a life of at least some luxury, although Eleanor knew how creditors could hound even the wealthiest of society. Possible creditors aside, something did not seem right with Caroline . . . and Eleanor wondered what it was.

Caroline sliced the cake she'd purchased for Eleanor's visit, and forced another smile. Truth be told, she wasn't certain why she felt strangely apprehensive, for surely Boston was all she'd hoped for and more.

Despite having not fetched her at the docks — a small oversight — her uncle had been the soul of benevolent generosity since her arrival. He'd talked with almost manic enthusiasm about Boston society, and how he intended for her to have a season the rival of any in London. 'You'll see the society in Boston is to be as good as any in the old country,' he boasted, 'or even better. Plenty of parties and balls to be had — we want you to be seen, of course. A pretty girl like you . . . you'll be snatched up in an instant!'

'Thank you, Uncle,' Caroline said quietly, and wondered why she was not more pleased. This was exactly as she dreamed, yet something did not feel quite right. Uncle Edward's joviality was at odds with the brusque civility he'd greeted her with on their last meeting. What had changed? 'I'll need new dresses,' she ventured cautiously, and Uncle Edward waved an arm in sweeping acceptance. 'Of course, of course. There is a modiste here that is all the fashion. You must visit her.'

Hope leaped within her, and Caroline smiled. 'That would be pleasant indeed.' Feeling emboldened, she added, 'I see you have not yet engaged a lady's maid for me.'

Edward frowned and then managed a small smile. 'Yes, well, we'll see about that. All in good time, of course.'

Caroline nodded, deciding for once to be happy with what she had. She wasted no time leaving Edward's calling card — she didn't have her own — at every house of quality she could find. No doubt everyone would see through her attempts as the beggar for society that she was, but Caroline didn't care. She was hardly able to meet anyone by simply walking in the park!

Uncle Edward continued to beam approval at her actions, and even went so far as to secure an invitation to a musicale for them both. 'I too know some people of import here, Niece,' he said in a preening way and Caroline had to admit he was right. Although she never enquired as to the nature of his business, it appeared that his work provided him with some useful contacts.

'Do have some cake,' Caroline invited Eleanor now, forcing her thoughts back to the present. 'I'm afraid it's bought from a bakeshop; the cook here is quite hopeless and I'll have to sort something out as soon as I can.'

'As hopeless at cookery as at hair?' Eleanor chuckled drily. 'Then you are in a sorry state, indeed.'

Caroline knew her friend was gently mocking her, and sighed. 'I don't mean to sound spoiled. I only wanted nice things for you. You will come to the musicale tonight, won't you?'

Eleanor glanced at the invitation card Caroline showed her. 'As it happens, I've already been invited to this musicale. Ian is attending with Isobel Moore, and they've kindly asked me along.'

'Oh! I didn't realize . . . !' Caroline said awkwardly and Eleanor smiled. Caroline's thoughts were plain on her face; she hadn't expected Eleanor to entertain the same society as she did. In truth, Eleanor had not expected it either. Ian's position in society was far more elevated than being a doctor warranted, and it was all due to his association with the Moores.

When Ian first showed her the invitation, Eleanor had baulked. 'I can hardly attend with you and Miss Moore,' she protested. 'I shall feel a third wheel, and that, dear Ian, is something I refuse to feel ever again.'

'The Moores wish for your company as much as I do,' Ian replied. 'And you must get out in society, Eleanor. You're young and pretty. Don't moulder away sewing my shirts and making butter as if you were a spinster!'

'I haven't made any butter yet,' Eleanor protested with a little laugh. 'And I like to keep occupied. You might like these soirées and such, but they're quite out of my element. The most entertainment I've had is a *ceilidh* at home, or a quiet card party in Glasgow. They hardly count!'

'Then it's high time you went to something proper. Besides, I'd appreciate your company. I . . . don't want to be with Isobel alone.'

Eleanor raised her eyebrows at this confession. 'Has she set her cap at you?'

'I wouldn't say that,' Ian said uncomfortably.

'You must put it to rights if she has,' Eleanor warned him. 'For you'll both suffer if anything improper occurs.'

'Eleanor!' Ian was scandalized. 'Nothing improper could ever occur, I assure you!'

'Perhaps not,' Eleanor allowed. 'But much happens in the minds of gossips.'

The thought of attending a social event thrilled her more than she cared to admit, even though in her mind she wondered which one of her few gowns would be suitable. None, probably. Perhaps she could quickly add some lace at the cuffs of one, or a fichu.

'If you like,' she said now, 'I could come here before, and dress your hair. Then we could go together, if that suits.'

'What about your brother?'

Eleanor did not miss the spark in Caroline's eye. 'As I said, he is escorting Isobel Moore. I don't wish to be a third wheel.'

'Is that how it is?' Caroline took a sip of tea, her expression carefully disinterested. 'Is he courting her?'

'I don't believe so,' Eleanor replied. 'But all the same, I think I shall meet them there.' She knew Ian wouldn't be pleased with this arrangement, but she'd no notion of ordering her life to suit his romantic tangles.

'Very well, then, it's settled.' Caroline smiled in satisfaction, thinking of the evening ahead, her first invitation, even if it had been issued to her uncle. Perhaps his presence would encourage him to take more of an active interest in society. They might even host a ball, or at least a dinner party! Caroline's hopes suddenly soared, given wings from her own imagination, and the apprehension she'd felt about her uncle evaporated.

She knew tonight was nothing but a small musicale, but excitement raced through her all the same. She couldn't help it; this was her first chance at any kind of entertainment. She certainly hoped Eleanor was as confident a hairdresser as she'd said.

'Ian, you seem hopelessly distracted.'

'Do I?' Ian glanced down at Isobel, realizing even as he spoke how accurate her words were. They were walking down Beacon Street to the evening musicale at a local matron's house. Despite the pleasant evening, the purple twilight and the bustling of carriages, his thoughts had been elsewhere. 'I apologize, Isobel, I was thinking of a case I had at the hospital this morning.' He paused, remembering. 'A man needed surgery, but so many of the procedures are too painful to be endured —'

'Ian, please!' Isobel shuddered. 'I cannot bear such talk of pain and disease. You must forgive me my delicacy.' She smiled prettily, no doubt expecting him to be charmed, and Ian managed a small smile back.

He hadn't really expected Isobel to share his interest, but could he marry someone who thought the hospital and all it implied indelicate? Ian sighed. He hadn't yet offered for Isobel, and he hadn't yet decided if he would.

He'd been hoping to delay such conversations as this by Eleanor's presence, but his sister had more spirit than he'd credited her with, and cried off.

He could hardly blame Eleanor for the tangle he was in; the threads had been drawn by his own blundering manoeuvres. He knew Isobel and her parents were waiting for his proposal — perhaps all of society was. Only the other day Margaret had remarked pertly, 'Dear Isobel. You must see her nearly every day, Ian?'

'A few times a week,' Ian corrected, and Margaret gave him a knowing look.

'Ah, yes. Only a few times a week.'

He didn't want to compromise her, Ian thought miserably. He just didn't know if he loved her. And even if he refused to be such a romantic as to yield to love, how could he know that Isobel would make a good doctor's wife?

'You're frowning.' Isobel touched his cheek lightly, flushing as she did so and then dropping her hand quickly. 'Is something wrong?'

'No, I'm sorry. My thoughts were elsewhere, but I promise to leave such worries behind. I'm looking forward to this evening's recitation.'

Isobel made a little pout. 'It's not a recitation, Ian. It's a musicale.'

'I apologize again. I gave my thoughts away, I see.'

'Perhaps you will give a few more away, before the evening is over.' Isobel glanced away, and Ian knew what her pretty jest really meant. She wanted him to propose.

'I'm at your command,' he said, his throat dry but his voice light enough for her not to take him seriously or so he hoped. What was he going to do?

'I'm looking forward to you meeting my

sister Eleanor,' he told Isobel as they strolled through the Common. 'My hours at the hospital have prevented me from presenting her to your family. She arrived a week ago and she's already had two invitations to this musicale, one by us, of course, and one by an acquaintance, Caroline Campbell, also new to this city. She's travelling with Miss Campbell, and we'll join up there.'

'I'm sure we'll get along,' Isobel said politely, but Ian sensed no real interest and his discouragement grew.

The musicale was in the drawing room of one of Isobel's acquaintances, and promised, Ian realized, a few rather unsteady performances by amateurs. Combined with the new awkwardness that had sprouted up between him and Isobel, he reckoned the evening would be dismal indeed.

At least Eleanor would be present, with her new friend Caroline Campbell. She'd already left for the Campbells' residence when he'd come in from the hospital that evening, but there'd been a note from her explaining her whereabouts. Ian scanned the mingling crowd in the salon, mostly matrons and their aspiring daughters, for a glimpse of Eleanor.

His gaze rested on a man who looked vaguely familiar, then his heart skipped a beat before pounding hard. Despite the white hair and gaunt lines of his face, there was no mistaking the man . . . Sir Edward Rydell.

Fury, white hot and consuming, surged through Ian as he broke from Isobel, who gave a little cry of surprise. He could see nothing but Rydell, hear nothing but the mocking laughter of eleven years ago when the man had swindled Ian's family property from his boyish grasp.

'I never thought to see you again, Rydell,' Ian said as he stood in front of the older man, his voice choked with anger.

Rydell raised his eyebrows, smiling coolly. 'Nor I. We're hardly likely to travel in the same circles, are we?'

'Thank heavens for small mercies. I wouldn't want to be in the same room with a man such as you.'

A shocked current rippled through the salon.

Rydell shook his head in warning. 'I'd be careful with your words, Ian, my boy. This is neither the time nor the place.'

'I'm not a boy any more, Rydell, not like when you cheated me out of my family home.'

Rydell's voice was low and controlled, but filled with menace. 'I told you to be careful.'

Ian took a deep, shaking breath. 'And I'm calling you a cheat.'

CHAPTER FIVE

The silence in the salon was taut. Ian stared at Edward Rydell, his breathing ragged.

'What did you call me?' Rydell asked in slow, deliberate tones.

Ian felt a hand on his sleeve, its warning pressure. Eleanor, who had come quickly to his side, shot him a pleading glance. He already knew this was neither the time nor the place for such a confrontation; indeed, his behaviour had already breached the code of a gentleman. 'I believe you heard me,' he said quietly, once he'd reined his emotions back under control. 'I've no need to say it again.'

'You owe me an apology,' Rydell demanded.

'Ian . . .'

'No, Eleanor. It's all right.' Ian raised his chin. 'I apologize for speaking to you in such a manner, and in such a place. But the business between us is not finished.'

'It was finished a decade ago, Crombie,' Rydell replied. 'You simply have not accepted it.'

Ian was conscious of the frank and curious stares of the people gathered in the salon. Next to him, Isobel was rigid with the embarrassment of being party to such a confrontation. 'No, I haven't,' he replied quietly. 'And I never will.'

Rydell smiled suddenly, his eyes glinting. 'If I didn't dislike you so much, Crombie, I'd admire your tenacity. I might even have a position for you in my offices. I could use a good clerk.'

Ian's hands balled into his fists and blood surged to heat his face. Rydell's smile widened, and even though Ian knew the older man was taunting him on purpose, he could barely keep himself from hitting him.

'Ian, he's winding you up,' Eleanor whispered. 'Resolve this another day. Not here, not now!'

The whispers and titters were growing louder, the stares emboldened. Ian let his hands drop to his sides. 'You've barely begun to grasp just how tenacious I can be, sir,' he said with cold dignity. 'And now that you are in Boston, I have no doubt that you will discover its full measure.' Without waiting for a reply, he turned, leading Isobel to a secluded corner of the salon. Eleanor, her face pale and worried, followed.

'Ian, what on earth was that about?' Isobel demanded in a furious whisper. 'You've made us both the talk of all society, no doubt!' She didn't sound pleased by the prospect.

Ian let out a shuddering sigh. 'Isobel, I'm sorry. I know I was out of place.'

'Who was that man?'

'An old adversary,' he murmured. 'I didn't expect to see him here.'

'That much I could garner on my own!'

'Ian, how could you?' Eleanor looked at him in despair. 'After all this time. . . .'

'It still rankles! Besides, a salon in Boston was one of the last places I expected to see Rydell. I thought he was mouldering back at Lanymoor House, or worse! What on earth is he doing here?'

'He was with me, as a matter of fact,' Eleanor said. 'I thought he looked familiar, but I'd no idea . . .'

'With you?' Ian stared at his sister in disbelief.

Eleanor sighed. 'Perhaps it is not for me to explain. We'd only just been introduced.'

'You forgot that bastard's name?' Ian asked, his contempt evident. 'After he destroyed our family?'

'No, Ian,' Eleanor said coldly. 'Sir Rydell did not destroy our family. You did that when you ran away, unable to face your own shame. And I'd thank you to watch your language with ladies present.'

Ian's face was chalk-white. 'You blame me for what happened?'

'It was an accident, I well know! But you shouldn't have run away, and you need to stop blaming Rydell for every injury or hardship our family has ever faced.'

'He tricked me!'

'Well I know it.' Eleanor drew in a ragged breath. 'Again, this is neither the time nor place for such a discussion. I have not even been introduced to your lady friend.'

Ian's pallor was replaced with a hectic flush as he realized how badly he had conducted himself, and in front of half of society, as well. He drew Isobel forward. 'I beg both of your pardons. Isobel, my sister, Eleanor McCardell. Eleanor, this is . . .' Ian floundered briefly, colouring even more. 'A dear family friend, Isobel Moore.'

Eleanor took Isobel's flushed face and bright eyes in one swift, appraising glance. She knew immediately whose affections were engaged, and whose were not, and wondered how Ian planned to extricate himself from such a delicate situation. 'I'm very pleased to have your acquaintance.'

'Likewise,' Isobel murmured, but her clouded expression told otherwise.

'That was quite exciting, to be sure!' Caroline's eyes sparkled mischievously as she joined their little group. 'I'd hoped to see you again, Mr Crombie, but hardly under such circumstances!' She smiled prettily, and Eleanor saw that Ian was not unaffected. She watched as Isobel's eyes narrowed at the intrusion of this unwelcome stranger. 'What on earth possessed you,' Caroline continued, 'to speak thus to my uncle?'

Ian made a choking sound. 'Edward Rydell is your uncle?'

Caroline's pretty manner dropped as she looked uncertainly between Ian and Eleanor. 'Of course he is. It's on his behalf that I'm in Boston at all.'

Ian shook his head slowly. Isobel clutched at his sleeve. 'I believe the musicale is about to begin,' she said pointedly. 'Shall we take our seats?'

'Yes, of course.' Ian nodded to Caroline. 'Good day to you, Miss Campbell.'

Caroline watched him depart with a childish mixture of annoyance and hurt. She turned to Eleanor. 'What is this about?'

'Your uncle and my brother had a falling

out,' Eleanor explained quietly. 'To tell the truth, I can't remember all the details. I was only a child at the time.'

'You mean they knew each other, back in Scotland?'

'Yes. A strange coincidence, is it not? Although perhaps not as much of one as we think, considering we both sailed from Tobermory.'

Caroline plucked nervously at the sleeve of her gown. 'Why was Ian — Mr Crombie — so angry with my uncle? I'd never seen him in such a rage!'

'You barely know him,' Eleanor reminded her a bit tartly, then sighed, the memories tumbling back in her mind, clouding her thoughts. 'I'm sure your uncle has his own story to tell, but I remember Ian coming home one day, filled with happiness. Then Harriet — my older sister — lit into him. She was furious. I'd never seen her so distraught.' Eleanor shook her head to clear the memory. 'The next day, Ian was gone, and Harriet told me that we'd lost Achlic, our farm.'

'I fail to see what that has to do with my uncle!'

'He was the one who took Achlic. We never spoke about it much after that. We left to live with Jane McCready, and Harriet went to the new world to find Allan.'

'Allan?' Caroline turned sharply, and then she laughed. 'Harriet! Harriet MacDougall! My pianoforte tutor! Of course. She was going to marry James.'

'Yes, she was,' Eleanor said slowly. 'I'd almost forgotten. So much has happened since then. It almost seems like a dream, another life. I never understood what happened, why she never did marry him, but I was always glad she went to find Allan . . . even if it left me alone.' Eleanor bit her lip, remembering that fateful day, when Harriet had said goodbye. She'd refused to cry, not wanting Harriet to feel guilty, yet there had been an aching loss inside her, and a terrible fear that she would never see Harriet or Ian again, that she'd lost them already to the chasing of their own dreams.

'She didn't marry James,' Caroline said, her eyes shining with a strange excitement, 'because I showed her the letters. James kept Allan's letters — hid them from Harriet! I discovered them, and showed them to her. And now she's married her sweetheart, hasn't she?'

'Yes.' Eleanor nodded. 'She has.'

'Oh, Eleanor! This makes us nearly sisters! It must be fate that has brought us together like this, our pasts so twined. Don't you think?'

Eleanor shook her head wearily. 'Perhaps, Caroline, but it hardly seems to be a matter of gaiety. The past is a troubled one.'

'I'm sure we can overcome any troubles! Uncle Edward will explain, you'll see. And Ian will forgive him! Perhaps that is why we sailed together, why we've become friends. So the past can be put behind us — truly!'

'Perhaps.' Caroline was still such a child, and a naïve one at that. One look at the rage simmering in Ian's eyes, and the cold sneer on Rydell's face, made it quite clear that there would be no forgiveness between the two men. Eleanor shivered, for she was afraid it would be much worse than that. There would be no mercy, no quarter given. She knew what Ian wanted, had always wanted. It had been in his letters, still hovered in his speech. Revenge.

She patted Caroline's arm, suddenly wanting to believe in her dreams, to dispel the coldness inside. 'Perhaps we can make it so. If you speak to your uncle . . . I'll speak to Ian.' She shivered again. 'They might see reason.' Although she doubted it.

Caroline nodded happily. 'Oh, they will, Eleanor! I know they will.' And Eleanor felt she could almost believe it.

Later that evening, back at their house, Eleanor plucked up the courage to speak to Ian. After changing into her nightgown and robe, her hair braided, she went in search of her brother.

She found him in his study, sprawled in a chair and still in evening dress, a tumbler and bottle of brandy at his elbow.

'Ian,' she said sharply. 'Is this any way to conduct yourself?'

'Can't a man have a drink in the privacy of his own home?'

'Certainly, but he should not attempt to drown his sorrows.'

'Don't lecture me, Eleanor,' Ian warned. 'I've heard enough from you this evening! It's clear whose side you've taken in this war.'

'A war, is it? I'd call it merely a scuffle.' Firmly, Eleanor took the brandy bottle and returned it to the cupboard. 'Ian,' she said quietly, 'if I were to choose sides, you know I would choose yours. Rydell is a cold fish, there's no doubt, and a thoroughly unpleasant character as well. I've no doubt his business dealings are suspect, but the truth will out, and in the meantime you must not damage your position here in Boston.'

Ian raised one sardonic eyebrow. 'Fearful for your own standing, Eleanor? What, do you want to snare a rich husband?'

'You are trying to be cruel.' Despite the hurt that flashed through her, Eleanor kept her voice steady. 'I came here to be with you, and it is you and your work I'm mindful of. Do you know how many people heard you call Rydell a cheat? Twenty years ago he could have called you out for a duel! You must think, Ian, and show some self-control. You've always had too hot a temper.'

Ian leaned forward, raking his fingers through his hair so it flopped across his forehead, making him look like the boy he'd once been. 'I never thought I'd see him again. I know I acted a fool, but I couldn't help it! All the old rage came rushing back. He cost me so much, Eleanor.' Ian looked up at her, his eyes bleak. 'So much.'

Eleanor knelt down and put her arms around him. 'You must put the past behind you, dear,' she said gently. 'It is the future which concerns us now. Achlic Farm is long gone. You wouldn't go back if you could, would you? Your life is here.'

Ian was silent for a long moment. 'Yes,' he agreed finally. 'It is.'

'Rupert!' Margaret MacDougall Moore embraced her younger brother warmly. It had been several years since she'd made the voyage to Prince Edward Island with Henry to visit him and her parents, and she gazed at him with fond affection. 'You've grown into a man.'

'I am twenty-three, Margaret!' Rupert returned, laughing. 'It's been some time since I was the little lad you remember.'

'So it would appear.' Margaret's eyes twinkled. 'Come in, I've set the tea things in the morning parlour.'

Rupert gazed around him in frank appreciation as Margaret ushered him into the Moore residence, one of the newer town houses in the South End of Boston. Although it couldn't quite qualify as a mansion, it was impressive enough indeed, with sumptuous rugs and furniture, and Rupert said as much.

'Henry's been fortunate,' Margaret said. 'As well as working hard. For my own sake, I'm glad he's not on the ships as much as he used to be, even if he laments his role in the offices a bit!'

'He's not enjoying life as a landlubber?'

'Well . . .' Margaret pursed her lips. 'I don't know if I would go that far. But if the wind blows a certain way . . .' she chuckled and shrugged. 'He gets that look in his eyes. Still, he's enjoying the profits of his business opportunities.'

She led him into the morning parlour, an airy room striped with the sun's rays that slanted through the elegant sash window. Rupert settled in a rose velvet chair, while Margaret perched on a settee and began to pour.

'We're so glad you've come, Rupert. I've missed having family near me, even though the Moores are so good to me. Henry feels very strongly . . .'

'About what do I feel so strongly?'

Margaret's gaze flew to the doorway, where Henry Moore now stood. He was the same as Rupert remembered, tall, fair, with creases around eyes that sparkled with humour.

'I was only going to say that you care about family,' Margaret said demurely. 'And you were pleased by Rupert's letter.'

'Indeed I was.' Henry grabbed a muffin off the plate and took a bite even as he reached to pump Rupert's hand. 'I know a sharp mind for business when I see one.'

'I don't know if I've proved myself yet,' Rupert objected with a little smile, and Henry shrugged.

'No, you haven't, but I'm sure you will with the right opportunity. You'll have to work for it, though.'

'I'm not afraid of hard work.'

'I thought as much.' Henry nodded his approval. 'Your letter in itself showed a keen grasp of the essentials. I didn't realize news of the Second Bank's struggles had reached there.'

'It hasn't, not really. I just keep my ear to the ground. And the news of any forgeries is always good for popular interest.'

'Of course, and it's likely to become a problem for us, the way things are placed.'

'I look forward to you keeping me up to date,' Rupert said seriously. 'I want to be an asset to any of your enterprises.'

'I see you're going to talk business,' Margaret interjected with a roll of her eyes. 'I've barely seen my brother, and you're already on to banks and forgeries!'

'We'll save it for later,' Henry promised. 'Let's talk of something else. Although the only subject on Margaret's tongue lately has been her charity school!'

Rupert turned to look enquiringly at his sister. 'I heard you'd involved yourself in some charities . . .'

'Nothing more than a bit of volunteering,' Margaret dismissed. 'But if Henry is willing to fund it, I'm hoping to start a small school for the city's poor. What with all the immigrant ships coming in, the city is very nearly overrun.'

'She's determined to turn into a crusader,' Henry added with an indulgent smile.

'Hardly,' Margaret flashed. 'You will not find me accosting people in parlours, or soliciting strangers for funds! I want nothing more than a small school, a few children . . .' she faltered, and glanced down at her teacup.

'And that you shall have,' Henry said quickly, filling in the moment's awkwardness. 'I was only funning you, love.'

Later, after an excellent dinner, Rupert retired with Henry to the library. It was a comfortable room, small but elegantly furnished, with nautical maps lining the walls, and a large inlaid leather desk occupying a handsome position by the bay window.

'I'll take you down to the shipping offices,' Henry told him as he handed him a glass of port. 'At the moment, I can use you looking over the accounts, which is dull work, I don't mind saying. There are three other clerks in the office, including Aubrey, my manager. You'll have to start at the bottom. I won't be accused of playing favourites. But if you keep your ear to the ground as you say you do, I should hope you might prove yourself.'

'I intend to.'

Henry sat down and stretched out his legs.

'I'm hoping my office here will grow, in time. I'm looking to invest, branch out a bit. Of course, merchant shipping will always be profitable, especially as I look to India and Africa. But there's opportunity in this country as well.' He sighed and took a sip of port. 'Although, with President Jackson's determination to close the Second Bank, who knows what will happen with the economy.'

Rupert had read about the Second Bank, the congress-approved, privately owned bank where Federal funds were deposited. 'I thought the Second Bank encouraged speculation and inflation,' he said. 'That's why Jackson is determined not to renew its charter.'

'He's determined because he's an old stick in the mud,' Henry returned with some heat. 'And he doesn't like big business. But what is the alternative? Every state and every county having its own banks, and worse, its own banknotes not worth the paper they're printed on! With all the different currency circulating, and not backed by gold, it's easy for anyone with a printing press and some engraving knowledge to make his own notes.'

'You mean forgery.'

'Exactly. I don't want to be caught with a

fistful of worthless paper, I can tell you.'

'You could only accept gold, or US bank notes,' Rupert suggested, but Henry shook his head.

'True, but that has become more difficult, especially when it comes to making investments. The gold simply isn't there.'

'Then it's likely we're prime for a depression, or at the least a panic,' Rupert said thoughtfully.

Henry nodded. 'Possibly, but business is booming at the moment, and I intend to profit from it. I don't want to stay in shipping for ever, at least not the way I am now. The face of shipping is changing anyway, and I won't be left behind.'

'I've no doubt of that.'

Henry grinned. 'Find me some good investments, Rupert, and you'll be well on your way up the ladder. But be careful, as well. None of us wants to be caught holding the bag.'

'Your uncle does not wish to be disturbed, miss.'

Caroline bit her lip in frustration as she stared at the butler's implacable countenance. Uncle Edward had been closeted in his study for most of the morning, but Caroline could wait no longer to confront him. 'I'm sure he does not, Taylor, but I've something pressing to ask him.'

Taylor's lips twitched, in irritation or sympathy Caroline could not tell. She fluttered her eyelashes just in case.

'I doubt he will appreciate such interference, Miss Campbell.'

'That matters not, either,' Caroline returned grimly. 'Now if you please.' She exchanged her role as simpering female for mistress of the household, even though she was no such thing. Despite the few evening entertainments she'd managed to dredge invitations to, she felt little more than a wraith, drifting around Edward's rented house, waiting for her life to begin. She lifted her chin, meeting Taylor's stony gaze with bold determination, even though her heart was thudding with anxiety.

Taylor stepped aside with a slight shrug, and Caroline pushed open the door.

'I said not to be disturbed, Taylor.' Edward looked up in annoyance, only to have it increase at the sight of his niece. 'For heaven's sake, Caroline! What do you want?'

'To ask you about Ian Crombie,' Caroline returned boldly. She hid her sweaty hands in the folds of her dress. 'At the musicale last night you exchanged sharp words.'

'He was in a dander, all right,' Edward's

eyes narrowed shrewdly. 'Although I hardly see how it concerns you.'

'Your conduct in Boston society will naturally reflect on me!' Caroline drew herself up. 'If I'm to contract an eligible husband, I need to concern myself with what passes in all the elegant drawing rooms.'

'Is that all?' The note of sarcasm cut through Caroline, and she felt herself flushing.

'Of course it is all! I have made Mr Crombie's acquaintance, and as you should know he is well placed in society. Nearly everyone is saying he will offer for Isobel Moore.' Caroline took a breath, surprised how this little revelation pained her.

'You've certainly made society's gossip your business,' Edward returned with a little malice, and Caroline shrugged.

'It *is* my business. It must be.'

'Indeed.' Edward ran a hand through his hair, sighing wearily. 'Very well. I certainly did not desire the boy to confront me in such a fashion. Such a palaver, over nothing! After ten years, you would think he'd have reconciled his fate.'

'I didn't realize Eleanor was Harriet Crombie's sister. Did you know of it?'

'Why should I? I'd never met the girl

before this evening.'

'But you remembered Harriet.'

'Of course I did! She was on the brink of becoming part of this family, although a more mismatched betrothal I'd never seen. It was just as well she cried off.'

'I don't think James ever recovered,' Caroline said quietly. After Harriet had broken off the betrothal, James had removed to London. Caroline hardly ever saw him any more, and only heard from him in brief letters. She had a vague suspicion that he was involved in little good, and had witnessed her uncle writing a bank draft for him, irritation and perhaps a little guilt in every hard line of his face.

'More fool him,' Edward said. 'He was far too smitten with the girl as it was. She never loved him.'

'What do you care for love?' Caroline scoffed, her eyes glittering.

Edward was quiet for a moment. 'More than you think. I know you believe me to be completely heartless, my dear, but I assure you it is not so. There was a time . . .' He shrugged. 'It hardly signifies now.'

Caroline was intrigued, but she held her tongue. Her uncle would not thank her for asking prying questions. 'What about Ian?'

'Mr Crombie to you. His family was in

dire straits. They wanted to sell some land, a back pasture. I offered to buy the entire farm, for a very decent price. Ian accepted.'

Caroline bit her lip. Something was wrong with her uncle's telling of the story, she was sure. How could Crombie be angry about that? 'It can't be that simple.'

'Well, I assure you it was,' Edward snapped. 'If the foolish boy didn't read the contract properly, it can hardly be my fault. He thought I was only buying the pasture . . . and for such a sum! He'd no notion of business at all.'

'His man of business must have known,' Caroline objected. She knew little about such affairs, but she could feel there was more to the story than her uncle would have her believe.

'He wasn't involved, and why should he be?'

'To keep you from taking advantage of him!'

'I hardly did that. I offered him every opportunity to look over the arrangements. It's his own fault for being careless, my dear niece, and that is precisely the reason he is so angry now.'

Still Caroline shook her head. 'But he was only a boy.'

'He was sixteen. I was managing affairs at

that age, I assure you. Now, I've had quite enough of this discussion.' Edward glanced down at the papers on his desk, frowning, before he shuffled them into a pile. 'You hardly have a head for business, so I don't expect you to understand the finer points of such a transaction,' he added, to Caroline's fury. He glanced at her knowingly. 'You've professed quite an interest in Crombie. I wouldn't go setting my cap at him, if I were you. He's hardly suitable.'

'Setting my cap . . . ?' Caroline flushed. 'I'm doing no such thing! His sister, Eleanor, happens to be a good friend of mine.'

'The Crombies are hardly likely to advance your social position in this city,' Edward remarked mildly.

'I told you, they are friends with the Moores, who are very well placed.'

'Beggars at the table. Hardly a position you need covet.'

Caroline shifted uneasily. She'd had her own notions of the Crombies' placement in society. If anything, she'd felt a vague but satisfying pity for Eleanor and her mended, out-of-date dresses, her pride in keeping a bourgeois little house. Still, she did not like to hear it put so crudely by her uncle. 'I'm sure the Crombies are well respected here.'

Edward raised his eyebrows. 'After the

little episode at that musicale, I wouldn't be surprised if Ian Crombie's reputation is a bit tarnished.' He smiled. 'Now, don't get into a huff, Caroline. The boy would hardly suit you. He's hot-headed, a penniless doctor, and the hospital isn't even pleased with his work, or so I've heard.'

'Where did you hear that? You didn't even know he lived here!' Caroline protested, her face pale.

'I have my sources. And as you said, he's dangling after Moore's daughter, so he isn't worth your time.'

Caroline found she was trembling. 'You keep your ear to the ground, I see.'

'It suits us both for me to do so. You've made it plain you want to contract an eligible match; I desire the same. So let us waste no more time discussing a foolish boy who cannot possibly help you fulfil such an aim.' Edward smiled, holding out his hands in supplication. 'I've arranged a treat for you tonight. Let's not spoil it with petty arguments.'

'A treat?' Caroline found herself unbending, despite her determination not to yield. Resting on high principles, especially for near strangers, *was* uncomfortable. 'What kind of treat?'

'We're dining out, with friends. A gentleman of my acquaintance will be one of our party. I think you might find him to be congenial company.'

'Perhaps,' Caroline returned grudgingly, but she was ensnared by her own curiosity, and Rydell knew it.

He chuckled. 'Go and put on something fetching. And why don't you order some new gowns from the modiste? You can hardly have a successful season here without a few frocks and fripperies.'

Caroline was astute enough to know she was being bought, and she fleetingly wondered why. She pushed the question out of her mind, for the prospect of new gowns was too tempting to resist. And she did need them, if she was to be seen in society at all. The fashions in Boston were quite different.

Caroline hurriedly bestowed a kiss on her uncle's cheek. 'Thank you, Uncle.' She left the room, determined to forget about Ian Crombie. He was a stranger, and a penniless doctor at that.

Caroline paused, recalling Ian's ready smile, his cheerful good nature. No, she barely knew him. And all things considered, perhaps it should stay that way.

Chapter Six

Rupert gazed out at the rain-washed streets of Boston and sighed contentedly. He'd been working for Henry Moore for only a fortnight, but he already loved his work and his adopted city.

'Have you finished those yet?' Aubrey, Henry's personal clerk and office manager, glanced at him with ill-disguised impatience. 'Accounts are dull work, I'm sure, but they must be done.'

'Far from dull,' Rupert replied civilly. In the last two weeks the other clerks hadn't warmed to him, and Rupert knew why. He was uneducated, from the backwoods of Canada, and he'd been given a job most promising young men would struggle for.

He also saw the glint of suspicion in Aubrey's eyes, the fear for his own job. There was no hiding that Henry favoured his brother-in-law, even if he insisted on giving him the most menial of office tasks. Whenever Henry came into the offices, he spoke with Rupert, joked with him even. The other clerks seethed.

'Compared to ploughing fields, this is positively scintillating,' Rupert added. As a joke, it fell flat, reminding the other man of his own inadequate background.

'Not a farmer, then, are you?' Aubrey sneered.

'No.' A pang of guilt assailed him, for he knew farming was honest work and worse, how much his father had longed for him to continue on at Mingarry Farm.

Rupert glanced down at his neat row of figures. Yes, he was happy tallying numbers for Henry, but his eye was on greater things. He spent his free time reading newspapers or listening to the talk on the docks, in the public houses, even outside the gentlemen's clubs. A word here, a tip there, and he found he was already discovering new investment opportunities. He looked forward to telling Henry of his plans, when the time was right.

'Ready?' Charles, one of the junior clerks, walked up to Aubrey. Rupert knew they were all going to the Union Oyster House, as they did every Saturday night. So far he had not been included. He wanted the amity of his co-workers, yet he understood why it was not forthcoming and he was honest to acknowledge that he valued his own ambition more.

'I'm finished.' Rupert pushed the figures towards Aubrey, who nodded shortly.

'I'll check them on Monday. It's too late now.' As if that were Rupert's fault, when the figures had only been given to him an hour ago.

He shrugged easily, refusing to be baited. Charles shifted uncomfortably. 'I don't suppose you want to join us, MacDougall?'

Aubrey glanced at the younger man sharply. No doubt Charles would pay for his moment of grace. Rupert smiled with regret.

'Another time, perhaps. I'm afraid I'm already engaged this evening.' Even if he were not, he wouldn't go with the other men. Not yet. Not till he'd proven himself, and won their respect.

Aubrey nodded. 'Of course. You're dining at the house, I suppose?' The sneer, Rupert knew, masked only envy, and who could blame him? If their positions were reversed, Rupert knew he would feel as Aubrey did. He wouldn't be able to help it.

'If you mean at the Moores, yes.' Rupert left it at that. No need to remind the other men he was family. They were hardly likely to forget it.

In fact, Rupert had been invited to the Moores' house along with Ian and Eleanor. It would be a reunion of sorts, Rupert thought with a smile. He hadn't seen Ian or Eleanor in over ten years, when they'd all been little more than children.

He remembered his little schoolboy adventures with Ian well enough; they'd boarded together for nearly two years. When Ian had run away, Rupert had kept his secret, even though his conscience had been sorely tried. Had he done the right thing? Rupert mused now. Perhaps; Ian had certainly done well for himself.

He could not remember Eleanor as much more than a pale slip of a child, with masses of hair and a gentle way about her. Harriet had told him she was widowed; he wondered what else the years had made of her.

He enjoyed the walk from Henry's offices near Quincy Market to the Moores' elegant row house on Tremont Street. Rupert didn't miss the new shops opening in this prospering section of the city, including a purveyor of pianos that claimed to produce four thousand of the instruments in one year, as well as a gourmet food shop, S.S. Pierce, apparently the first in Boston.

'I'd no idea Boston residents required so many pianos,' Rupert told Margaret with a twinkle as he entered their drawing room, divested of his hat and top coat.

'Of course they do,' Margaret replied without missing a beat, her cheek pressed to his for an instant. 'It's a sign of prosperity, no doubt.' She looked, as always, elegant and refined without any of the excess frippery so many of the wealthy society women favoured. Her dress was rose silk, the hem flounced a good six inches, not the two or more feet most society women preferred, and her waist was cinched tightly with a belt in deeper rose.

'Indeed.' Rupert gazed out at the purple-hued skies meditatively, his mind turning once more to the pianos he'd seen and the prosperity they indicated. 'Indeed.'

A few minutes later Ian and Eleanor Crombie were admitted to the drawing room. Rupert pumped Ian's hand enthusiastically. Ian had grown up to look quite distinguished, he thought. Tall and thin, with auburn hair and vivid green eyes like Harriet, he was dressed in an excellently cut tail coat with the points of his collar nearly brushing his cheekbones.

Rupert immediately felt every inch the country boy he was in his ill-fitting frock coat and modest collar. There was no need for such fine clothes on the island, and he'd only managed to buy one new suit on his modest salary.

Ian looked preoccupied and drawn, and Rupert wondered if one of his cases at the hospital were troubling him.

He turned to Eleanor, who had been no more than a dreamy child when he'd left. The woman in her place bore little resemblance to the placid-natured girl he remembered.

Eleanor stood by the drawing-room door, her hair caught into a neat bun and covered with a modest cap, making her look older than her years. Her green brocade dress was plain, the sleeves not nearly as full as fashion required, although the belt cinched at her waist showed it to be admirably trim. Her brown eyes were alert with interest, yet her hands were folded modestly over her middle.

Caught between matron and maid, Rupert thought immediately. And who could blame her, a widow at twenty-three years of age?

Henry came in to greet his guests, and soon they were all being shepherded to the dining room for an elaborate meal.

'This is an up-and-coming neighbourhood,' Rupert remarked as he started on his pigeon pie. 'The homes look quite elegant.'

'Yes, the South End has quite a bit of promise,' Henry replied. 'The South Cove Company has plans to fill in some of the bay and extend this area by seventy acres.'

'Indeed.'

Margaret chuckled. 'You look so thoughtful, Rupert! What are your plans?'

'Well, since you ask . . .' Rupert put his fork down, his expression serious. 'It seems to me that all the opportunity is in this country. Admittedly England and other parts of Europe are looking to the East for expansion and trade, but as Americans I think we should look to the West.'

'You've been here a week and you consider yourself an American?' Eleanor asked, her expression dubious and a bit scornful.

Rupert met her gaze directly, surprised by the hungry interest flickering in her hazel eyes, before it was quickly cloaked by a veil of civility.

'I certainly do. America is a young country, and after the Revolution —'

'Don't you mean the Rebellion?' Henry interjected drily, but Rupert shook his head.

'Revolution,' he said firmly. 'I told you, I'm an American now. As I was saying, America is poised to expand. They weren't able to before because of the war for independence, and then the second war with

England, but now they're prime.'

'Prime for what?' Eleanor now looked curious, as if Rupert were some kind of unusual specimen she was studying. Rupert felt a prickle of irritation, even though he was gratified by her interest.

'Prime for new business opportunities, and expansion. If you read the papers . . .' he gave a little cough. 'Excuse me, I'm behaving terribly to control the conversation in such a way. And I know well that ladies of breeding aren't meant to read newspapers!'

'Oh, really?' Margaret, leaning back in her seat, looked amused. 'Not in this house, I'm afraid. We all read the papers, and quite avidly.' Rupert ducked his head, and she chuckled, waving to him to continue. 'Go on, Rupert. You've caught my interest.'

Rupert resisted the urge to tug at his collar. He was certain of his ideas; on fire for his beliefs and yet . . . despite the old acquaintance of everyone in the room, they were little more than strangers. He barely knew Henry at all, and he hadn't seen the others since he was little more than a child. His heart beat with anxiety and excitement; he saw Eleanor looking at him again with that peculiar expression on her face, interest and even need masked by diffidence.

'Well, since you read the papers,' he continued after a moment, 'you'll see loads of companies springing up everywhere. There are plans to build canals, mills, even railroads.'

'Railroads!' Eleanor was thunderstruck. She leaned forward, and Rupert noticed how interest made her cheeks glow, her eyes sparkle. 'Engines are so noisy and smelly from what I've heard, not to mention dangerous. Surely it won't catch on.'

'I think there will be a railroad from one end of this country to the other, before fifty years are out,' Rupert declared. 'Perhaps no more than twenty. You'll be able to travel from the Atlantic to the Pacific, all from the comfort of a train!'

'Oh, Rupert, that must be nonsense,' Margaret protested. 'Settlers have been in America for two hundred years, and nothing like that has happened. Most of the country is wild, and filled with Indians.'

'The Indians are being removed,' Henry said quietly. 'A tragedy in itself, but the Black Hawk war has opened up the Illinois territory to us.'

'Where do the Indians go?' Eleanor asked, her brow wrinkled, and Henry shrugged.

'Reservations mostly. Wherever they can. Many die under the conditions.'

'And that's the price of expansion?' Eleanor said in a thoughtful, quiet voice. Rupert's prickle of irritation intensified.

'There always has to be a price,' he said and Eleanor looked at him sharply.

'As long as you don't pay it!'

'You can't tell me you care for the Indians,' Rupert persisted. 'You've never even met one, and if you saw one, you'd think it savage.'

'Oh, would I?' She raised one eyebrow, a quiet challenge.

Rupert shifted uncomfortably. 'I only meant you are new to this country.'

'As are you,' Eleanor returned. 'Newer than I by a fortnight, or so I recall? Yet you seem to have formed your own strong opinions. Allow me the same liberty.'

'Bravo, Eleanor!' Margaret clapped her hands lightly, amused as always by debate of any kind. 'You must not discount Eleanor's wisdom, Rupert. She's been an observer for most of her life; she has much to offer us.'

Rupert knew Margaret meant it as a compliment, but by the way Eleanor flushed and looked down at her plate he knew she regarded it as a slight. *An observer of life.* He put that thought in the back of his mind, to be taken out later and examined at leisure.

'Let us not argue about Indians,' he said smoothly. 'Surely there is enough interesting discussion without resorting to unpleasant debates.'

'Tell us about the railroads, then, Rupert,' Margaret said.

'There are already plans to build a railroad to Chicago, a small settlement in the Illinois territory Henry mentioned. And that's just the beginning.'

'It surely couldn't be true,' Eleanor said dubiously, her eyes raised briefly from her plate.

Rupert subjected her to a penetrating stare. 'Are you saying that because you can't believe it, or because you merely don't *want* to believe it?'

Eleanor bristled. 'What are you implying?'

'Many people are afraid of change.' Rupert spoke quietly, even gently. He realized he was afraid of hurting her, and yet he couldn't let her words go unchallenged.

A shadow flickered in Eleanor's eyes. 'I'm not,' she said after a moment. 'As long as it doesn't impinge on comfort.'

Rupert chuckled. 'Change will always do that, I'm afraid. But if Henry will let me, I'd be happy to look into investments . . .

not abroad, but in this country.'

'You might have me persuaded,' Henry said affably. 'In time. But surely that is enough business talk over the dinner table. Margaret, have you told Eleanor your plans for a charity school?'

Eleanor's eyes lit with interest. 'Charity school?'

'Something small,' Margaret demurred, 'to alleviate the orphan problem.'

Rupert sat back in his chair, watching Eleanor as Margaret explained her school plans. Animated as she was now, she looked quite pretty. He wondered why she resented change, when she'd obviously embraced it in her own life. Marrying a soldier, moving to Glasgow, and then travelling unchaperoned to the new world . . . He would've thought she had a more adventurous nature, but perhaps it was well hidden.

He felt a pang of regret for goading her. He was an evangelist for opportunity, he knew, and he would need to use more tact and grace to convince people of his plans . . . his dreams.

His gaze moved to Ian, who was gazing moodily into his wine glass. The man was obviously troubled, and Rupert wondered why. From all accounts Ian had made a success of his new life. Why then, did he look as if he carried the world on his shoulders?

'Perhaps you and Henry can come with us to look for suitable premises,' Margaret said, bringing Rupert back into the conversation.

'That would be delightful,' Rupert said. He glanced again at Eleanor, and saw her look quickly away. He looked forward to getting to know her, he realized, and understanding the puzzle she seemed to present.

Allan glanced at his full barn in satisfaction. The hay and barley were harvested, and their farmhouse fairly burst with the fruits of the summer: ropes of onions, fat hams, and barrels of dried apples, salt and flour. Enough to last them the winter, he thought with thankfulness, for although it was only the end of September there was a chill in the air, and dawn had already shown a blanket of silver frost on the ground.

Harriet wrapped her shawl around her shoulders, joining Allan by the barn. 'A good summer,' she said quietly. 'We should do well this winter, I hope.'

'As do I.' Allan turned to embrace her lightly. 'I'd planned to travel to the mainland before the waters freeze up. There might be letters, and I could do with a few bits and pieces. We're low on nails, for a start.'

‘Of course. Perhaps Rupert will have time to write us, now he’s settled.’ Harriet was pensive. Rupert had left after the wheat had been gathered in, taking a ship from Charlottetown to Boston. It was considered a short and safe journey these days, which amazed her when she thought of her own harrowing crossing eleven years ago.

‘I thought we should visit Mingarry before winter sets in,’ Allan continued, breaking into Harriet’s thoughts. ‘Mother’s been so poorly this last winter, I have a care for her for the next.’

‘Of course,’ Harriet murmured. ‘I know Rupert’s leaving took them hard.’

‘Yes, Father especially.’ Allan sighed. ‘All of his sons found their calling elsewhere. I can’t help but feel that has been a sore disappointment to him.’

‘You came back,’ Harriet reminded him. ‘And have been a credit to him for ten years, Allan MacDougall. There’s no need for regrets, not now.’

‘I suppose not. It will be good to see them, though. There can be no mistaking they are getting older, as we all are, and who knows how many more years Providence will grant them, or us.’

Harriet shivered as the evening breeze picked up. ‘Many, I trust. And I’d like to see your parents as well.'

'Then it's settled.' Allan smiled. 'As soon as we can make ready.'

The next few days were taken up with preparations for travel, as well as continuing to ready for winter. When Maggie and George learned they were to spend a few days at Mingarry Farm, they were delighted, and seemed to spend even more time asking endless questions and getting underfoot.

'Will Uncle Rupert be there?' George asked eagerly, and Harriet shook her head.

'No, you know I told you Rupert has gone to Boston.'

'Boston?' George looked at her in confusion, and Harriet well knew how bewildering it was. Who would have ever thought, their family scattered to the corners of the earth in such a fashion? Her hands stilled over the bread dough she was kneading as she was assailed with a sudden, fierce pang of longing . . . longing for her family to be together, safe, under one roof. The desire was replaced by sorrow as she realized how unlikely that was to ever happen.

'Mamma, there's a man coming from the river!' Maggie announced from the window. 'And he's got such a long face!'

Harriet turned from her work to look outside. 'It's John McPhee,' she said, worry sharpening her tone. 'Your grandparents' hired man.' She frowned, drying her hands on her apron, and hurried outside.

John McPhee climbed up from the river, the colour of pewter in the cold, overcast day, his face as grim as the sky above him.

'John, is something wrong at Mingarry?' she called. 'We've just been planning a visit there, before the cold weather comes.'

John nodded gravely. 'Aye, it's bad news, I'm afraid, Mistress MacDougall. Mr MacDougall's taken poorly these last few days, and is laid up in bed.'

Harriet's fingers clenched around the fringes of her shawl. 'How poorly?'

John looked even more serious. 'The mistress asked me to fetch you at once, for we don't know how long he'll hang on.'

'Hang on?' Harriet repeated numbly. She saw Allan come round the house from the barn, his boots muddy and his expression one of alarm as he saw John.

'It's Father, isn't it?' he asked quietly as he drew up to them, and Harriet could only nod.

Allan's expression hardened and he nodded once, firmly, in decision. 'I'll get the horses ready. We'll come at once.'

Chapter Seven

Harriet pulled her shawl tighter across her shoulders as she clung to the seat of the wagon. It was raining steadily, the roads turned to muddy ruts.

The journey from their own farm to Mingarry usually only took an hour, and yet in this weather Harriet knew it could take twice or even three times that. She suppressed a sigh, drawing a fractious Anna closer to her. 'Hush, little one. Hush.' She glanced at Allan, the rain dripping from the brim of his hat, his hands tight on the reins, his face grim, as it had been since John McPhee had brought the news of his father's illness.

Harriet put a hand on Allan's sleeve, and he gave a small smile, reaching over to pat her hand with his own. She watched the rain sluice over their intertwined fingers, chilling them to the colour of bone. Her fingers curled and tightened instinctively. 'It will be all right.'

Allan sighed heavily. 'I pray so.'

'Mamma? Are we there yet?' George and Maggie's pale, anxious faces peered from behind.

'Soon, darlings, soon.' Harriet silently prayed that the rain would not give them a chill and create even more illness. Travel in this weather was dangerous for anyone. She wondered inwardly if the journey was worth such a price, but Allan would not be dissuaded.

'He needs me,' he'd argued, his voice low but firm. 'John wouldn't have come if Father wasn't truly ill. If you don't want to travel in the rain, I'll go alone.'

And leave her to travel by herself, with three children? She held little hope that Allan would return once he'd arrived at Mingarry. The needs of his parents would keep him busy, Harriet acknowledged silently, they would come first. 'Nonsense. A little rain won't hurt us. We'll stay together.'

'Look, Mamma, Mingarry!' Maggie pointed at the clump of birches, their leaves now a deep gold, that marked the beginning of the older MacDougalls' property. Harriet murmured a prayer of thanks.

It was another half hour before they actually reached the farmhouse, sodden and shivering. The house was dark, strangely lifeless, and Harriet felt a chill of foreboding that had nothing to do with the freezing rain. 'There's no smoke from the chimney.' The words came out before Harriet could stop them, and with a muffled oath Allan swung down from the wagon.

Harriet gathered the children together, Anna pressed close to her chest, and followed her husband up the steps to the wide front porch.

Inside the house was dark, the damp penetrating even to the hearth. Harriet glanced quickly for signs of life, but the grate held nothing but dead ashes and it looked as if no food had been prepared for some time.

'Mother.' Allan started forward as Betty emerged from the bedroom, a shawl draped over her stooped shoulders, her mob cap askew on her thin, white hair.

'Oh, Allan, thank Providence you've come.' Betty leaned into her son as he put his arms around her.

'How is Father?'

'He fell yesterday morning, while out in the barn. I didn't see it happen, of course, but John came running in. He's been in bed since, but he hasn't stirred or even had a bit of broth to drink.' She glanced helplessly around the cold, dark room. 'I fell asleep . . .'

'It's all right, Mother.' Harriet tried to smile reassuringly even as her heart sank. It was much worse than either of them had feared. Quickly she settled Anna in a fleece-lined basket, set George to gathering firewood, and Maggie to washing the few crusted dishes left forgotten in a basin of dirty water.

While Allan tended to his parents, she would have to deal with the practicalities of life. She accepted it with a determined pragmatism; busy hands meant less time to think, to worry.

Within an hour there was a cheerful fire, a pot of stew with dried meat and root vegetables simmering over the flames, and the water barrel had been refilled.

Maggie leaned into Harriet's side, her hand bunched in her skirt like a much smaller child. Harriet put a comforting hand on the girl's shoulder. It was disconcerting to her, she knew, to arrive at a Mingarry changed beyond all recognition. The last time they'd been here, it was spring; the windows had been thrown open to the warm air, fragrant with lilac, and Sandy had played his fiddle. Maggie had lifted up her skirts and danced, Harriet had as well, and Betty had tapped her foot to the music, her fingers busy knitting a gown for little Anna. How horribly different this dark, dank place was, smelling of sickness. Harriet gave Maggie a little nudge. 'George has found the box of spillikins, there by the fire. Go have a game before supper.'

Maggie went dutifully enough, although once the little sticks were spilled out, she involved herself in the game, and Harriet tended to Anna, her troubled thoughts still at bay.

Allan returned from the bedroom, where he'd settled Betty and looked in on his father, and glanced in approval at the changes. 'Thank you, Harriet. It's good to see it as it was. As it should be.'

She shrugged his words aside. 'How is your father?'

'He doesn't stir. If his chest didn't rise and fall with breath, I'd think him dead.' Allan sat at the table, wearily running a hand through his hair. 'Mother's taken it hard, as I'm sure you can see. I didn't realize how frail she'd become. She's not capable of the household chores, and the girl who was helping with the heavy work left a fortnight ago to marry a lad from Charlottetown. I didn't even know.'

Harriet pressed her lips together and silently served Allan a bowl of stew and tankard of ale. Maggie and George left their game of spillikins by the fire, subdued by the prevailing mood of the house, and joined them at the table.

It was only after supper, when the children were asleep in the spare bedroom, that Harriet and Allan were able to resume their conversation.

'What shall we do?' Harriet asked quietly. She'd found the mending basket and started on it with resolute determination. Allan gazed bleakly into the fire.

'I can't see there is much choice. Mother and Father can't cope on their own, and there's no one to help.'

Harriet focused on threading her needle. She didn't want to see the despair in Allan's eyes which she knew would be mirrored in her own. 'They could hire someone to help in the house. And John in the fields. . . .'

'John can't labour by himself.' Allan paused, and Harriet glanced up, almost recoiling at the anguish in his eyes. 'Harriet, I can't leave them now, not like this. It wouldn't be right.'

'I know.' It didn't need saying, she knew, for the decision had been made the moment they'd crossed the threshold and seen the empty fireplace, the bare shelves. They would stay and help.

'What shall we do with our own holding?' Harriet asked. 'The house?' She thought briefly of the comfortable house they'd left, snug and ready for winter.

'I'll go back tomorrow and get the things we need. I can close up the house, and the fields will lie fallow. It might be good for the land, for a year.'

Or more, Harriet added silently. How long would they be here, away from their own lives?

'John can come with me, help bring our livestock over here.' He touched her hand briefly. 'It might only be for a little while . . . the winter, which is lonely as it is. You'll be glad of the company.'

'Yes.' Harriet resumed sewing, not trusting herself to say more. She knew Allan felt guilty for the time he'd spent away from his family, pursuing his own dream. No amount of faithful service afterwards would erase that guilt. She also knew that Sandy was not going to get better with any haste. If they left in spring, it would be because he'd passed on, and she couldn't wish that. Not now, not yet. She raised her eyes and smiled at Allan. 'It will be all right.'

He nodded, managing a small smile back. 'I pray so,' he said. 'It's the least I can do, after . . .' he trailed off, shaking his head.

'I know, Allan,' Harriet replied softly. 'I know.'

Caroline smiled in satisfaction at the sight of at least a dozen boxes neatly piled by the door of the modiste's. She'd spent an agreeable morning charging an outrageous sum to her uncle's account, and there would be two new evening dresses, as well as three day gowns, to collect in a fortnight's time. Meanwhile, she was able to take home no small number of gloves, hats, handkerchiefs, spangles, and other fripperies she'd firmly decided she could not do without.

'Why don't you put these in the carriage, Jackson,' she said airily, 'while I take a turn about the park?'

Jackson, her uncle's hired driver, shuffled his feet in obvious reluctance. Caroline knew she had succeeded in charming him with a few well-placed winning smiles and demure looks, but it didn't keep him from doggedly going about his duty. 'I hardly think it is fitting for a female such as yourself,' he stammered. 'Ladies in Boston don't walk by themselves.'

'Oh, but surely this is an agreeable place for ladies?' Caroline enquired with an air of innocence. 'The houses seem quite pleasant, and I'm certain I saw a few ladies taking the air.'

Jackson mumbled something unintelligible, and Caroline smiled in implicit acceptance. 'I'll be back shortly.'

Before he could offer any more objections, she left the shop, snapped open her parasol, and walked briskly down the street. She longed for a moment's freedom, away from her uncle's servants who often seemed like her gaolers.

Taking a deep breath, she looked around the fashionable neighbourhood. She was charmed by the row of town houses, the neat front gardens and wrought-iron fences, and the general air of genteel prosperity.

There were some ladies strolling down the pleasant, tree-lined street, but Caroline noted they were accompanied by matrons, governesses, or other suitable chaperones. A few of them glanced her way with speculative interest, for while it was clear she was a young woman of some quality, they no doubt wondered at her boldness in strolling unaccompanied.

She sighed inwardly. Although it was perfectly proper for her to reside in her uncle's house, a surly housekeeper and taciturn butler were hardly respectable companions for a girl intent on making an advantageous alliance.

A sudden feeling of disquiet infringed on her earlier sunny thoughts. Although her uncle resided in an affluent part of Boston, and was clearly invited to some respectable occasions, Caroline could not help but feel there was something amiss in the house — and society — he kept. She thought briefly of the dinner party to which he'd escorted her a week ago, with the promise of charming company. Charming indeed!

The evening had been a sore disappointment. The party had consisted of herself, her uncle, the odious Dearborn she'd met back at Lanymoor, and his rather foppish son whom even she found insipid.

Uncle Edward had ordered a private table at one of Boston's finer establishments, and Caroline had endured Frederick Dearborn slobbering over her extended hand — thank goodness she had worn evening gloves! — and his inane and irritatingly adoring chatter.

More bothersome than Frederick's attentions, however, were those of his father's. Never overt or overbearing, Matthew Dearborn still managed to convey an intensity of interest which left Caroline queasy and uncomfortable. She often felt his eyes resting on her, and felt as if she were mentally being devoured. The elder Dearborn did not address her once the entire evening, which somehow made it worse. It was as if, she thought later, she were of no consequence because he had already decided what to do with her.

Which was ridiculous, because Caroline intended to have nothing to do with either of the Dearborns. She'd made as much clear to her uncle in their carriage on the way home.

'If that is your idea of a treat, Uncle, you are sorely mistaken in what you think pleases me.'

Edward, preoccupied and brooding, barely glanced at her. 'What pleases me should please you, Caroline.'

'Well, it does not!' After several hours of the unendurable company, she could not help but be pettish. 'Do you think to propose a match with Frederick Dearborn? Because I will not have him. I do not care how rich he is.'

Her uncle merely raised his eyebrows. 'Have a care, Niece. Your dowry is modest and you are unknown in this country. You should treat any offers you receive with due consideration and sobriety.'

'I won't marry him,' she repeated shrilly, her hands clenched into fists.

Edward laughed drily. 'Never fear. I won't

have you wasted on that dandified character. His brains do not reside in his head, of that I assure you.' He resumed his moody staring out of the carriage window, and Caroline was left feeling that the conversation had been concluded most unsatisfactorily.

'Caroline! That is, Miss Campbell.' Caroline whirled around, a smile lighting her features as she saw Ian Crombie behind her, his hat in his hands, looking handsome as well as delightfully uncertain.

'Mr Crombie! I am surprised to see you here. Do you reside in this part of town?'

'No, but my sister-in-law does. I was visiting her. And you?'

'I was at the modiste's,' Caroline admitted with a little smile, her head cocked to one side. She saw Ian's gaze sweep her form with appreciation, and then he flushed and looked down in obvious embarrassment.

'A delightful occupation of one's time, I am sure,' he said after a moment. He paused, the blush that stole across his cheeks making the freckles on his nose stand out. 'I wanted to apologize, Miss Campbell, for my conduct towards your uncle the other evening, at the musicale.'

Caroline wrinkled her nose and said pertly, 'Then perhaps you should make your apologies to him.' She did not want to discuss her uncle, even if it provided a possible avenue for flirtation.

Something in Ian's face hardened. 'I am afraid that is quite out of the question. However, I did not mean to subject a lady of your sensibility to such a scene, and for that I am indeed contrite.'

Caroline's hands tightened on the handle of her parasol. She felt torn between her desire to be pleasing and gay, and the confidences of her uncle, which had tried her sorely. 'I'm not sure I should accept such an apology,' she said quietly. 'Considering the offence given to my uncle.'

'He's regaled you with his side of the story, I see.'

'He has explained things.'

'Then you know he swindled me out of my family's home, as well as my own inheritance,' Ian said, bitterness spilling forth and spiking his words.

Caroline thought of her uncle's explanations. 'You signed the contract,' she said, her voice strangely whispery. 'That's hardly a swindle!'

Ian shook his head. 'I should've known you would take his side. What recourse could you possibly have? I only wanted to apologize for my conduct, that is all.' He sketched a bow and turned to leave.

Caroline found herself taking a step forward, involuntarily, and her parasol clattered to the paving stones.

With a little, ironic smile, Ian picked it up and handed it to her.

'Thank you.' Caroline stumbled over the simple words. 'I don't mean to offend you,' she blurted. 'You're angry. I didn't want that.' She felt as gauche as a country maid. She'd wanted to flirt with Ian Crombie, entice him a bit, but she realized what a foolish desire that was. The feud between Ian and her uncle was long and deep; a few moments of trifling conversation would not heal the still-open wounds of long ago.

'I'm not angry at you,' Ian said. 'Only with a feud that has not let me go these last ten years. You're right, Miss Campbell. I signed that contract. I was a boy intent on being a man. I wanted to handle affairs quickly, and be done with it.' He paused to draw in a long, ragged breath. 'Good day to you.'

Caroline watched him leave, the dejected set of his shoulders making her want to cry out, ask him to explain. She stiffened her own stance. It was better this way. If Ian Crombie was a penniless doctor *and* intent on marrying Isobel Moore, they had no business conducting this conversation in the first place.

■ ■ ■ ■

Eleanor had not realized how Boston was growing. It was, she thought as she surveyed the newly built Quincy Market, a city under construction. The market was an elegantly proportioned structure of granite and brick, with a domed roof. A few years ago the place where it now stood had been the centre of Boston harbour; workers had filled in the harbour to allow Boston to grow, and now the market was a busy, colourful place, full of food stalls and the sounds of barter and trade, over which could be heard the mournful lowing of cattle being led to slaughter.

Even Beacon Hill, the land where the most prosperous homes were located, was being transformed. Henry had informed her that builders were taking the dirt from the hill to fill in Back Bay, an area of water adjacent to the Moores' neighbourhood.

'So the lofty souls who look down their noses at us from the hill will be lowered?' Eleanor said with a little chuckle, and Henry nodded, eyes twinkling.

'Exactly so.'

'Eleanor,' Margaret interjected, laughing as well. 'You do know Henry's family live on Beacon Hill?'

Eleanor's hand flew to her mouth as her eyes widened. 'Oh! No, I'm sorry!'

Henry joined in the laughter. 'Nonsense. They approve of the scheme, I assure you.'

'The city is growing,' Margaret continued Eleanor's train of thought, 'because of the population increase. There are more and more immigrant ships coming in to port every day.'

'And more business,' Henry added. He gestured to the Quincy Market. 'This market built, and six new streets besides, all filled with new business! It makes me thankful I started when I did.' Henry looked up and smiled. 'Ah, Rupert's here. I told him he could take the afternoon off work to help us look for your school premises.'

Eleanor found her insides experiencing a strange tightening as she saw Rupert enter the Moores' drawing-room. He wore his usual dusty frock coat and rather worn hat, and his hair was still as unruly as a farmer's. Yet, Eleanor was forced to admit, there was something vital and exciting about Rupert, about the jauntiness of his step and the quickness of his smile, the way his eyes lit up when he spoke. She wished she could feel that interested — that passionate — about, well, *anything.*

'He's as new to the city as I am,' Eleanor found herself blurting out. 'What could he know about a suitable place for a school?'

Henry glanced at Eleanor, his eyes bright with speculation, and she blushed. 'Rupert has a good eye for things, and he is Margaret's brother. I trust you don't object?'

'No, of course not,' Eleanor mumbled.

'Eleanor's just put out because Rupert ruffled her feathers the other evening,' Margaret said with a mischievous grin.

'That's absurd . . .' Before Eleanor could continue, Rupert approached, interrupting.

'Me? Ruffled whose feathers?' He kissed Margaret and shook hands with Henry, bowing slightly to Eleanor in acknowledgement.

'Eleanor's, of course. You were teasing her mercilessly about the Indians.'

'Teasing, was I?' Rupert shot an inquisitive glance at Eleanor, who was looking pointedly in the other direction. She felt her face flame and her gloves were damp as she clutched her reticule.

'I thought we were merely having an intelligent discussion.' Eleanor glanced quickly at him, thinking he meant to tease her once more, but he looked quite serious.

'Is there a difference?' Henry joked, and the conversation moved on to suitable premises for Margaret's charity school. Henry suggested they take his carriage to a building that was for rent near the wharves in the North End.

'Is that a safe area?' Rupert asked, and Henry smiled grimly.

'Not at all. The block nearest the harbour is called the Murder District. You can't even get a policeman to go there.'

'And you're sending your wife?' Rupert was incredulous.

Henry glanced wryly at Margaret. 'I don't really think I have much choice. But I don't intend to have her or Eleanor ever go alone — our driver is a burly man in possession of a trustworthy flintlock.'

'Still . . .'

'The proposed site of the school is several blocks away from this Murder District,' Margaret interjected with a smile. 'I'm sure it's perfectly safe if not precisely respectable. A Mr Edward Taylor, a Methodist minister, has established a seaman's mission in North Square, near the building.'

'Why not have the school closer to your home?' Eleanor asked. 'Surely it would be safer as well as more convenient.'

'You couldn't place a charity school on Beacon Hill, or even in the South End,' Henry said quietly. 'There'd be far too much fuss.'

Eleanor flushed, embarrassed that she hadn't realized something so obvious. 'That's not fair,' she protested all the same.

'No, it isn't, but you'd find the pupils wouldn't come either. It isn't just the wealthy who want to be off on their own.'

They soon all climbed into Henry's smart black carriage, Rupert taking Eleanor's elbow as he helped her up. She wanted to jerk away — even more so when he sat next to her, his knee practically touching hers. It was terribly inappropriate and she sat there stiffly while he grinned, his eyes twinkling knowingly.

'It's a bit close in here, isn't it?'

'Yes,' Eleanor agreed tersely. She saw Margaret give her a speculative look from under her lashes, and she straightened, her hands clasped tightly in her lap, and looked out the window.

I'm acting like Henrietta McCardell. The thought and image of her fussy mother-in-law gave Eleanor a jolt. She'd never considered herself to be prim and proper, and yet her behaviour towards Rupert was like that of an old spinster.

I *feel* like an old spinster, she thought. She couldn't remember John any more, couldn't remember how it felt to be loved.

Held, touched. Desired. And every time she looked at Rupert, saw him looking back at her with that quiet, knowing smile, as if he could guess her every thought, the hot tangle of emotions within her seemed to threaten to spill over into — what?

Eleanor didn't want to find out.

The carriage rolled to a stop, and Eleanor saw that they were in the North End neighbourhood. The tang of salt water was in the air, and gulls shrieked overhead. The buildings were a mixture of large brick warehouses and dilapidated row houses, the cobblestone streets going without repair and refuse piling in the corners.

It seemed hard to believe that the shining new Quincy Market bordered one end of this neighbourhood, and in the heart of it stood the new North Congregational Society church, designed by the celebrated architect Charles Bulfinch, with its bell cast and hung by Paul Revere himself.

It was, Eleanor considered, as if Boston was growing new and old at the same time.

Henry took Margaret's arm as they walked down the pavement, the street bustling with carriages and wagons full of merchandise headed for the market place, from country produce to sacks of fine cotton, brought from Lowell and other mill towns that were fast springing up all over the state.

It fell naturally to Rupert to take Eleanor's arm, and she accepted reluctantly. 'We haven't seen each other in a decade, Eleanor, and yet we're almost family. Is there a reason you're uncomfortable with me?' Rupert asked quietly, after Henry and Margaret had walked a bit ahead. 'I trust you don't dislike me?'

'No, of course not. How could I? I barely know you.' Eleanor looked away, pretending to study a woman selling apples on the street corner. The obvious hunger and despair in her eyes made Eleanor turn away uncomfortably.

An urchin darted out but Rupert stepped smartly between her and the ragged little child, and he darted off again.

'A pickpocket,' he explained, then took a coin from his pocket. He gave it to the old woman and then gallantly presented Eleanor with an apple, polishing it first on his coat.

'I didn't want . . .' she began, but then shrugged and took it, her fingers clasping around its smooth surface. 'Thank you.'

'Is it so hard to accept a gift, even a modest one like an apple?'

'Of course not.'

'Then why are you so prickly?'

'I'm . . .' Eleanor stopped. She was being ungracious, and she didn't even know why. Rupert was so full of life, buzzing with ideas and energy. It scared her, yet she could hardly tell him that. 'I'm tired from my sea journey still,' she finally said, which was true. 'It was very taxing.'

'Yes, I heard from Margaret how you had to nurse the other passengers. Very admirable of you.'

'I know you would have done the same,' Eleanor responded with a dismissive shrug.

'Thank you.' Rupert's eyes sparkled with humour.

Eleanor managed a small smile. 'This city feels very new,' she said after a moment. 'Growing old before it's even properly begun! I know it has history, from America's colonial days, and of course the Rebellion. And yet . . . there's so much life here.'

Rupert's hand squeezed her elbow, his expression intense. 'I know. I feel it as well. There's opportunity here, far more than there ever was in Scotland, or even Prince Edward Island, where the only chance a man had was to clear a forest and build a cabin, farm a few fields that could be gone after one bad harvest. Here . . .' Rupert spread one arm towards the street with its broken cobbles, the market place, the harbour sparkling in the distance. He turned suddenly to Eleanor, smiling at her in a way that made her heart lurch. 'I'm going to make my fortune here, Eleanor. I know it.'

Looking into his determined face, Eleanor had to agree with him. And yet it made her wonder about her own ambition, or lack thereof. Rupert might be set to make his way in this new world, but what about her? What was she going to do?

'Ether, you say?' Dr Collins looked dubious. 'I've heard rumours, of course . . .' He shook his head. 'We've used ether to treat pulmonary inflammation, but during surgery? It's questionable, lad. Questionable indeed.'

Ian bit down on his frustration. Sharp retorts were no way to convince his superior of the need for hospital research into the use of ether. 'Dr Wells of Hartford, Connecticut has been experimenting with the use of ether for several years,' he told Dr Collins patiently. He shifted uncomfortably in the hard wooden chair, struggling not to lean forward in eagerness. 'It has proved quite successful. I've received —'

'With small animals, yes, I know. But a full-grown man? Dr Crombie, the risk is simply too great.'

'What risk?'

'The risk,' Dr Collins snapped, 'of injury, even death, from the use of a questionable substance!'

Ian strove to maintain his calm. This topic was too important, and too close to his heart, to forsake it for the satisfaction of a quick rejoinder. 'Surely such a risk is much smaller than the surgery itself? With an anaesthetic in use, there would be no need to hurry, perhaps make mistakes . . .'

Dr Collins drew himself up, indignant. 'Speed is the hallmark of a good surgeon. In and out, my boy, in and out. Why, Dr Jackson says he can remove a tumour in less than two minutes.'

'Ninety seconds,' Ian replied wearily. 'And the patient usually bleeds to death anyway.' He'd spent too much time at Massachusetts General Hospital to be unaware of this attitude.

Yet how many people died because surgeons were in such a rush, and became clumsy? To voice that concern was tantamount to slapping a surgeon in the face, and Ian valued his position too much to issue a direct challenge.

Dr Collins must have sensed his mood for he smiled stiffly and said, 'We took you on the hospital staff on the recommendation of

Stephen Moore, a colleague and friend. So far you've proved yourself capable. However . . .' Dr Collins trailed off delicately, and Ian froze.

'However?' he repeated coolly, and his superior shrugged.

'You are not irreplaceable, Crombie. You're young and rash and while we appreciate what you do for this hospital, realize it can very well tick over without you.'

Ian felt cold. He knew this was as close to a threat as the elegant Dr Collins would come to, and he accepted it with as much good grace as he could muster. 'I understand, sir.'

Just in case he didn't, Dr Collins added, 'Let us have no more talk of ether, in the hospital or out of it. Keep on with what you are doing, and forget these newfangled notions. They can only turn your head, to no purpose.'

Ian nodded stiffly in acceptance, if not agreement. He thought of his fleeting dreams of being funded for research, perhaps being the first doctor to actually perform a surgery with ether.

Now his dreams were already ash. He'd spoken too soon.

He was thankful he'd not mentioned to Dr Collins his proposed visit to Dr Wells in

Hartford. He'd written to the dentist several weeks earlier, and had received a reply in the affirmative only today.

He slipped his hand in his coat pocket and felt the comfortable crackle of parchment. The letter, he'd hoped, would be evidence in support of his research. Now he knew it would just condemn him. The doctors of Massachusetts General Hospital were not ready for change.

'Good day to you, Dr Crombie.'

Ian stood up, taking his hat and sketching a slight bow. 'Good day.'

Ian let himself out of the hospital. Twilight, purple and velvety soft, was settling on the common and he stopped for a moment to enjoy the peaceful scene. He knew there was a stage coach leaving Boston for Hartford every other day. At the next opportunity, he planned to be on it.

His frustration with Dr Collins abated for a moment, only to be quickly replaced by other concerns. Isobel. He was due at the Moores' for supper the following evening, and then afterwards he was meant to escort Isobel to a party. He'd fallen in with the plans without completely being aware of them, and now he felt a twinge of apprehension.

There could be no mistaking the glimmer

of intent in Stephen Moore's eye, or Isobel's, for that matter. Yet why should it disconcert him so? Isobel would make a fine wife. She was honest and affectionate, they enjoyed an affable friendship. And she was certainly beautiful.

Yet still . . . for a moment Caroline's laughing face came into his mind's eye, and he nearly started in surprise. Caroline Campbell was spoiled, childish, charming. Even worse, she didn't believe her uncle was to blame for the Crombies' loss of Achlic Farm eleven years ago. Just her relationship to Rydell was enough to cool their brief acquaintance. 'Hardly suitable,' Ian muttered to himself as he hurried across the darkening park. 'Hardly suitable at all.'

The party Ian was escorting Isobel to was at another home on Beacon Hill, a handsome town house ablaze with lights, its windows thrown open to admit the balmy air of early autumn.

Even from the pavement they could hear the sound of the quartet hired to play the waltzes, and the accompanying tinkle of laughter and clink of crystal.

Isobel alighted from the carriage, smoothing the silk of her evening gown. 'According to Monsieur de Tocqueville, Boston ladies are every bit as fashionable as those in

Paris,' she said with an air of satisfaction. 'He was particularly impressed with our command of the French language, and said our taste in music was far better than the ladies of New York.'

'Indeed?' Ian had already heard about Alexis de Tocqueville, the Frenchman who was currently travelling around America to learn about democracy. Considering the recent political upheaval in France, he thought, it was most likely a wise decision to absent himself from the country.

While the men of Boston had been eager to discuss politics and trade, the ladies nearly swooned to the side of the handsome young Frenchman. It appeared Isobel was no different.

'You've been so involved at the hospital,' Isobel continued with faint reproach, 'that you haven't even met him. Perhaps he'll be here tonight. He's only in Boston for a few more weeks, and he's been in attendance at all the best parties.'

Once inside the town house, Ian and Isobel were swept into the festivities. Isobel was soon gossiping with other ladies about the popular Monsieur de Tocqueville, who had not yet put in an appearance.

Ian was alone, and he found himself searching the crowds for a familiar, impish face. Caroline. Why was he looking for her? He was afraid to form an answer, even in his own mind.

Then he caught sight of her, looking resplendent in a lemon yellow silk gown with deep flounces, her dark hair pulled up and framing her face in curled clusters. She clutched a silk fan, and waved at her face with airy and obvious pretension. He smiled, for something about the obvious gesture was strangely endearing, as was the flush on her cheeks and the excitement making her eyes sparkle. She was like a child surveying a table full of puddings.

He started forward, then checked himself. She was speaking, quite animatedly, to her uncle. She was the relative and ward of Edward Rydell — how could he have forgotten for even one moment?

He watched the older man, the tight line of his jaw, his hard eyes, listening with impatience to his niece even as he scanned the ballroom with obvious unease. Looking for him? Ian wondered sourly. He turned away abruptly, frustration and anger roiling within him.

On the other side of the ballroom, Caroline clenched her fan and tried not to glare at her uncle. 'I cannot see the purpose of such activity,' she said between her teeth.

Her smile and excitement had quite disappeared in light of her uncle's request, or rather, demand.

Edward smiled grimly. 'Mr Dearborn is an important business acquaintance of mine, and it would suit us both well if you were kind to him.'

'Him, or his idiotic son?' Caroline snapped.

'Both, if you wish it,' Edward retorted. 'Remember, dear Niece, that you are here at my sufferance. If you want to remain in society, you had better heed my advice.'

'Sufferance!' Caroline gasped. 'Are you telling me you will cast me out if I do not act according to your wishes?'

'If you wish to put a bald face on it,' Edward agreed. He nodded pleasantly to an acquaintance passing by. 'Watch your tone, my dear. You hardly want to gain the reputation of a shrew.'

'Why would it matter to your business dealings if I give my attentions to Mr Dearborn?' Caroline asked. She felt faint and sick, as if she were probing a sore tooth, and she wasn't certain she even wanted to know how deep the decay truly was.

'He's taken a fancy to you, as it happens. You know he is widowed, and looking for a wife. He's a powerful man, Caroline, worth a fortune. He can be quite charming when he chooses, and he is well respected in the business world here. Marriages have been built on much less.'

'Are you saying . . .' Caroline's fingers tightened convulsively around her fan. 'Are you implying . . . ?'

'I imply nothing.' Edward's tone was deliberately bland. He glanced at Caroline's pale face, and smiled with what seemed to be true kindness. 'My dear, you look quite unwell. Perhaps you should get some air.' He paused, laying a hand on her arm. 'You are free to do as you please, Caroline. If you conduct yourself with propriety, of course. You know that, my dear?'

'You just informed me you would have me cast out at your merest whim!' Caroline retorted in a gasp.

'Naught but heated words. You mustn't mind everything I say. Why don't I fetch you some punch? It's rather warm in here.'

Edward disappeared, and Caroline sagged visibly. What was her uncle getting at? One moment he was threatening and cold, the next he was all solicitude. She was afraid to discover which of his fronts was the real one.

'Miss Campbell, you're alone.' She whirled around to see Ian Crombie smiling at her uncertainly. 'I did not want to exchange words with your uncle.'

'He's left for a moment.'

'Then may I take this opportunity to ask you to dance? That is, if your card has not been filled?'

Caroline didn't want to admit to the truth, that she was not yet well known enough to have any dances on her card marked. She was also not sure if she should dance with Ian Crombie. She glanced around, saw her uncle was nowhere to be seen, and smiled recklessly.

'I would like that very much,' she said, and placed her gloved hand in Ian's. She refused to think of her uncle's reaction at seeing her dance with Ian Crombie. She would not think of her uncle at all.

As Ian took her in his arms for a waltz, Caroline shivered. She'd never danced so close to a man — in Scotland, the waltz was still considered faintly scandalous.

Ian danced wonderfully, holding her lightly and yet with an obvious tenderness. Secretly, Caroline thanked Providence that Uncle Edward's generosity had extended to dancing lessons. If it hadn't, she would have been marked a green country girl for certain.

'I wanted to apologize for the sharp words

I spoke when we met in the street the other day.'

Caroline stiffened, but managed to keep her voice light. 'You apologized at the time, Mr Crombie. You needn't do so again.'

'Then perhaps you would let me explain a bit more, the circumstances which caused your uncle and I to quarrel so severely?'

'I don't know if that is wise.'

'Perhaps not, but I cannot bear for you to think me a liar or worse.'

Caroline found she thrilled to these softly spoken words. She hesitated still, glancing around, expecting to see her uncle bearing down on them, coldly furious. He was still nowhere in sight. 'We can hardly conduct such a conversation during a waltz,' she said a little breathlessly.

'Then may I suggest after this dance we take some air? The view from the terrace is quite lovely, and perfectly respectable.'

As if timed to his words, the strains of music faded and Caroline was left in a quandary. She still could not see her uncle. 'If you must,' she said, reluctance and anticipation mingling equally.

Ian took her elbow and led her to a secluded balcony overlooking the back gardens. Candles and torches had been lit throughout, giving it the look of an enchanted grotto.

'Now, may I tell you how it came to pass?' Ian asked gently. 'I can't help but think your uncle left out a few salient details.'

Caroline nodded, her face pale, and he continued. 'Rydell met me outside my solicitor's offices. He was alone, he must have known where I was going and why. He had a better business offer, or so he claimed. I was young, I didn't even know he wanted our land. So I agreed to meet him.'

'And then what happened?'

'He showed me the contract, the better price. He even knew the price our solicitor was going to suggest! How he discovered such information, I'll never know.'

'Uncle Edward said he didn't even know you believed to be selling only part of your land,' Caroline protested numbly. 'He said the price was too high for that. He assumed you knew it was the whole property.'

'He has an interesting memory, then. I remember him saying quite the opposite.'

'No.' Caroline didn't know why she refused to believe it. She'd never been under any illusion that her uncle had particularly high morals, or even that he wouldn't scruple to use questionable methods in business. Yet Ian's relentless, factual accounting of their transaction was making her feel faint and sick. It was as if this changed everything . . . yet why should it? It was only business, and ten years old at that.

'He said,' Ian continued clearly, 'that no one else would offer such a price "for a field".' His face was contorted into harsh lines of bitterness. 'I couldn't believe my fortune. He told me to look over the contract, of course, said I ought to, it was the decent thing. But he also said he couldn't hold the price for too long. There were other fields, you know.' Ian shook his head. 'I was barely sixteen, a green boy, I can admit that. I thought I was saving my family from ruin, and instead I was leading them *to* it!'

He turned half away from her, bringing his anger under control. 'So perhaps now you see why I haven't forgotten. Why I vow to regain my family's land.'

'You want the farm back? In Scotland?' Caroline said in disbelief. 'But your life is here, in Boston!'

'For now. One day I want to return to Mull, to Achlic. I dream of it.' The look in his eyes was distant, soft. 'With my wife. I want to raise my family there, where I was raised. I *will* do it.'

'Why are you telling me this?' Caroline asked helplessly. She felt ensnared, and yet also drawn by Ian's magnetic blue gaze.

'I don't know.' Ian gave a little smile. 'I honestly don't, except I wanted you — you especially — to understand.' He paused. 'Do you?'

Caroline nodded. 'Yes. Yes, but . . .' She shook her head. 'What can I do about it? I have no influence over my uncle, or very little.'

'I'd hardly ask you to exert your influence on my behalf!' Ian sounded insulted at the very thought. 'I wanted you to understand because . . . well, because. I suppose I care for your regard.'

'You are too forward, Mr Crombie.'

'I apologize.' His manner was stiff, and Caroline wished she hadn't spoken so rashly. 'Perhaps you will be so good as to heed my warning, Miss Campbell. Your uncle did not hesitate in taking advantage when it behoved him once. He's likely to do it again.'

'Are you suggesting I might be in some kind of danger?' Caroline demanded. In the ballroom another waltz struck up, and she heard a peal of feminine laughter.

Ian shrugged. 'I suppose it depends on what you consider to be dangerous. I'll take you back to the ballroom. I doubt your uncle would be pleased to see us here.'

'No, he wouldn't,' Caroline agreed. 'And I

don't think Miss Moore would either!' She bit her lip, wishing she hadn't sounded so shrewish.

Ian looked at her in surprise. 'What do you know of Isobel?'

'Only what rumour has reached me. That you intend to offer for her.'

'I intend no such thing!' Until he said it, Ian hadn't realized he'd made the decision, but now he saw he had. He could not marry Isobel. As perfectly suitable as she was, he didn't love her. He never would.

Caroline narrowed her eyes. 'Does she know that?'

Ian pressed his lips together. 'I have made no mention of desiring her suit.' He shrugged impatiently. 'I must take you back to the ballroom. You'll be missed.'

Caroline let him escort her back, barely aware of his murmured courtesies, for her mind was in turmoil. Ian was not engaged to Isobel, and more importantly, she believed what he said about her uncle. She pressed her hands to her flushed cheeks. He was so very, very unsuitable.

Eleanor had never been to balls. A few country dances and *ceilidhs* was the extent of her social outings, and she found herself shrinking to the side of the ballroom in typical wallflower fashion. Margaret and Henry had been insistent that she accompany them, along with Rupert. Since Ian had already secured an invitation courtesy of Henry's parents, it seemed sensible.

Only now, she wasn't so sure. Her gown was one of Margaret's cast-offs, of good quality but obviously of last year's fashion, the bodice hastily taken in to accommodate Eleanor's more modest bust.

Eleanor was conscious of the other guests' speculative and even pitying looks, and they made her shrink further towards the potted palm she was now half-behind.

'Care to dance?' Rupert stood before her, a hint of challenge in his smile. 'Unless you're a bit too attached to the greenery?'

Eleanor swallowed. 'I don't dance.'

'I'll show you.'

'What would you, a farmer's son, know about society dances?' she snapped, nettled.

Rupert only chuckled. 'Mamma showed us all, when we were little. She had a coming out in Edinburgh as a girl, you know.'

Eleanor nodded. She remembered hearing about Betty MacDougall's family connections. Her distant relation to the Rydells had allowed Sandy to be tacksman.

'Please?' Rupert held out his hand. 'You're the only lady present I am acquainted with.'

'What about Margaret?'

'My sister? I'd rather dance with you.'

'Even if I step on your toes?'

'I'm wearing boots. Still a farm boy at heart and foot, you know. I can't abide some of these dandified fashions.'

Smiling a little, Eleanor allowed herself to be led to the floor. Rupert took her into his arms, and she was surprised to realize how solid and warm he felt. She fancied she could feel his heart beating even though only their arms were touching.

'See? This isn't so difficult.'

And actually, it wasn't. Eleanor allowed Rupert to lead her, and felt as if she were floating. Even in a gown borrowed from Margaret, and slippers that were at least a size too large, she felt like a princess.

'I shouldn't dance with you again,' Rupert said after a waltz, 'or we'll have all the tongues wagging here. Shall we get some air?'

He led her out to a terrace, the branches of a few potted plants bearing candles, making Eleanor feel as if she'd stumbled into a fairy tale. The faint strains of music came from the windows, and Eleanor shivered suddenly.

'Shall I fetch your shawl?'

'No. I'm not cold. It's just so . . .' she shook her head. 'So magical. I've never seen anything like it, been anywhere like this.' She thought briefly of her stifled existence in Glasgow, the life she'd once hoped to live with John a vague memory.

'You didn't have much of a girlhood, did you?' Rupert asked softly.

'What do you mean?' Eleanor's voice was sharp, and Rupert smiled.

'Only that you missed the dances and parties most girls dream about. Being married, and widowed, so young.'

'There are plenty of women in my position,' Eleanor said with a shrug. 'And in these dangerous times, back in Scotland at least, there are few parties.'

'I know. Every letter we ever received from the old country spoke of the clearances.' Rupert was silent for a moment. 'But I wasn't talking about everyone, I was talking about you.'

Eleanor turned to face him. 'You don't need to pity me.'

'I don't.' Rupert put his hands on her shoulders, pulling her gently towards him. 'I promise you, I don't.'

Eleanor gazed at him in soundless surprise as he gently lowered his face to hers and kissed her.

Chapter Eight

Eleanor pulled away from Rupert, her eyes wide, one hand touching her lips. 'Why did you do that?' she asked in a low voice.

Rupert smiled, bemused. 'I don't know.'

Hardly courtly words, Eleanor thought, flushing a dull red. She turned away. 'You shouldn't have.'

'I'm sorry, Eleanor . . .'

'I know what you think,' she continued, unable to meet his eyes. 'You feel sorry for me, poor widow that I am, with no home to call my own. I suppose you thought a stolen kiss in the shadows would cheer me to no end!' She turned to face him, her expression suddenly fierce. 'Well, you're wrong, Rupert MacDougall. I have plans for my life, and they don't include being made a fool of by you!'

Rupert didn't say anything for a moment as Eleanor glared at him, feeling both indignant and slightly foolish. A trill of feminine laughter drifted through the opened windows. 'I apologize for my conduct,' he said quietly, 'if it was indeed unwelcome to you.'

'If . . .' Eleanor repeated, eyes blazing with indignation.

'Please know that I hold you in the highest regard,' Rupert continued, as if she hadn't spoken, 'and do not think of you as a poor widow, as you said, in need of my attentions.' He paused, and there was the glimmer of something like mischief in his eyes, despite his sombre expression. 'However, Mrs McCardell, I think that *you* may think of yourself in such a fashion.'

Before Eleanor could gather her wits to form a suitably scathing reply, Rupert had bowed and left her alone on the terrace.

'You have terrible manners,' Eleanor muttered, even though he couldn't hear her. Leaving her alone was quite ungentlemanly. And yet her own conduct had been like that of a fishwife! She sighed, and the sigh quickly became a shiver of remembrance. No man had ever kissed her, save John, and now Rupert. She could hardly believe he'd taken such a liberty, or that she'd allowed it. She would forget that kiss, she told herself. She must.

On the other side of the ballroom, Caroline found her uncle had disappeared again, and was looking around nervously for some pleasant society. Indeed, she was presently in danger of becoming a wallflower herself.

'Will the gossips talk too much if we dance again?'

Caroline turned in surprise to see Ian Crombie standing in front of her, looking abashed and wonderfully uncertain.

'I doubt they will fail to notice.' What she didn't add was her sudden and complete indifference to the gossips, or indeed all of Boston society at that moment.

'I believe the coast to be clear,' Ian said softly, 'in regards to your uncle.'

Caroline knew she should decline rather coolly and turn away. But she was alone, and she loved the way Ian looked at her with almost bewildered longing, and so she placed her gloved hand in his.

'You keep me on your toes, Mr Crombie,' she told him after a moment on the dance floor, for the intensity which pulsated between them scared her just a little, and she sought to lighten the mood with some harmless flirtation.

'Why are you frowning, Miss Campbell?' Ian asked softly and Caroline looked up at him, blushing.

'No reason, really,' she half-mumbled, not

wanting to mention her uncle or anything to do with Scotland again, for surely such talk could only lead to bitterness.

Ian, however, needed no explanations. 'I fear my association with your uncle will spoil our own friendship,' he said.

Caroline's heart beat quickly. 'Have we a friendship?' she asked, meaning to sound teasing and a bit coy, but it came out breathlessly anxious instead. Hopeful. She blushed all the more, silently wishing that Ian Crombie did not affect her as he did, reducing her to a twittering schoolgirl.

'I would hope so, but I might be presumptuous,' Ian replied with a little half-smile. 'Admittedly, our acquaintance is short, but the truth is, Miss Campbell, I can't get you out of my mind.' He'd manoeuvred her to a quiet corner of the ballroom, and their steps were merely a semblance of a dance. 'Does such an admission shock you? I hope not.'

Caroline, at a loss for words, could only shake her head.

'I find it most inconvenient,' Ian continued, humour lurking in his eyes even though his expression was serious. 'At work, in surgery, in the street, even. I always seem to be seeing your face, hearing your laugh.'

'How vexing,' Caroline said, choking back

a laugh. 'I daresay.'

'Indeed.' Ian paused thoughtfully. 'Especially so, if my cause were hopeless. Do you suppose it is?'

Caroline swallowed. Her head felt as if it were swimming, her thoughts floating in a sea of feeling. What was Ian asking of her, and dare she reply? 'No cause is truly hopeless,' she finally answered, avoiding his gaze. 'I would think a man such as you would enjoy a . . . a challenge.'

'Ah.' Ian lifted her hand, bringing it close to his lips. 'Do you intend to present such a challenge?'

'I fear my circumstances do the task for me,' Caroline replied, mesmerized by the sight of her own gloved hand, lily-white and strangely limp, hovering near Ian's mouth.

His eyes filled with silent laughter, as well as something deeper, and more dangerous, he lowered his mouth to kiss her fingertips, only to be stopped by a coldly furious voice.

'A charming scene, to be sure, but I fear I must interrupt.'

Caroline turned to see her uncle staring them both down, his hands clenched into fists at his side. She felt dizzy for an entirely different, and far more unpleasant, reason. There was a metallic taste in her mouth, and she realized it was fear.

'Uncle Edward . . .'

'Caroline, you have yet to dance with me,' he continued, avoiding Ian's gaze. 'Permit me to take your hand.'

Slowly, purposefully, Ian brushed Caroline's fingers with his lips and then let go of her hand. 'Save one more dance for me, Miss Campbell,' he said with a bow.

Caroline watched him walk across the crowded ballroom before Rydell grabbed her wrist and pulled her roughly into a dance. 'That impudent pup! I suppose he thinks he can annoy me by grasping for your affections?'

Caroline looked sharply at her uncle. 'I don't think Mr Crombie concerns himself with your feelings on the matter.'

'Hah! If he doesn't, he hasn't learned much in these last ten years.' Rydell regarded his niece shrewdly. 'Don't fool yourself, my girl, into thinking that lad cares a tuppence for your fine feelings. He's using you to get at me, that's all.'

Caroline lifted her chin, not trusting herself to reply, and certainly not wanting to hear any more of her uncle's thoughts on the matter.

'And what do you think you're about,' he continued furiously, 'making a cake of yourself over the Crombie lad, when I asked you to attend to Dearborn? He's far more likely to offer for you than that penniless doctor.'

'I assure you, I do not wish Dearborn to offer,' Caroline replied through clenched teeth.

'Perhaps I should send you back to Lanymoor,' Edward said musingly, although his eyes were narrowed and glittering with suppressed rage.

'I imagine that one would be as preferable as the other,' Caroline replied coldly.

So quickly Caroline could only blink, Rydell changed tactics. 'Of course such measures are not necessary,' he said in placating tones. 'All I ask, Niece, is that you lavish some of your pretty charms on a business acquaintance. He is widowed, he finds you diverting. Is that so much to ask?'

Caroline pressed her lips together and shook her head minutely. Put that way, it was certainly a small favour, and . . .

She knew her uncle had plans for her that he was not divulging. And at that moment, with her fingers still burning from Ian's light kiss, she was too afraid to ask.

'Mamma, are you all right?'

Maggie stared anxiously at her mother as Harriet pressed a hand to her middle and shook her head. 'I'm fine, *cridhe,* just tired. This damp weather makes me feel a bit achey, that's all.' Harriet swallowed her queasiness, and, as briskly as she could, tied her apron round her middle.

She glanced around the room, Anna gurgling happily in her basket by the fire, the breakfast dishes still on the scrubbed pine table.

Sandy and Betty were both still abed and George was in the fields with Allan, supervising the last of the harvest, although with the poor weather, Harriet wondered how much there would be. Worries pressed against her, giving her a headache. Wearily she pressed her hand to her eyes before smiling at Maggie. 'We've lots to do, haven't we?'

Betty's kitchen garden, usually a sight to behold, was tangled with weeds, the tomatoes lying ripe and rotting on the ground. Harriet was determined to save what she could, even as she thought of her own garden going to waste.

Allan had already brought their livestock to Mingarry Farm, and he'd managed to salvage some of their crops and garden, enough, God willing, to see them to winter.

Yet Harriet still ached to be in her own neat kitchen, showing Maggie how to pick the firmest tomatoes, how to bottle fruit and make jam.

It wasn't the same here, even though Harriet knew they were needed. It was the right place to be, and that was a better lesson for Maggie to learn than any homemaking skill. Harriet sighed. Still, it was a hard lesson.

The morning passed in a flurry of chores, and it was nearing noon when Harriet carried a tray of tea and toast into the MacDougalls' front bedroom. She suppressed a shiver at the sight of her father-in-law, lying as pale and still as a corpse on the bed, his eyes closed and his hands folded on his chest. Betty stirred in her chair, gazing at Harriet with flat, despairing eyes.

'You're too kind, too good to me . . .' she trailed off weakly, looking out the window, the bright glass panes once her pride and joy.

'Nonsense.' Harriet set the tray on the table and handed Betty a steaming mug. 'You need your strength, Mother. Really, you do.'

Betty plucked fretfully at the fringe of her shawl. 'I can't eat.'

'Just a bite of toast, then. Perhaps some broth.' Harriet spoke firmly, but her own spirits were sinking. Betty's skin was papery thin, her eyes faded and lost. Her hair lay flat and white under her mob cap. She was, Harriet thought, a living ghost.

Glancing at the bed, she wondered if she could even say as much for Sandy. She sat down, pulling a chair next to Betty's.

'Come join us in the great room,' she urged. 'The fire's warm in there, for such a damp day. And the children may cheer you. Anna babbles constantly, it's like a song.'

Betty only shook her head. 'I must stay here, in case he wakes. . . .'

Harriet glanced at the bed once more. 'You could hear from the next room. Surely such a constant vigil isn't needed.'

Betty shook her head again, as petulantly as a child. 'He needs me. I must be the first thing he sees.'

'As you wish, Mother, of course.' Harriet paused. 'But you'll do him no good, wasting away like this, with not a bite to eat. For his sake, Mother, you must keep up your strength.'

Betty nibbled a bit of toast before dropping it dispiritedly on to the plate. Harriet bit her lip, clinging to her patience. 'At least let us take turns,' she said. 'I can sit in here with Anna, Allan can take a turn in the evening.'

'No, it's my duty.' Betty straightened her slumped shoulders. 'My burden.'

'But it can't be good for anyone,' Harriet persisted, only to stop at the sight of tears trickling down Betty's withered cheeks.

'This is all I have left,' she whispered. She turned to gaze blindly out the window. 'I know it's not likely he'll recover, Harriet. At least not completely. He'll never be the man he was. I realize that.'

'We can never know what God has in store for us,' Harriet protested, even though she recognized the truth of Betty's words.

'This is all I have now,' Betty repeated. 'Please don't take it from me.' The tea tray forgotten, Betty kept staring out the window, her back to Harriet.

Silently Harriet rose and returned to the kitchen fire. She felt helpless and hopeless in the face of Betty's sorrow. *What about us?* she wanted to ask. *You could come and join the living. You have us.*

She saw Allan and George, both looking tired and muddy, come in from the fields and she took a steadying breath. At this moment, Harriet knew she couldn't indulge in the self-pity that Betty wallowed in. Right now, she felt like she was the only thing keeping this family from plunging into complete despair.

'Do you like it?' Margaret asked as she

stood in the centre of the room, circling slowly.

Rupert glanced at the sunlight bouncing off the bare walls, catching the dust motes in the air. 'It's perfect.'

'It needs a good deal of work,' Margaret continued, 'but nothing a bit of soap and water can't cure. And the location is perfect, or so Henry assures me.'

'Near the docks, you mean? But not too near?'

Margaret nodded. The building was the fifth she and Henry had looked at in the North End, and she was finally satisfied. Even better, so was Henry, with his wife's safety in such an unsavoury location.

'More and more immigrants are pouring into this city every day,' Margaret said. 'We must get this school started.' She glanced out one grimy window, her expression slightly troubled.

'And not all of them will be treated as you plan to,' Rupert said quietly. 'I've only been here a short while, and I've already heard grumblings against the immigrants.'

'I'm sure you've seen the "No Irish" signs in shop windows,' Margaret said, her eyes flashing. 'People are scared of strange accents. They refuse to accept what they can't understand.'

'It doesn't help that these poor people come off the ships dirty, coughing, and crawling with lice,' Rupert added drily.

'That's hardly their fault!'

'Don't you think I know that? We were the lucky ones.' He paused. 'I'm proud of you, Margaret, starting this school. I suspect it will be a great boon to this city, as well as to your own life.'

'What do you mean by that?' Margaret turned, her profile haloed by the late afternoon sunlight.

Rupert smiled softly, understanding in his eyes. 'Only what I said. You've always had causes, Maggie, even when we were children. You wanted lessons more than I did when I was being tutored, you were furious when McAllister refused to teach you.'

'I remember it well,' Margaret said tartly. 'At least here girls and boys will be educated alike.'

'If they come.'

Doubt shadowed Margaret's eyes briefly. 'You don't think they will?'

Rupert shrugged. 'It's hard to say.'

'Eleanor and I are going to put leaflets around,' Margaret said. 'Advertise. She's quite as dedicated as I am.'

'I believe it.' There was a pause, and Rupert saw the question about to be asked in his sister's eyes, for he continued hastily, 'People are proud, though. Remember what Allan told us? Father wasn't willing to accept help when he first arrived on the island, he'd have rather kept himself apart, starving and homeless, than accept another's hand. I imagine many people are the same. They come to this new world to prove themselves, not take handouts.'

'Perhaps,' Margaret agreed softly. 'Perhaps, for the fathers. But mothers are different. Mothers will do anything for their children.' She was silent, her eyes dark with remembered pain, and Rupert gently touched her arm.

'Maggie?'

'It's silly, really.' Margaret forced a smile. 'To be sad, even now. Henry and I have been married nearly ten years — since I was seventeen — and there have been no children. I haven't quickened, not once, not even to lose it. By now I should accept the truth.'

Rupert was silent, his gaze steady, and Margaret turned away with a little laugh. 'I suppose I'm embarrassing you with such womanly talk!'

'Not at all. I'm a farmer first, remember.' He paused. 'Perhaps this school will ease that need.'

'That's what Henry hopes. I was brooding, you know. We'd — we'd set up a nursery early on, when we thought there'd be children. Henry wanted a whole house full. I'd go up there sometimes, sit in the rocking chair, just to think. I know it sounds horribly maudlin, but I felt as if I could imagine myself a mother better there, and perhaps if I could, it would truly happen . . .' She trailed off, blinking back tears.

'It still could, you know. You're young yet, Margaret.'

'Rupert, ten years is a long time.' Margaret sighed and dusted her hands on her apron. 'No, it's time I accepted the truth, that there won't be any children. This school is my nursling now, the pupils my children. That's the way it has to be.'

There was a steely glint of determination in her eyes that Rupert recognized from childhood. He nodded, willing to let the matter drop. It was not his concern, even if his heart ached for his sister. He knew about impossible dreams.

'I can help shift the bits of furniture,' he said as he glanced around the room, 'but surely you aren't going to do the cleaning by yourself? The walls need to be whitewashed, and the floors . . .'

'Oh, no, I shan't,' Margaret smiled, her

expression almost arch. 'Eleanor is going to help me. I'm determined to have her teach with me, you know. She needs something to keep her busy.'

'I daresay.' Rupert turned away, his expression carefully neutral, but Margaret only chuckled knowingly.

'Don't you have an opinion about Eleanor?'

'Should I? I suppose she's old enough to shift for herself.'

'Of course she is.' Margaret was dismissive. 'She's been a widow for a year!'

'Then why should I have an opinion?' Rupert asked, but Margaret only laughed again.

'Oh, Rupert, I see how you watch her. Why, you couldn't keep your eyes off her when you dined with us! And at the party the other evening. . . .'

'Margaret . . .' He spoke warningly.

'I saw the two of you disappear on to the terrace,' Margaret continued, deliberately ignoring him. 'Quite improper, you know! And you left separately, with Eleanor put to the blush! What did happen, by the way? I haven't been to ask her yet, but I'm dying of curiosity.'

'It is none of your concern!' Rupert was torn between amusement and irritation at his sister's perceptiveness.

'It would be good for Eleanor to have someone to love,' Margaret said thoughtfully. 'I don't think she had much of a marriage with that soldier, he was off in India half the time. She's always lived in other people's —'

'Stop.' Rupert held up one hand, speaking firmly. 'It's not for you to tell me of Eleanor's marriage.'

Margaret's eyes flashed. 'I wasn't gossiping!'

'I didn't say you were. But if Eleanor wants me to know about her marriage, she can tell me herself.'

Margaret's ire was replaced with a little smile. 'You are smitten, aren't you?'

Rupert grinned, although he couldn't have identified the surge of feelings he had when he thought of Eleanor, her spirit, her timidity, and her sweetness. 'Don't jump to conclusions. We barely know each other.'

'You grew up together!'

'Margaret, it's been ten years. Much has passed, for Eleanor, and for me.'

'Very well, then.' Margaret smiled knowingly. 'I'm content to wait . . . and watch.'

Rupert chuckled, shaking his head. 'As you wish, but I'll thank you kindly to stay out of our business.'

'You have business together?' Margaret enquired with raised eyebrows.

Rupert threw up his hands in exasperation. *'Margaret!'*

Eleanor stood in front of the Moores' residence on Beacon Hill, her hands tightly gripping her reticule. Only that morning she'd had a note from Isobel Moore, inviting her to take tea with them.

She was glad for the invitation, although there had been a slight hesitation to her acceptance. Her few meetings with Isobel Moore had been far from friendly. In point of fact, the other girl had been haughty and even a touch cold. Eleanor sighed, inwardly steeling herself. If she wanted to make a life for herself, she had to start by making friends. This was as good a place as any.

A parlour maid ushered her into the drawing-room, which was empty, although a piece of embroidery lay next to a small, silk-covered chair. Eleanor stood in the centre of the room, admiring its elegant proportions and yet feeling entirely out of place.

'Eleanor! I'm delighted you could join me.' Isobel came into the room with a whisper of her silk skirts. Eleanor turned, admiring the austere beauty of the younger girl. Her hair, a deep blue-black, was swept up from a pale, striking, face. She was smiling, hands outstretched, and clumsily Eleanor went to meet her.

'Miss Moore,' she murmured as Isobel gently clasped her hands. 'Thank you for your kind invitation.'

'Oh, but won't you call me Isobel?' Isobel released her hands and moved to a chair, gesturing for Eleanor to take the seat opposite. 'I do hope we become friends — good friends — considering.'

'Considering?' Eleanor asked as she perched on the chair, hands in her lap.

Isobel raised her eyebrows in surprise. 'Has Ian not told you? He is one for secrets, isn't he?'

'Told me . . .' Eleanor had a feeling she should tread carefully here. Isobel was smiling, but there was a high colour in her cheeks, and her hands were bunched in her skirt. 'To be candid, we haven't had much time to talk about each other's affairs. He is so busy at the hospital, and I . . .' Eleanor broke off, wondering just what she could say had kept her occupied. 'I'm starting a new school for immigrants, has Henry told you about it? His wife, Margaret, is behind it, and she's asked me to help her.' Even if they hadn't really started yet, that counted for something.

'A worthy cause, I'm sure. It's a pity Margaret hasn't any children of her own.'

Eleanor felt rather than heard the criticism in the words, and she bristled. 'If she did, she wouldn't have the time to devote to the school, so badly needed and such a worthy cause, as you said.'

'Indeed.' Isobel was silenced for a moment by the arrival of the tea tray. She dismissed the maid and poured for them both, handing Eleanor a cup of delicate porcelain. 'Of course, I admire her. I speak only for myself in wishing a nursery full of children when Ian and I are wed.'

Eleanor jerked in surprise, slopping tea on to the saucer. She set her cup down on the table. 'I had no idea things had advanced so far. May I offer you my congratulations?' Her mind was racing. Had Ian actually offered for this girl, with not a word to anyone? She thought of how he had danced with Caroline only a few nights before, and wondered if there were more to this story. Her brother, she knew unquestioningly, was a man of honour.

'Congratulations might be premature, if only slightly,' Isobel replied, her smile firmly in place. 'He hasn't spoken to my father yet, but I've no doubt.' She lifted her chin. 'Ian has been by my side since he came to this country, Eleanor. He'll not leave it.' As if sensing the implied threat of these words, Isobel continued. 'He loves me, of that you can be sure. When we marry, we plan to set up house here on the Hill. Papa has it all arranged. He's going to buy a town house on the next street for our wedding present.' Isobel bit her lip, at once looking as guilty as a child caught with a forbidden sweet. 'Only you mustn't tell Ian, it's meant to be a surprise.'

Eleanor could only nod, unable to form a reply. She wondered how Ian would take to being given a stately home, when he was working so hard to regain his own lost property.

'He *will* marry me,' Isobel said in almost a whisper, and her eyes shone with tears before she quickly blinked them back.

Eleanor was moved to sympathy in spite of herself. 'I have no doubt he holds you in the highest regard.'

'He's spoken to you of me?' Isobel asked eagerly, and Eleanor almost winced.

'As I said, we've had so little time to talk properly,' she began, only to see Isobel's face fall. 'But he has mentioned you with affection, to be sure.'

Like a sister, perhaps, but that could grow into something more, Eleanor thought. Who was she to say? Her love for John McCardell had been that kind of affection. If he hadn't died, who knew what deeper love might have taken root?

'When we're settled in our new home,' Isobel continued brightly, 'you will of course make your home with us. I would not like to think of you alone.'

'Thank you,' Eleanor murmured, her hands shaking as she picked up her teacup once again. She could see pity in Isobel's eyes, glittering almost venomously.

'Perhaps you will find yourself better situated in time,' Isobel continued in a kindly tone, 'but you must always feel at home with us.'

'Thank you,' Eleanor murmured yet again. She'd no doubt Isobel's invitation was merely a pretext to staking her claim on Ian. Eleanor knew she would have to talk to her brother. Had he any idea what plans were afoot? She feared he had at least an inkling, and knew he shared some blame in not dashing Isobel's hopes as he should have.

Unless . . . Eleanor gazed at Isobel. She was beautiful, wealthy, charming. Surely she wouldn't have the audacity to summon her fiancé's sister here without some hope of an offer?

Perhaps Ian did love her, and was just

clinging to his bachelor days. It suddenly seemed entirely, and unpleasantly, possible.

Her spirits sank. If Ian and Isobel married, once again she would be the third wheel, an outsider looking in, with no real life of her own. She couldn't stand the thought of living with Isobel and Ian; it would be repugnant, a widow residing with newlyweds! Isobel would have control of the housekeeping; she would be the poor and pitied spinster relation. It was not to be borne! She couldn't do it; she would rather return to Scotland.

And yet what awaited her there? The McCardells didn't want her back; Jane MacCready had no room. She could travel north to live with Harriet and Allan. Eleanor knew they would make her welcome, just as she knew her life would soon fade into days of endless drudgery, helping on a small farm with no prospect of change.

At least in Boston there was a chance of . . . what? Romance? She thought of Rupert, and quickly dismissed him. He was not interested in her beyond a mild, pitying flirtation. He'd made that clear the night of the party.

No, she was not going to hold out hope from that quarter . . . as if she would!

'Yet where does that leave me?' Eleanor

whispered, not realizing she'd spoken aloud until Isobel glanced at her strangely. She smiled back, trying to collect her thoughts.

The answer was plain. It left her nowhere . . . again.

Chapter Nine

Eleanor didn't find time to talk to Ian until several days later. His long hours at work and many social engagements — some of which Eleanor declined — left them with few evenings at home.

Finally, towards the end of October, Eleanor found herself in the sitting room with Ian across from her in front of the fire. It was a cozy, domestic scene, with the night falling outside and the rattle of branches against the window pane.

Inside the fire was cheering, the little room comfortable and warm. Of course, it was nothing like the elegant proportions of the Moores' residence, but Eleanor was proud of the way she'd fashioned the rented furniture into something resembling a home.

'An excellent dinner, Eleanor,' Ian said as he opened the newspaper with a rustle of stiff pages.

It had been leftover mutton and potatoes, but Eleanor didn't bother contradicting him. She prided herself on her economy, and the way she could make a few thin ingredients stretch to an appetizing, if not elegant, meal. It was a skill learned from childhood.

She picked up her sewing, reluctant to disturb the contentment of the evening. Then she put it down again. Disturb it she must. 'Ian . . . I wonder if you would be so good as to tell me your intentions towards Isobel Moore.'

She sensed rather than saw or heard Ian stiffen. Slowly he put down his newspaper. 'Why do you ask?'

'I'll tell you in a moment, if it seems appropriate,' Eleanor replied crisply. 'Right now, I wish you to tell me.'

'Eleanor . . .' Ian spoke warningly, then sighed. 'I have no intentions.'

'You are not going to marry her?' Hope and a new compassion for Isobel flared within her.

Ian's expression hardened for a brief moment. 'No.'

'You might wish to apprise her of the fact.'

'It has not arisen!'

'Perhaps not with you, Ian,' Eleanor nearly snapped, 'but it has with me!'

The silence was ringing. Ian put down his newspaper. 'Isobel has spoken to you? About me?'

'She told me you were to be married, and I could gladly make my home with you once you were wed.'

'Good Lord!' Ian jumped up from his chair, raking a hand through his hair as Eleanor watched, strangely satisfied.

'I suspected you felt this way, but when Isobel summoned me . . .'

'She had no right!'

'And you, Ian, have no right to trifle with her affections.'

'I have never . . .' Ian glared at her. 'I have never given her reason to think . . .' He trailed off at Eleanor's look of obvious scepticism.

'You think she's delusional, then?'

'Don't be absurd.' Ian sank back down into his chair. 'What should I do?' His legs stretched out, his mouth turned down in a pout, he looked like a sulky schoolboy.

'Ian, you cannot run away from your problems,' Eleanor said gently. 'It didn't solve them before, and it certainly wouldn't now.'

'I'm not running away.'

'Aren't you?' Eleanor raised an eyebrow. 'Only yesterday you informed me you are planning to take the coach to Hartford for some business. Beyond the indelicacy of leaving me to my own means for several weeks, you are dropping the problem of Isobel Moore like a hot coal, and when you return you hope it will have died to ash.'

Ian was silent for a long moment. 'My trip to Hartford is to do with work, research,' he finally said. 'But I daresay there is a bit of truth in what you say.'

'Then speak to Isobel before you leave. Otherwise you might come home to a terrible storm of gossip, brewed in your absence, and creating more heartache and ill feeling than you care to deal with.'

He grimaced. 'Eleanor, I can't! The Moores have done so much for me, brought me into their home like a son. To reject their daughter out of hand, especially when they've taken my gestures of brotherly affection as something more . . .'

'Then you must be prepared to marry her,' Eleanor replied.

Ian closed his eyes briefly. 'I can't.'

'Why not? She's suitable, she's pretty, she's kind. You'd be well situated for life.'

'I'm not a money grubber!'

'No, but one must be practical. Do you love someone else?'

Ian's tormented silence was enough to

give Eleanor pause. She looked up from the industrious stitches she'd been sewing. 'You do? Who is it?'

Ian shrugged. 'Love is a strong word. But my affections have been recently engaged — elsewhere.' He stared broodingly into the fire.

Eleanor was silent for a moment, her mind whirling. She wasn't sure what she'd expected when she'd started this conversation, beyond doing her duty and making her brother do his. Now she felt the full, sticky extent of their quandary. 'It's Caroline Campbell, I suppose?'

Ian looked up, his mouth twisting in a bleak smile. 'How did you know?'

'You danced with her twice at the Emersons' ball, and the two of you were stuck in a corner for far too long. More than one pair of eyebrows was raised at that bit of brazen conduct, I assure you!'

'Caroline is not brazen.'

'No, she's charming and lovely,' Eleanor replied calmly. 'And quite spoiled and vain.'

Ian looked as if he wanted to leap up and defend Caroline's character, but after a moment he looked away, sinking back into his chair. 'I'll grant you she can be silly and girlish,' he said after a moment. 'But to me, that is part of her charm. Eleanor . . .' Ian spread his hands out. 'We cannot choose who we fall in love with. Yes, I suppose it is love. If I could choose, I would have Isobel in an instant, for I know she'll make me a good wife. But I would make her miserable, loving someone else.'

Eleanor gazed at him, lips pursed. 'Have you ever considered that it might be nothing but a flirtation? An obsession, even? Caroline may tire of you, you may tire of her.'

'Yes,' Ian admitted after a pause. 'I suppose I would have to consider that possibility.'

'And then what?'

He shrugged. 'I don't know. But I can't marry Isobel in my present state.'

Eleanor shook her head grimly, twitching a thread. 'Then you'd better work to get Isobel well situated. If she is the one who cries off —'

'I haven't proposed!'

'Oh, Ian, enough! She is expecting it any day, as is the rest of society! I've been in Boston less than a month and even I am aware of events.'

'All right,' Ian agreed quietly. 'But who? Everyone I know in society is through the Moores, and they would not court Isobel under my nose.'

'No,' Eleanor agreed. 'They wouldn't. So we'll have to think of something else.'

But what that would be, she had no idea.

'Miss Campbell is not at home,' Rydell's butler sniffed disapprovingly.

Ian bit down on his impatience. 'Could you tell me when she might return? Only I'm leaving this afternoon for business, and I wanted to speak with her before my departure.'

'I could not say, sir,' the butler replied. 'But it is not Miss Campbell's habit to entertain strangers in her uncle's home, at any time of day.'

Ian forced a smile. 'I'm glad to hear it.' It was a mistake to have come here, he knew. Caroline Campbell was guarded jealously by her uncle, like a prize, and Ian Crombie was not even remotely in the running for it. Yet the need to see her — speak with her — had been almost unbearable.

Since confessing his regard for Caroline to his sister, Ian had experienced a burning urge to declare it to the woman herself . . . and discover if she felt the same.

'If you could leave a message . . .' he began, only to have the door firmly shut in his face. Ian bit down on the curse he wanted to shout, and turned away.

'Who was that at the door, Taylor?' Caroline hurried down the stairs, her hair half undone, her skirts crumpled. She'd been trying to write a letter to her brother James, only to have stopped in a fit of impatience, and then rather inopportunely dozed off. The insistent knocking on the front door had awakened her, filling her with a fresh hope.

Perhaps today he would visit . . .

'No one to concern yourself with, miss,' Taylor replied coolly.

Caroline's brows snapped together. 'I believe I shall be the judge of what concerns me, or not,' she said. 'Who was at the door?'

'Your uncle said . . .'

Without another word, Caroline pushed past the butler and opened the front door. She saw Ian walking slowly, sadly, down the street. *'Ian!'*

'Miss! This is not seemly!' Taylor's voice was sharp, but Caroline barely heard it.

Ian turned, his face suddenly suffused with happiness, and he hurried towards her. 'Caroline! I was trying to see you.'

Heedless of propriety, Caroline ushered him into the house. 'Come into the drawing-room. Taylor will send for tea.'

'Miss, I cannot condone . . .' the butler began, but Caroline turned to him, her earlier fury now replaced with charming sweetness.

'Oh, dear Taylor! You know how my uncle wants me to be in good society. It's perfectly proper for Mr Crombie to visit, he's the brother of my dear friend Eleanor who took tea here the day before last. Now, please do fetch us something. I'm sure Mr Crombie is parched, and my uncle would be furious to know we're not being hospitable.'

Taylor looked as if he disagreed entirely, but for propriety's sake resisted tossing Ian straight back into the street. He sighed. 'Very well, miss, but I hope your uncle does not come to hear of it.' He turned to the kitchens, and Caroline led Ian into the drawing-room, where a fire crackled merrily.

'You've wrapped him around your little finger,' Ian said admiringly, and Caroline chuckled.

'I can't be *completely* useless.'

'I hardly think that.' He paused, taking off his hat. 'I had to see you.'

Caroline's breath caught in her chest. 'Why?'

'Because I haven't stopped thinking about you since we danced together.'

She moved to the back of a chair, her hands gripping it tightly. 'You'll quite turn my head, Ian Crombie.'

'You've already turned mine.'

Caroline laughed breathlessly, stunned and delighted by his boldness. 'This is all highly improper, you know.'

'Not if I have honourable intentions,' Ian countered softly.

Caroline gasped. 'What are you saying? You barely know me . . .'

'I know, it's insensible,' Ian agreed. 'I've told myself a thousand times you're completely unsuitable, but my heart just doesn't listen.'

'Ian . . .' Caroline shook her head slowly. This was more, much more, than she'd ever envisioned, imagined even. It left her breathless with both delight and terror. 'I don't know what to say.'

'There's nothing to say, not now. Not yet. Just give me a little time. So you can come to know me, and I can court you properly.'

'My uncle . . .' Caroline faltered. She couldn't begin to imagine the extent of his rage, if he were to learn she was entertaining Ian Crombie's suit! It truly did not bear thinking about.

'Let's not think of him now.' Ian moved closer to her. He reached down to one of her hands, gently uncurling her fingers from their grip on the chair. Her palm lay in his, and he kissed her fingertips. 'May I kiss you?'

'You just did.'

'Again, then.' Dumbly, Caroline nodded. Ian brushed his lips against hers, and she closed her eyes, her heart overflowing.

There was a knock on the door, and Caroline jumped back as if scalded.

'Tea, miss.'

'Yes. Th— thank you.' She was blushing and stammering like a schoolgirl, and she couldn't help herself. Ian smiled at her, eyes twinkling.

'Shall I pour?' he suggested.

Caroline recovered herself to say sharply enough, 'I think I am quite capable, thank you, Mr Crombie!'

The maid left, and Ian chuckled softly. 'You delight me, even when you're cross.'

'Don't patronize me,' Caroline replied a bit tartly, and Ian's eyes were warm.

'I would never. I have too much regard for you, Miss Campbell.'

Breathlessly she handed him a cup, relieved that her fingers did not tremble and slosh the tea into the saucer.

The next half hour passed pleasantly enough, with the conversation far less charged, although Caroline started to feel uneasy about her uncle interrupting them.

She was almost relieved when Ian finally took his leave.

'I regret to say I cannot stay, as much as I want to. I have business to take care of out of town, but as soon as it is concluded, I intend to see you again . . . if you'll allow me.'

'Yes.' Caroline swallowed, her throat felt so dry. 'Yes, I will.'

'Till then.' He kissed her fingertips once more, and then he was gone.

Several hours later, still in a haze of happiness, Caroline decided to beard her uncle in his library. Blinded by her own delight, she convinced herself that he would understand the affection between her and Ian, and want her happiness. The feud between Ian and her uncle was a decade old . . . her marriage to Ian could finally put it to rest.

Filled with such happy daydreams, Caroline went to open the library door, only to be stopped by the sound of low voices.

'You're sure?'

'She's a young girl, give her time.' Edward Rydell's voice was unctuous, almost wheedling.

'She did not seem very happy in my company at the party.' Caroline recognized Dearborn's raspy, strident tone.

'She's shy, retiring. I promise you, you'll

have her affections.'

'I could choose another wife, you know, Rydell,' Dearborn warned. 'You seem to think the chit is a pawn in your possession, but I assure you it's not so. I've taken a liking to her, it's true, and I need a wife. But I could find others, just as I could find other — business partners, if the present ones don't seem to be satisfactory.'

'I don't like threats,' Rydell said coldly. 'But I assure you, my niece will marry you . . . whether she likes it or not.'

CHAPTER TEN

The words echoed in Caroline's mind, making her feel faint and dizzy. She leaned her head against the study door frame, listening for Dearborn's response.

He chuckled, an unpleasantly indulgent sound. 'I don't want an unwilling bride, Rydell,' he said. 'I'm not a monster, you know.'

'Unwilling? I think not.' Rydell laughed as well, but it was without humour. 'You know how silly young girls can be. They are liable to get all sorts of notions into their heads. No, all my niece needs is to see sense. A marriage to you, a prominent businessman, will, of course be advantageous for her in every way that matters.'

'I should think so.' A pause, and with her heart thudding wildly, Caroline heard footsteps coming towards the other side of the door she was pressed against.

She stumbled backwards, crashing into a

planter which rocked on its legs. Then, without a backward glance, she turned and fled upstairs. She barely saw where she was going, tripping over her skirts as she ran, her fist pressed to her mouth.

She only felt safe when she was in her bedchamber, the key turned into the lock with shaking fingers.

She flung the key on the bed. Dear God! Marry Dearborn, a man old enough to be her father? She thought briefly of his glittering eyes, his gaunt face, and shuddered. Never! She would never do it . . .

And I don't have to. Caroline thought of Ian; the vision of his smiling face, his eyes warm with affection and even desire, gave her some much needed calm. She needn't act like a pitiful heroine from some gothic melodrama. No one could force her to marry Dearborn, no matter what her uncle thought. He couldn't drag her to the altar.

I loved once. Her uncle had admitted as much. Perhaps if he could not see reason, she could appeal to sentiment. He didn't know she loved Ian, but if he did . . . if he understood . . .

If only there wasn't this feud! Caroline pressed her fingers to her temples, as if she could induce a solution from her own thoughts.

'Very well,' she said aloud, her voice not quite steady. 'They simply will have to put this feud of theirs aside. It is old, pointless now — there are more pressing matters.'

If her uncle could see that she loved someone, even if it was Ian Crombie, he would surely not ask her to marry another man! She knew he had some finer feelings, beneath his cold demeanour, beneath the veneer of contempt.

Dusk was falling before Caroline saw Dearborn take his leave of her uncle's house. She watched his black carriage pull away, the leaves fluttering and swirling in its wake, and then turn the corner before she tidied her hair and dress and went downstairs.

'Taylor, do you know where my uncle might be found?'

'He's in the library, miss. I don't know if he wishes . . .'

She shot him a cool smile, hoping she looked more confident than she felt. 'Never mind, Taylor. I need to speak with him.'

'Of course, miss, but I should advise —'

Caroline felt a prickle of irritation. To be thwarted by the butler . . . ? 'I tell you, he will want to hear what I have to say.' Actually, she feared the exact opposite, but she was not going to confide in Taylor of all people.

With a swish of her skirts, she opened the library door and closed it firmly behind her, her heart beating like a wild bird trapped in a cage.

Her uncle was looking at some papers on his desk, his back to her. 'Put the brandy on the table, Taylor, and leave me.'

'It is not Taylor, Uncle Edward, but Caroline. Your niece.' Caroline was relieved to hear her voice sound steady, almost normal.

He whirled around, his face suffused with ready anger. 'What? You are not to enter without knocking, you brazen chit!'

Caroline had meant to be calm, meant to be the mature young woman she knew she could be, that she hoped Ian *believed* her to be, but somehow her temper escaped, flew out of its cage, surprising them both. 'And you are not to auction me off like a slab of meat at the butcher's!'

'What did you say?' Rydell's eyes narrowed dangerously. 'Did you eavesdrop, you nosy minx?'

'I was coming in here to tell you . . . something,' Caroline said, suddenly not wanting to play her trump card, her love for Ian. Who knew what her uncle would do with that information in his current mood?

'I could not help but overhear! And I was disgusted by the pair of you, bartering for me like a cow or ox.'

Rydell smiled unpleasantly. 'You may choose to draw such comparisons, my dear, but the truth remains. It behoves you to do as I wish and marry Matthew Dearborn.'

Caroline threw her head back. 'And why on earth would I consider such a deplorable thing? As if I loved him — or even *knew* him!'

'You have been too long carried away with ridiculous romantic notions. Marriage is not about love. It is not even about knowing someone! It is a business contract in which both of you come away with something satisfactory.'

'Oh, indeed?' Caroline retorted. 'Then tell me what Dearborn gains from such a contract! My dowry, I'm sure, is hardly bait for which he'd dangle.'

'Don't be crude.' Rydell's nostrils flared in distaste. 'I know not why he cares for the alliance except that he's taken a liking to you. You divert him, amuse him, although you would hardly do so in your present state, scowling and shrieking like a misbegotten shrew.'

'If I behave in such a fashion,' Caroline snapped, striving to regain her calm, 'it is because I have been goaded beyond all resistance.'

'Then you need to develop a bit more moral character.' Rydell smiled in triumph, as if he knew he'd successfully retrieved the upper hand.

Caroline drew in a long, shaky breath. She knew she needed to stay calm, strong, if she wished to win this one skirmish. There would be other battles. 'I amuse him. Very well.' She nodded, accepting the fact, repellent as it was. 'What is in it for you, dear uncle? For you obviously desire the match very strongly.'

'Ah, now you're trying to be clever, I see.' Rydell nodded, almost admiring her deduction. He decanted the brandy and poured himself a generous amount. 'I'll tell you as much. I have business with him, important business, and your marriage would seal our bargain nicely.' He paused and took a sip. 'You might have noticed I had not been as generous to you with your dress allowance and such amusements when you resided at Lanymoor House. It was not spite, Caroline, but economy. My investments and properties have been hard hit in these dangerous times, and so I turned to America for new opportunity. Dearborn has provided it admirably, and I would hate to see all our newfound wealth — *your* newfound comforts — disappear in a trice.'

Caroline felt a ripple of unease at her uncle's vague words. She almost asked what kind of business, but she didn't want to be diverted from her purpose. 'I don't care about such things,' she said after a moment, and Rydell laughed.

'Oh, indeed not? You might think differently if that dress were stripped off your back, and you were handed a char brush and pail and told to work for your living as a skivvy!'

Caroline's eyes widened at the image. She shook her head. 'You exaggerate to shock me.'

'If only I did.' Rydell turned to face her, his expression suddenly savage, something like fear in his eyes. 'What if I told you that a marriage to Dearborn is the only thing that keeps this roof over your head, the clothes in your wardrobe, the shoes on those pretty little feet? What if I told you that such a marriage is the only thing standing between you and humiliation and scandal in front of all of Boston society?'

Caroline stared at him, her mind frozen by such a pronouncement. She was not afraid of scandal, at least she didn't think she was, but bankruptcy — poverty — those chilled her. Her father had been a gambler, her mother impoverished, and she was close enough to the pauper's state, kept only by her uncle's variable generosity, that the poverty her uncle threatened her with seemed all too possible.

And yet . . .

Surely her uncle was exaggerating. They lived in comfort, they moved in nearly the best society. There could not be such a thin line between respectability and despair! Not now, not ever.

'It cannot be,' she said, shaking her head. 'You are trying to frighten me into agreeing. I know it!'

Rydell shook his head slowly, his expression bleak. He looked suddenly old, old and tired, his hair white, his face haggard. 'If only, dear niece,' he said wearily. 'If only that were true.'

For the first time, Caroline gave credence to his words, and she felt cold all over, as if she'd been doused in ice water. Just what kind of trouble had her uncle got them both into?

'Are you saying,' she said in a whisper, 'that if I marry Dearborn, he will save us from ruin?'

'Yes, if it is possible.'

'And if I don't? What will he do?'

Rydell smiled grimly. 'The opposite, of course.'

'But then he is a monster! A monster you would have me marry!'

'He is selfish, certainly,' Rydell answered. 'He is concerned with his own gain and prosperity, as any merchant would be.'

'But why,' Caroline nearly wailed, 'has he taken such a liking to me?'

'Be glad he has. It is the only thing which saves us from debtor's gaol.'

'There are no debtor gaols in this country!'

'What would you prefer? To flee out west and live in a mud hut? Or worse, be scalped by a savage?'

Caroline's hand clawed at her throat. She felt breathless. 'Don't say such things!'

'I've spared you the worst of it, for your own sake. You could do far worse than Matthew Dearborn, Caroline. He is wealthy, he is respected in his trade, and he would, I believe, treat you kindly. He is not a monster, and neither am I to encourage this match.'

'What if . . .' Caroline bit her lip. She wanted to speak of Ian, yet she feared that to mention his name now would be near ruinous.

'Leave me now,' Rydell said tiredly. 'There

is nothing more to say. Nothing that we will not regret, at any rate.' He turned away from her, shoulders slumped, and Caroline knew there was no point in finishing the conversation. For now, it was a very short reprieve. At least there were no plans to see Dearborn . . . at least no plans she knew of.

She walked slowly back to her room, her mind spinning. She didn't know what would happen. Would her uncle truly expect her to suffer Dearborn's attentions? If what he said was true, and she now feared it was, he would certainly not leave it at that. It could only be a matter of weeks — perhaps days — before her dilemma returned afresh.

And, she realized hollowly, her uncle would not take kindly to the fact that she loved another, especially if it jeopardized Dearborn's interest. No, he would likely fly into a rage.

Caroline shivered. What on earth should she do? Then it came to her. She would write to lan. He always seemed so certain, so wise. He would know what to do.

She laboured over a letter, trying to choose her words carefully and present a calm, dignified appearance. Then all sense left her as she imagined her fate, married to Dearborn, his skeletal hands on her . . . and panic set in. Nibbling her thumbnail, Caroline scrawled a quick missive: Ian, I have spoken to my uncle and I'm afraid for the future — mine, and certainly ours, if anything is to pass between us! Please call on me at your earliest convenience. Caroline Campbell.

Too melodramatic? she wondered. Perhaps, but she felt the need for drastic measures. She wanted to take action, and at once. She craved salvation.

Caroline knew better than to trust any of her uncle's household to deliver the message, so she paid a boy in the street a penny to take it to Ian's house, and return as quickly as he could with the reply.

She sat by her window, her forehead pressed against the cool glass, watching the street below. The little season was almost over, and the leaves were tinged with red. Caroline had heard of America's harsh winters, and she suppressed a shiver.

The fire in the grate had turned to ashes, but she was too highly strung to bother with summoning a servant to tend to it.

Finally, as dusk was beginning to settle, Caroline saw him, his smudged face half hidden by a dirt cap, dragging a stick along the iron fence.

She threw a shawl around her shoulders

and hurried outside. 'Well? What news have you?'

'I took the letter, mum, as you told me,' the urchin said. 'But the lady in the house said the master had gone away, on business, to Hartford.'

Caroline's spirits sank. She'd forgotten that Ian was away on business . . . all the way in Hartford! He could be gone for days, weeks, perhaps even longer. Surely, though, he would have told her if he intended to stay away for very long?

'Did Eleanor — the lady — say when he would return?' she asked.

The little boy nodded. 'Sorry, mum. Not for a fortnight at least, she said.'

Ashes to ashes, dust to dust. It would happen to them all, Harriet thought, as it had happened to so many before them. She stood in front of the little trio of headstones, a wave of sadness sweeping over her.

First Archie, then little James, taken when he was but a bairn, and now Sandy. She leaned back on her heels, the ground hard with frost beneath her.

Sandy had clung to life for six weeks since the accident, six long weeks of Betty likewise fading away, of Harriet wondering what the future held — could hold — for any of them.

She rested a hand on her middle. Six more weeks for this new life to grow, to one day be welcomed into a world that was both harsh and wondrous.

Harriet rose and headed back to the farmhouse. She'd promised Betty, since Sandy's death two weeks ago, that she would tend his grave since Betty was too weak to do it.

She sighed wearily, wondering if Betty would be in better spirits today. They had to move forward from this place. Winter would be coming on, and Allan had boarded up their own house for the season. It broke Harriet's heart to think of the home she'd made for them all now empty and lifeless, but she knew it was for the best. It was how it must be.

'Mamma, you look tired.' Maggie, looking older than her years, gave her mother a worried frown.

Harriet tied her apron around her waist and smiled. 'I am a bit, but it's for a good reason, Maggie.'

Maggie shook her head in confusion, and Harriet held a finger to her lips. 'I'll tell you soon. I must talk to your father first.'

She did not find a moment alone with Allan till that evening, when the children and Betty had gone to bed.

'I think we're mostly set up for winter,' Allan said as he stretched his feet towards the fire. 'What with this early cold spell, I reckon it's a good thing I closed up our own stead early.'

'Yes.'

He glanced at her, his eyes shadowed with concern. 'I know this has been hardest on you, Harriet, taking the burden of the household along with Mother . . .'

'It's not that.' Harriet sighed. 'Well, partly perhaps, but I know needs must. There's something else, Allan . . . good news, I hope, if unexpected.' Self-consciously she rested her hand on her middle, and Allan started in surprise.

'You mean . . . a child? You're expecting?'

She nodded. 'April, I think. Perhaps May.'

Allan moved to her side, putting his arms around her shoulders. 'But that's wonderful news! How could you doubt? I'm delighted, my darling.' He kissed her, and Harriet rested her head against his shoulder.

'I know we'd always hoped for more children, but in these times . . .'

'This is but a season, Harriet. Now that Father has died . . .' Allan's face darkened for a moment, before he smiled tenderly. 'There is no reason not to sell this farm, and bring Mother home with us. We can weather the cold season here, and return home in spring. It would be better for us all.'

Harriet wondered if Betty would agree, but she was too eager to grasp this thread of hope to dwell on it for long. 'Yes,' she said, smiling. 'In spring.'

The next day Harriet decided to tell the others her news. The children were delighted, as she expected them to be, but it was Betty's reaction which surprised her the most.

Her worn face broke into a smile, and it was as if the sun had finally broken through a dense fog. 'A child! A wee bairn! Oh, Harriet, how glad this makes me.' Betty bent her head. 'I thought there was no life within me, and yet . . .'

Harriet knelt next to her mother-in-law, her hand on her shoulder. 'You see, there is much yet to live, and to give thanks for.'

'Yes.' Betty patted her hand. 'Yes . . . and it comforts me so to think of a child again in this house. Sandy would be delighted, I know it!'

Harriet held her tongue, not wanting to spoil the first moment of Betty's happiness. Secretly, though, she hoped they would be back at their own farm come spring as she and Allan had discussed. Would Betty be willing to go?

Harriet knew the woman, fragile as she was, could dig in her heels. Perhaps she wouldn't want to leave the house she and Sandy had built together. Perhaps Allan would be tied here, as he had been so many years ago. Perhaps they all would.

Chapter Eleven

The trees outside Rupert's window were blazing with colour, and it suited his mood perfectly. In the four months since he'd been in Henry's employ, he felt he'd shown himself admirably.

The other clerks in the office were reluctantly accepting him, due to his relentless friendly cheer and good humour, even though they had initially resented his presence.

Henry had been careful not to show Rupert any favouritism in the office, even though Rupert dined regularly at his residence and was treated as a brother there. In the office, he was but another clerk, adding sums and checking figures, finding a way to prove himself.

And the time had come, Rupert thought, to prove that he was capable of more than playing with numbers on a page. He didn't want to be a clerk for ever, hunched over a desk in a cramped office, toiling for his dollars. No, he wanted to be a businessman, to make his own fortune in this new age of opportunity and enterprise. He just had to find a way to get started.

With a sigh, Rupert opened the cash box. One of his duties was to tally the amount in the cash box with the figures on the page, and make sure they were equal before depositing the money in the Massachusetts Bank.

He knew most people mistrusted banks, reflected in President Jackson's recent decision not to renew the Second Bank's charter. As Rupert feared, the loss of a national banking system had led to hundreds and even thousands of state banks creating their own notes, with different designs, shapes and denominations. Even worse, many of these banks didn't have gold or silver backing their paper.

The Massachusetts Bank was dependable, fortunately, and Henry believed in keeping his money there. Rupert looked forward to the day when all banks were safe and reliable, instead of rogue operations that the average man was wary or even frightened of.

Rupert paused in his counting of the various bills and coins. Henry was usually meticulous about only accepting proper coin — silver, gold, or dependable notes. It was becoming more and more difficult to keep such standards, however, and lately Henry had started accepting notes from various state banks.

With narrowed eyes, Rupert examined a note from the Bank of New York. The ink on the bottom left corner looked slightly smeared — or was he imagining it? Would Henry appreciate his concern about possible forgeries, or consider it too much meddling?

'It's getting late, MacDougall,' one of the other clerks said in a surly tone. 'The bank will be closing. What are you doing there — wool gathering? Or perhaps you're considering taking a bit for yourself?'

'That would hardly be wise,' Rupert replied curtly. He turned back to his figures. The amount of cash in the stronghold equalled the accounting books, which was fortunate, but Rupert still carefully separated the Bank of New York notes. Each one of the bills had a smeared corner — not impossible for a printing press to create, he acknowledged, but still suspect.

'I'm going to the bank now,' he told the other clerks, and with the box under his arm, he headed out.

He'd been given the job of taking the money to the bank not because they considered him trustworthy or deserving of special responsibility, Rupert knew, but because if the money was stolen on the way to the bank, no one wanted to be blamed.

He sighed, wishing things could be different, that the other clerks could accept him fully, but knowing they never would. He was set apart by his relationship to Henry, even if he worked hard at what he did. It would always be seen as favouritism.

Once inside the bank on Park Street, Rupert deposited the money, accepted the slip, and then quietly asked to speak to the manager.

'The manager, sir?' The clerk behind the grille looked at him in surprise. 'He's quite a busy man.'

'I'm sure, but this is a matter of some import,' Rupert replied easily, although his eyes were hard. 'And of no small concern to his own interests, you may be assured.'

Reluctantly, yet intrigued, the clerk left to find the manager. A few minutes later Rupert was seated in front of the man's desk, spreading the notes out for him to see. 'You see that bit in the corner, smeared? It could be a faulty printing press, of course, but perfectly legitimate, as legitimate as any of these state banks are now,' Rupert said with a little conspiratorial smile. 'But I feared the worst, that they're counterfeit, and I thought it prudent to consult an expert before speaking with my employer.'

The bank manager gazed through a monocle, examining each note with careful precision. 'A wise decision,' he said after a moment. 'These notes are indeed counterfeit.'

Eleanor carefully stacked the worn reading primers on the desk. It had been another busy morning at the First School, which was the rather innocuous name Margaret had come up with.

'I don't want anything with "charity" or "immigrant" in it,' she'd said. 'That will send them away in droves.'

'If they even come in the first place,' Eleanor interjected, knowing she sounded a dismal note but unable to help herself.

Yet they *had* come. Nearly a month into the school year, the ground now touched with frost, and they kept coming. The classroom was full of eager students willing to learn, little ones whose parents were grateful to have them occupied during working hours, and older children, even adults, whose faces were hungry for knowledge as much as for food.

'Learning is power to them,' Margaret had said once. 'The difference, perhaps, between making matchboxes and making a living. A *life.*'

And Eleanor had to agree.

'You will come to supper tonight, won't you, Eleanor?' Margaret asked as she tidied the classroom. Henry's manservant, Wallers, waited discreetly by the door. Despite the school's busy location on North Square, next to the sea mission, it was still too close to Boston's Murder District for Henry's comfort. Wallers guarded the school the entire time it was in session.

'With Ian away so much,' Margaret continued, 'I don't like to think of you alone.'

'He sent a letter from Hartford. He should be home in a few days.'

'Whoever imagined he'd stay away so long! He spoke once of some experiments he was interested in, but I'd hate to see his position at the hospital put in jeopardy.'

'You are a pioneer in your own field,' Eleanor replied with a little smile. 'Let Ian be one in his.'

'Oh, of course! Never let me be one to stand in the way of progress. I just don't wish you to be lonely.'

'I'm not,' Eleanor said simply. Or at least,

no lonelier than she ever had been. In truth, she'd enjoyed being mistress of her own domain, even if it was but a charade for a few weeks. She was also grateful for a respite from the tension which had thrummed between Ian and her ever since she'd confronted him about Isobel. A situation, she realized with a suppressed sigh, he'd done nothing to address before his departure.

'I shall come to supper, if the invitation is true,' she added. 'I fear my larder is empty, and your table is always excellently laid!'

'Good.' Margaret couldn't resist a teasing little smile. 'Rupert shall be dining with us, you know.'

Eleanor shrugged. 'I shall look forward to it.' She knew Margaret was not so subtly trying to push them together, and she also suspected that Rupert resisted such interference. She'd refused to rise to Margaret's insinuations, well meaning as they were.

Rupert was ambitious and determined, with a bright future ahead of him. Why, they'd barely spoken since that kiss on the terrace — a kiss Eleanor had re-lived more than once. She doubted Rupert gave it even a passing thought. He was ambitious, worldly, and according to Henry, he was likely to go far. He wasn't interested in a woman like herself.

What are you like, then? Eleanor asked herself. She felt as if she'd never really had her own home, her own life, to discover her true self. *And at this rate, you never will.*

She pushed such gloomy thoughts aside, determined not to wallow in self-pity. It was becoming far too comfortable an occupation.

That evening, Eleanor enjoyed the easy conversation around the Moores' dinner table. Margaret regaled them with tales from the classroom, and both Rupert and Henry were eager listeners.

'It certainly sounds like a success,' Henry commented. 'I know Rupert intended it to be!'

'What?' Eleanor exclaimed in surprise. 'That is, what do you mean?'

Henry raised his eyebrows, shrugging. 'Rupert went around the neighbourhoods, didn't you know? He chatted the school up quite a bit, spoke to the fathers. Seemed to think a man's influence would help sway them, and I do believe he was correct. Rupert?' Henry looked questioningly at his brother-in-law.

Rupert shrugged in dismissal. 'It was but a small thing.'

Eleanor looked down at her plate. She didn't know whether to feel irritated or grateful, and the truth was she felt both. *How dare he interfere,* her self-righteous self cried, even as her heart acknowledged, *he took an interest.*

'We're certainly thankful for your interest,' Margaret said, giving Eleanor a curious look. Eleanor looked up and smiled.

'Yes, indeed, why did you not tell us before?'

'It didn't seem important.' Rupert moved the discussion on to other topics, and Eleanor was glad for the reprieve.

You are being a ninny, she scolded herself silently. This is about the school . . . the school only!

After dinner, they all retired to the drawing room. Henry and Margaret sat by the fire, playing spillikins, while Eleanor sat by the window, watching the spill of moonlight on the garden outside.

Rupert came and sat down next to her. 'You seem vexed, Mrs McCardell.'

'I believe we know each other sufficiently to use our Christian names,' Eleanor replied tartly.

'Very well, then, use mine.'

Eleanor looked up suspiciously. Was he making fun of her? With Rupert, she could never tell. 'I am not vexed, Rupert.'

'Are you quite certain?'

'It surprised me, that is all.'

'What did?'

'Your . . . involvement in the school.'

Rupert sat back, looking genuinely surprised. 'Is that it? But I only wanted it to succeed.'

'Indeed, and as Margaret said, we are grateful.'

Rupert chuckled. 'No, as I recall, Margaret said she was grateful. You, however, seem quite the contrary.'

'I assure you I am not.'

Rupert lowered his voice. 'Perhaps, then, you are vexed about something else?'

'I do not know what that could be.' Eleanor concentrated on her teacup, as if the act of raising it to her lips was one that required consummate skill.

'Perhaps you are still vexed by the kiss we shared over a month ago now.'

Eleanor saw Margaret shoot them a quick, searching look, and she knew their private game was no mistake, but an intention to afford her and Rupert some privacy . . . the last thing she needed!

She drew in a shaky breath. 'You are wrong,' she said quietly. 'And you are wrong to tease me about it.'

Rupert held out a hand, then dropped it. 'Eleanor, I am not teasing you. If the truth be told, that kiss still vexes *me.*'

Eleanor felt her face flame. 'I do not know why it should,' she said curtly.

'Can't you guess?'

Eleanor's heart beat faster, and a thin tendril of hope curled to life within her. Was he suggesting he had feelings for her? But she was too fearful of being embarrassed, her own raw feelings exposed, to challenge him. 'No, I cannot.' She rose from her seat. 'Margaret . . . Henry . . . I must go. The hour is late.'

'Rupert could take you home,' Margaret offered, and Eleanor shook her head, not daring to look at him.

'No, he must not trouble himself. If your coachman would escort me, that will do admirably.'

Margaret looked to protest, but Rupert sketched a little bow. 'As you wish. I assure you, it's no trouble, unless it might trouble yourself.'

'It does,' Eleanor snapped, and with that, she hurried out of the room.

I acted like a fool, she berated herself in the coach on the way home. Why couldn't she laugh and flirt like Caroline Campbell, like any normal young woman? Why must she always be so prickly, so nervous?

Eleanor sighed. She'd never had a proper

flirtation, a real romance. John McCardell's courting of her had been a steady, stolid affair. Admittedly, they'd shared an awkward sort of friendship, but her heart had not beat faster, she had not dreamed of him kissing her. Mostly, Eleanor realized, she'd just wanted to escape her life on the farm.

She closed her eyes, willing the memories away. If Rupert truly cared for her, he wouldn't play these games, trying to force her own hand. He would be a gentleman, and declare himself.

Until that happened, Eleanor decided, she wouldn't give Rupert any more opportunity to tease — or humiliate — her.

A few days later, Eleanor arrived at the Moores' home to find Henry and Margaret in a blazing row.

It had been her custom to call for Margaret on the way to school. They often discussed the planned lessons, the individual pupils and their concerns, on the way to the school building.

Now Eleanor stood uncertainly in the hallway, Margaret and Henry glaring at each other.

'It's madness, Margaret. I've told you before. You must not.'

'You would forbid me, then?'

Henry raked a hand through his sandy

hair in frustration. 'I would not forbid you anything! But for my sake, as well as yours, I ask that you exercise caution!'

'And what of the children, waiting for us? What of the parents, who live with this kind of risk everyday? You think me so selfish?'

'I think myself so selfish,' Henry shouted. 'I don't want to lose you.'

There was a moment of silence as they stared at each other, Margaret still stormy, Henry beseeching.

'What is the matter?' Eleanor asked faintly.

Margaret turned on her, eyes glittering, cheeks flushed with temper. 'There has been an outbreak of typhoid by the docks, in the immigrant neighbourhoods. Henry wants us to close the school until it passes.'

'But isn't that . . .' Eleanor trailed off before Margaret's obvious anger. 'Most schools close in the face of pestilence,' she said quietly.

'Not ours.' Margaret shook her head. 'Eleanor, it's hardly likely a child with typhoid could make it to school! The contagion is kept in the homes. And what of the children who would be in school, if we are there? What of the children who will stay at home, and perhaps catch the disease, because we closed our doors?'

'There is no need to put your own lives at

risk,' Henry muttered.

Margaret turned away, almost near tears. 'God help those mothers, losing their children . . . their babies! I will not add to their suffering, not one jot.' She turned to Henry. 'Please, Henry.'

Henry shrugged, defeated. 'I said I will not forbid, but for heaven's sake, Margaret . . .' he held his hands out. 'I love you . . .'

'I know. I love you as well. But you must let me . . .'

Henry only nodded.

'If you feel so strongly, of course I will accompany you,' Eleanor said quietly, and Margaret gave her a grateful look. Eleanor suppressed the qualm of fear she felt at the thought of being exposed to the dreaded typhoid. If Margaret could face it, then she would as well.

The number of pupils in their school was not too depleted, and Eleanor was glad she'd agreed to go, despite the obvious dangers. She put her arm around a shy four-year-old, the girl's head leaning against her shoulder. Sometimes the First School felt like the only place where she was completely wanted and necessary.

Margaret smiled wearily as the pupils filed out at the end of the day. 'You see? What would have happened to all these children if we'd closed the doors?'

'I concede the point,' Eleanor replied with a little smile. 'I only hope the dangers are not too great. You look a trifle peaked.'

'Merely fatigued,' Margaret replied. 'It's been a long day.'

'Are you quite certain?' Eleanor placed a hand on Margaret's forehead. 'You seem warm.'

'Eleanor, don't fuss! You are as bad as Henry, thinking I shall come down with the typhoid if I so much as take a breath. Please, I'm fine.' Margaret ushered her out and locked the school room door. Wallers fell in step behind them. The sky was iron grey, the leaves turning to deep yellow, and a cold wind blew in from the bay. Margaret shivered and drew her shawl around her shoulders.

'Margaret . . .'

'Don't,' Margaret said. 'I can't bear any more fussing, really I can't.'

They climbed into the carriage Henry always had waiting, and Margaret leaned her head against the cushions and closed her eyes.

Eleanor bit her lip. She wouldn't fuss, but she was still worried. Margaret looked drained.

They rode in silence for some minutes. Eleanor watched Margaret. She hadn't opened her eyes once, and a hectic flush was already spreading across her cheeks. Eleanor reached out a hand and touched Margaret's shoulder. It burned.

'Margaret!' she cried, and her friend did not stir.

The carriage ride became a blur of frantic activity. Eleanor rapped on the door to alert the driver, biting her knuckles in anxiety, wishing the carriage had wings.

Henry had already opened the front door when the carriage pulled to a stop, as if he knew.

'It's Margaret,' Eleanor gasped. 'She's ill!'

Henry's face drained of colour, but his eyes were angry. 'I knew it! I knew this would happen!' He snapped at the coachman. 'Run for the doctor!'

Eleanor helped Henry take Margaret inside. She undressed her herself, laying her between cool sheets. Margaret moaned, her eyes opening.

'Margaret . . . dear . . .'

'You mustn't let Henry fuss,' Margaret said, her voice somewhere between a croak and a whisper. 'I'm just worn out. I know I am.'

'Of course,' Eleanor murmured. The doctor stood in the doorway, his face grave. 'The doctor's here to see you, Margaret, just to make sure you're all right.' But Margaret had already slipped back into unconsciousness.

Downstairs, in the drawing room, Henry stared bleakly out at the darkness, a tumbler of whiskey clenched in one fist. 'I told her . . . I *told* her . . .' He turned to Eleanor. 'Do you think it is the typhoid? Might she not just be fatigued?' he asked, his voice tinged with desperation.

'I pray it's only that,' Eleanor said quietly. There was no need to say more.

A quarter of an hour later, the doctor joined them. 'I'm afraid it's what I expected,' he said, his face grim.

'Expected?' Henry looked pleading, as if there was still a chance for good news.

'Your wife is very ill, Mr Moore. She has typhoid.'

Chapter Twelve

Ian leaned his head against the seat cushions and sighed in weary satisfaction. It had been four weeks since he'd left Boston, and he hadn't meant to be away so long. Now, as he jolted along in the stage coach, he wondered what kind of reception awaited him at home.

His conscience gave him an uncomfortable twinge, as he thought of both Isobel and Caroline. He'd promised Eleanor he would speak to Isobel, and yet he hadn't. How could he dash hopes she had not actually voiced? He feared it would ruin his friendship with the Moores; worse still, it could ruin Isobel.

And Caroline . . . he closed his eyes. Her impish smile and frightened eyes had followed him to Hartford. She was such an innocent, naïve and yet endearingly coy, trying to play the elegant lady.

As the stage coach bumped along the rutted road, his mind turned to Dr Wells and his experiments with ether.

He'd arranged to visit the controversial doctor when he'd read of the dentist's experiments with both ether and nitrous oxide as surgical aids. Ian had planned a conversation only, perhaps some observation, but Dr Wells had been so delighted in having an ally that he'd invited Ian to stay and work with him in his investigations. Ian was thrilled, his obligations in Boston, as well as Isobel and Caroline, forgotten in the thrill of discovery.

'Medicine always means risk, if we are to advance,' Wells told him one evening. 'I know there are many who consider what I'm doing the actions of a madman, or a fool.' He shook his head, smiling in self-deprecation. 'Administering a dangerous substance to squirrels and rats? Sometimes I wonder myself.' He paused reflectively. 'The obvious thing to do, of course, is find someone willing to administer the ether to me.'

Ian's mouth dropped open in shock. 'Is that safe?' Despite his passion for the cause, he knew well the medical community's doubt of ether's ability to render a patient unconscious for severe surgeries.

'It's been safe on the squirrels and rats,'

Wells replied with a little shrug.

'Yes, but . . .' Ian's mouth was dry. The dangers of an unauthorized procedure were manifold. Besides the obvious danger to Dr Wells, Ian knew his own medical licence could be revoked. He would be forced to retire in shame and ignominy.

'If you prefer, I could administer it to you,' Wells continued, his eyebrows raised, a shrewd look on his face.

'I honestly don't know which I prefer.'

Wells leaned forward. 'Do you believe in this, Dr Crombie? Because if you don't, you are wasting my time and I am wasting yours.'

Ian thought of what ether promised . . . surgeries performed without a patient needing to be subdued, writhing in agony or falling into unconsciousness because of the pain. New operations could be attempted that surgeons merely shook their heads at, because it was too painful, too impossible, would take too long. 'Better they die,' Ian had heard a cynical, or just weary, doctor remark more than once.

'I do believe in it,' he said in a low voice and Dr Wells sat back, satisfied.

'Well, then.'

Safely ensconced in the stage coach, Ian still had to suppress a shudder of raw fear when he remembered the procedure. He'd agreed to administer the ether, holding the glass ball and flute above Wells' face, so as only to give him the few crucial drops.

His hand had been shaking, he'd been scared he would grip the flute too tightly and shatter it. Dr Wells had quickly become insensible, muttering and seemingly delirious.

Wells had instructed Ian to make an incision on his arm, to see if he felt the pain. Ian hadn't wanted to do it . . . a needless cut, pointless injury! It went against everything he believed in as a doctor.

And yet . . . this experiment represented all his hopes and ambitions in the medical field.

He'd made the incision and stitched it, then waited apprehensively for Dr Wells to come round again.

It took at least half an hour, every minute feeling like an age, until Wells' eyes fluttered open and he smiled sleepily. Ian sagged with relief.

Dr Wells had been ebullient. 'It worked! I felt nothing . . . perhaps a small scratching. It was as if I were dreaming. Almost pleasant, really.'

They spent the rest of the evening discussing the experiment, and planning for Ian to present their findings to the board of surgeons at Massachusetts General Hospital.

At this thought, Ian's mouth went dry. He was a young doctor, considered by many to be untried. He'd already been warned by his superior. If Dr Collins discovered his journey to Hartford was not the pleasure trip he'd indicated, he could be dismissed, never to work again.

Would anyone, he wondered bleakly, welcome his findings? How else would medicine advance?

Wells had been adamant. 'If you do not present these findings, the opportunity will never arise! People — doctors especially, it seems — have to be dragged into this new dawn. Just think, Crombie — if you operate on me at the Bulfinch theatre! What a coup for medicine, and your own career. Your fortune, sir, will be made.'

'I'm not a surgeon,' Ian protested. His mind whirled. He saw the sense of Wells' suggestion; if they didn't take their research forward, it would be in vain. He just didn't want to sacrifice his position and livelihood to do it.

Yet Ian knew he would take the risk. If he didn't, he would be ashamed of himself, of failing to stand by what he believed, and Wells would be unbearably disappointed.

The stage coach rumbled forward, jostling him as it made its way across southern Massachusetts' rutted roads.

Ian's thoughts drifted again to Caroline, and he felt the tingling of trepidation and excitement. He had left her nearly a month ago, declaring his intention to court her. What would she think, when he'd virtually disappeared immediately afterwards?

He'd sent her a note, of course, as he had to the hospital, but he wondered if a scribbled missive had appeased her, if it had even reached her?

Ian knew all too well what her uncle was capable of, and keeping a letter from his niece would be the least of his sins.

If he were truthful, Ian thought, he'd stayed away in part to test Caroline . . . to see if her feelings changed, or if his did.

He knew the appearance she lent to the world . . . a scatterbrained girl, beautiful but flighty. He believed there was more to her than most would think, yet how could he be sure? She'd not been tested. She'd not had to prove her strength or courage.

And yet, he acknowledged, it was unfair to administer such a test himself. He wouldn't blame her if she turned her back on him, declared him unworthy. He *was* unworthy! Yet he longed to see her again, even to hold her in his arms. . . .'

All he could do was wait. Ian closed his eyes, resigning himself to the journey. He would wait . . . wait and hope.

Eleanor ran the damp cloth over Margaret's flushed face, trying to cool the fever that raged within her, rendering her weak and often unconscious.

It had been nearly a week since the doctor had made his dreadful announcement that Margaret had contracted typhoid. Eleanor thought she would never forget the look on Henry's face as he stood, silhouetted by the drawing-room's curtains, his face drained of all colour.

'You will need to nurse her,' the doctor continued with ruthless detachment, 'Preferably around the clock.'

Henry's mouth was working, as if he were trying to form a response, yet could think of none but outright denial of the diagnosis. Eleanor had never seen him at such a loss.

'I'll do it.'

The doctor turned to her in surprise. 'It is not generally considered the responsibility of a gently bred lady,' he said repressively, and Eleanor raised her eyebrows.

'Oh, you would prefer a woman of questionable morals? Or a sluggard?'

His face reddened. 'Of course not. I am merely suggesting that you might find it beyond your abilities.'

'I see, you don't consider me up to the task?' Eleanor's eyes flashed even as she nodded in apparent understanding. 'I feel no need to assure you that I am.'

'Eleanor . . .' Henry protested, glancing between her and the doctor.

The doctor gave Henry a significant look. 'Of course, it is your decision,' he said quietly. 'I'm sure you have quite a vested interest in who nurses your wife.'

Eleanor looked down; she hadn't meant to start an argument with the doctor, especially with Henry looking on. She wasn't even sure why she was so angry; she wasn't normally this shrewish. Her worry for Margaret seemed to have manifested itself as anger; her fists were clenched. She realized she wanted to do more than simply occupy herself; she wanted to help, even to change things. To have a purpose, no matter how short the time.

'I believe Eleanor will make an admirable nurse,' Henry said quietly. His face was still pale, but he managed to smile at her. 'I think that's what Margaret would have wanted.' As if realizing how he spoke of his wife, he said quickly, 'She *does* want it, I mean to say, she will . . .' He trailed off, turning away, and Eleanor felt a swift pang of sympathy for the naked pain twisting his features.

The doctor laid a hand on his shoulder. 'I'm sorry, Henry. I'll come tomorrow to see how she fares.'

After the doctor had gone, Henry went to sit with Margaret. He'd sat there every day, for as long as he could, before Eleanor forced him to eat, or sleep, or at least get some fresh air.

Her admonitions about getting the disease himself, or becoming too worn out to be of any use to anyone, fell on deaf ears. Henry sat by his wife, holding her limp hand as if he could somehow transfer his own health and well-being to the woman he adored, lying feverish and unconscious in her bed.

The doctor had been as good as his word, and come every day to check on Margaret's — and Eleanor's — progress. She'd grudgingly won his respect with her diligence, although he warned her that she was at risk of contracting the disease as well.

'I've always had a strong constitution,' Eleanor replied briskly, but inside she felt a lurch of fear. She didn't want to be ill. No matter how bleak her prospects sometimes seemed, she did not yet want to die.

Now, with the doctor gone, Henry downstairs for the moment and Margaret sleeping, Eleanor wondered what the future held . . . *could* hold. It had been a week, and though Margaret's fever had diminished at times, it had never truly broken. The future, for her at least, was frighteningly uncertain.

As Margaret dozed, Eleanor's thoughts turned to the immigrant neighbourhood where the typhoid raged, and the school which had been forced to close since Margaret's illness.

They must keep the school open, Eleanor thought. She knew it instinctively. If the school failed the people now, the pupils wouldn't come back. They would feel betrayed, their trust taken and stamped on.

It was what Margaret would want.

And yet . . . how? Eleanor was not willing to relinquish her role as Margaret's nurse. She knew others could perform the service capably, but it seemed a matter of honour to her, to be with Margaret, to see her through this. She believed Henry took comfort from it as well, thankful he didn't have to trust his wife's care to strangers. He could do the job himself, she thought wryly, and often did.

As for the school, the only other option

then, she told herself with forced practicality, was to find a new teacher. But who would be willing to take the risk?

'The doctor's just left.' Henry stood in the doorway, pale and haggard as he had been since Margaret fell ill. 'He says it's still up to Providence, of course. . . .'

'Something we all know,' Eleanor replied bracingly.

Henry's smile flickered and died. 'I asked him . . . he said he had some hope that she might pull through yet.' He paused, thoughtfully. '*Some* hope. What do you think that means, Eleanor?'

'It's better than none.'

'It's not much.'

'Henry, you must keep your spirits up.' Eleanor kept her tone purposely severe. 'You cannot fall into self-pity now. Margaret needs you strong. We all do.'

'I know.' Henry swallowed, choking back emotion. 'Thank you, Eleanor, for what you've done. If Margaret knew . . .'

'She will, quite soon, I think,' Eleanor replied briskly. 'When the fever breaks, she'll come out of her delirium.'

'You sound so certain.'

'I am certain.' But Eleanor averted her eyes, for she didn't want Henry to see the shadow of doubt within them. The truth was, she didn't feel certain at all . . . about anything.

'I'll sit with her,' Henry said, his voice bleak. 'You need a rest.'

So did Henry, but Eleanor didn't argue. He drew some comfort from being with her, she knew.

Eleanor made to leave the sick room, the wave of exhaustion that she'd held at bay now sweeping over her. She was tired, dirty and sweaty, and terribly hungry. She hadn't slept, eaten, or bathed properly in days.

With a sigh, she took off her apron and hung it by the door, making a mental note to remind the housekeeper of the need for a fresh one.

Although most doctors would insist dirt didn't matter to an ill person, Eleanor could hardly believe this was true. There had to be some reason diseases such as typhoid bred in crowded, squalid places. She didn't hold with the belief that it was the immigrants themselves that caused the disease.

She was just coming down the stairs, tucking a stray tendril of hair back into her bun, when the front door opened and Rupert stood there.

Eleanor's heart bumped in her chest even as she fought to keep her face impassive, indifferent even. If only she didn't look so dishevelled! But that could hardly be helped when she'd spent the last week in a sick room.

'Eleanor!' Rupert looked up at her, a smile breaking through the worry shadowing his face.

'Hello, Rupert.' Eleanor forced herself to sound calm, unconcerned. 'Are you here to see Henry?'

'Yes . . .' Rupert admitted. 'Though I wanted to see you as well. You're still nursing Margaret?'

'Yes.' Eleanor smoothed the front of her dress, a futile gesture, she knew, to improve her appearance. 'For as long as she needs me. . . .'

'I don't think you should do it,' Rupert said abruptly, a deep frown on his face, and she stared at him in astonishment.

'Is that so? Then, I'm glad your opinion is not my concern.'

'Don't take that tone with me,' Rupert retorted irritably, and Eleanor had trouble to keep herself from gaping at him.

'And don't treat me like a wayward child! I shall do as I please, and in this instance, all I can to help Margaret.'

Rupert turned away, his shoulders hunched as if he were struggling with himself. Eleanor stood there uncertainly, unsure whether she should smartly leave, or wait for Rupert to say something . . . perhaps even apologize.

'Eleanor,' he finally said, his back still turned to her. 'I'm not saying this because I think you are like a child . . .'

'And very glad I am to hear it!'

He turned around, his eyes blazing. 'Would you please stop snapping at me and listen? I fear for your own health.'

'I assure you, my constitution is strong.'

'You needn't shoulder the burden alone,' Rupert insisted. 'There are others who could take over, give you rest. You will help nobody if you work yourself into the ground!'

'I'm well aware of that.'

'I don't want you to become ill.' Rupert stared at her helplessly, and Eleanor felt a queer fluttering in her chest, as if something long buried, thought dead, was just stirring into life again.

'Why not?' she asked quietly.

'Are you mad? I wouldn't want anyone to become ill!' he exclaimed.

'I see.' Eleanor looked away, the fluttering inside her quieting again.

'Especially you.' The words were almost forced out, and Eleanor appraised him coolly.

'Very touching, I'm sure.'

Rupert looked annoyed, and then suddenly, as if transformed, he grinned. 'You're right. I'm not good at this. I've gone about it all wrong.'

Eleanor said nothing. She waited, hardly daring to hope . . .

'Eleanor, I care for you. I . . .' Rupert took a breath. 'I love you.'

Eleanor felt her face blush, although inside her heart filled with joy. She kept her features composed as she met his gaze. 'Then you will have to trust me, won't you?' Rupert opened his mouth in surprise, and Eleanor smiled. 'I'll fetch Henry.'

And with that, not daring to say or reveal more, she left for the kitchen.

Rupert stared after her, frustration and admiration mingled within him. She had courage, he thought with a little smile, courage and daring. Had he expected her to fall in his arms, swooning?

No. Not Eleanor. Yet he still wished she'd said something . . . given him hope that she returned his affections. His smile widened. He would just have to do what she said. He would have to trust her.

'Rupert?' Henry came down the stairs, running a hand wearily through his hair. 'I thought I heard your voice.'

'I'm sorry to disturb you at this time,' Rupert said, and Henry shook his head.

'It's not easy. I haven't put my head to business in days, I know . . .' He sighed. 'Life goes on, doesn't it? Business must. You mentioned in your note that you had something to discuss with me regarding the accounts?' Rupert nodded, and Henry ushered him into the study. 'I know it's a bit early in the day, but . . . ?' He gestured to the whiskey bottle on the sideboard, and with a shrug, Rupert nodded.

Henry poured two healthy measures, handed one to Rupert, and gulped his down. 'All right.' He sat at his desk and looked up. 'There is a problem, I assume?'

'Yes. A forgery.' Briefly Rupert told him of the Bank of New York notes, and how the smear of ink had made him suspect the money was counterfeit.

'And you had it confirmed at the bank?'

'Yes. I also looked in the office ledger. The money, I believe, was received from a local wine merchant in payment for shipment on the *Julia Rose.*'

'I believe I remember it.'

'What shall we do?' Rupert asked, his expression direct, and Henry let out his breath in an irritated whoosh.

'I don't know, Rupert. I haven't dealt with this before, you know. And I hardly have the presence of mind to deal with it now!' He stood up, striding across the room with restless energy. 'Right now the health of my wife is more important than a pile of fusty bank notes.'

Rupert was silent, unwilling to argue the point. Henry shrugged in something like apology. 'I'm sorry. You should not have to bear the brunt of my temper.' He paused. 'Forgery is usually handled by a marshal, although I'd prefer to keep the law out of it for the moment. From what I've heard, marshals have not got the best results, and they often scare the forgers into hiding without actually finding them. Besides, if word gets around, it could be damaging to the business, not to mention dangerous.'

'Dangerous? How?'

'Forgers are not nice people.' Henry smiled wryly, although there was a hard, flinty expression in his eyes. 'Some of the larger forgery rings have been involved in a good deal more than copying bank notes. They have, on occasions, resorted to murder. Or so the newspapers report.'

Rupert drew himself up. 'What do you suggest we do?'

'I'm not sure.' Henry glanced out the

window, his expression shuttered. 'As I told you, I don't have the time — or desire, frankly — to deal with it myself.'

'Of course. I'm happy to put any plan you might suggest into action.'

'Are you?' Henry glanced at him shrewdly. 'What I'd suggest is to investigate it quietly, but it wouldn't be easy or safe.'

'I don't mind that.'

Henry looked at him directly. 'I cannot put you in danger.'

'You aren't, if I volunteer.' Rupert shrugged, smiling, and Henry shook his head.

'Why are you so eager to put yourself in danger?'

'I'm eager to see justice done. And, I don't mind admitting, I intend to rise in this world, and that starts with proving to you and anyone else what I'm capable of.'

'You think you can catch these forgers?'

'Yes, I do.' Rupert wished he was as certain as he sounded, but he had no doubts that he intended to try. This was his opportunity, bald and staring, and he would grasp it with both hands.

'Very well. I give you leave to begin an investigation. You can report to me anything you discover. And for heaven's sake, Rupert, be safe.'

'Thank you, Henry.' Rupert clapped his brother-in-law on the shoulder, his expression sombre. 'And God be with you, and Margaret.'

'Yes,' Henry agreed quietly. 'God be with us all.'

As Rupert left the house, he felt the mingling of excitement, determination, and a little bit of fear, like a taste of iron in his mouth. He swallowed, keeping his eyes straight ahead. He would solve this forgery, and he would show Henry — and who knew who else — just what he was made of . . . no matter what it cost him.

The obvious place to start, of course, was the wine merchant's. Rupert doubted the merchant knew the bills were forgeries. It was unlikely to be such an easy discovery, and any criminal with even a modicum of common sense would not pass off so many of the bills so directly. Yet, perhaps he would be fortunate.

The wine merchant's offices were over his warehouse, near the docks. It took Rupert the better part of an hour to find them, and then finally to corner the merchant in his private office.

'Rupert MacDougall, of Moore Shipping Enterprises. May I have a word?'

The merchant, Ben Phillips, a small, dark

man, looked up with a mixture of curiosity and unease marring his features. 'Yes, if you must.'

Not the most promising beginning, but Rupert smiled easily. 'We recently brought a shipment of Madeira to you, for which you paid —'

'Handsomely,' Phillips interjected, looking a bit irritated.

'Are you suggesting the price was unfair?' Rupert smiled pleasantly.

'Of course not. I wouldn't have paid it if it had been. I just don't see what your business is, tracking me down. The payment was in order, wasn't it?'

'Actually, it wasn't.'

Phillips' face suffused with colour. 'What do you mean, it wasn't? I supervised the handling of the money myself.'

'There was enough money,' Rupert hastened to assure him. He paused, significantly, while Phillips waited, irritated and uneasy. 'Unfortunately, the money was counterfeit.'

Phillips' face, once mottled red, now drained of colour. 'All of it?'

'Yes.'

As if realizing his error in making such an admission, Phillips began to bluster. 'How do you know it was from me? Perhaps you're just looking for a scapegoat!'

'Very well.' Rupert leaned back in his chair. 'Why don't you tell me what banknotes you gave in payment to Moore Shipping. That should be a simple test.'

Phillips paused, seeing the trap. 'Well, I can't be certain. . . .'

'Surely that sort of thing is written down? I assure you, it's in our ledgers, we gave you a receipt.' He shrugged. 'I imagine that would be enough for a court of law.'

'How dare you threaten me!'

'The truth is, Mr Phillips, I could have the law here in under an hour, searching your offices, your cash boxes. Are there more of those fake notes? I imagine so, and from what I hear marshals these days aren't concerned with catching the printer, that's too difficult. They're happy to arrest anyone with the notes in their possession, and that means you.'

'How was I supposed to know they were counterfeit?' Phillips mumbled. His shoulders were slumped in obvious despair.

'Of course, I'm sure you had no idea,' Rupert said smoothly. 'However . . .'

'What?' Phillips looked up, cornered and angry again, reminding Rupert of a rat. 'What is it you want, anyway?'

'An excellent question. Moore Shipping,

of course, wants the money back, not forgeries.'

'That'll mean I pay double!'

Rupert shrugged, the expression on his face delicately implying that was not his concern. 'We also want to find the printer.'

'The printer?' Phillips looked, for the first time, genuinely afraid.

'Yes. The printer. To stop it once and for all. And that's where you can help.'

'Why should I?'

'I believe I mentioned the law . . .' Rupert pressed the tips of his fingers together, as if waiting.

'Are you threatening me?' Phillips demanded.

'No, I'm merely informing you of the consequence of possessing counterfeit money.'

Phillips made a sound like a growl. 'Very well. I'll have to look in the ledger.' He stood up as if to leave the room. 'It may take some time.'

'Fortunately, I have no pressing engagements.' Rupert smiled. 'Why don't I come with you?'

They left the cramped office on top of the warehouse for a more spacious, albeit dingy room, down below, crowded with shelves and drawers, and a spotty young clerk bend-ing over some figures.

'Dobson,' Phillips snapped to the clerk. 'I need the ledger with the figures for transactions in . . .' he paused, shooting Rupert a quick, speculative glance. 'The last month.'

What was that about? Rupert wondered. He doubted Phillips was part of the forgery ring; he didn't seem brave or clever enough for that. Yet the man might know more than he was letting on.

It took Phillips the better part of half an hour to go through his ink-splotched ledgers, laboriously squinting over each transaction detail. 'There.' He pointed to an entry in the book. 'Bank of New York notes.'

Rupert smiled slightly; he had never said the notes were from the Bank of New York, yet Phillips knew the notes in question. Was he, perhaps, one of the members of the ring, lower down on the rungs of power? If so, he should fear his betters in crime even more than the law.

Rupert felt a stirring of unease. He wasn't afraid of Phillips; the man was small, greasy, but easily handled. There were others, though, whom he had not yet met, who would hear of his inquiries and take action. He needed to be careful.

'Who were the notes from?' Rupert asked brusquely.

Phillips paused before answering. 'Summers. That's his name. He bought twelve cases of port.'

'That's quite a lot, don't you think?'

Phillips only shrugged.

'And if I tell this Summers that you gave me this information?' Rupert asked.

'What should I have to fear?' But Phillips did not quite meet his eyes.

'Do you have Summers' address?'

Phillips gave it; it was another warehouse near the docks, which seemed suspicious. What could another merchant want with so much port?

'I'll be back,' Rupert warned. 'After I've spoken to Summers. So I hope you are not thinking of going anywhere.'

The wine merchant smiled rather unpleasantly. 'And where would I be going?'

Dusk was falling as Rupert left the warehouse. He turned his collar up against the cold, wishing there were more people in the street. He felt vulnerable, walking the rough cobbles on his own. Easy pickings. He picked up his pace.

He heard the footsteps behind him, light and quick as a cat's, but before he could turn or move at all, he took a crashing blow on the back of his head and fell to the ground.

Spots danced before his eyes, and he fought to retain consciousness as rough, grubby hands turned him over and grabbed the lapels of his coat.

'That's a warning,' someone growled, inches from his face. 'Stop your prying, if you know what's good for you.'

A face swam in and out of focus before Rupert was dropped back on the sharp cobblestones. The last thing he heard was someone hurrying away before he blacked out completely.

Chapter Thirteen

Eleanor stared up at the front of Stephen and Arabella Moores' residence. Imposing and regal, she'd been impressed by the house's elegant proportions the last time she'd visited, to take tea with Isobel.

Isobel had taken the opportunity to inform Eleanor of her intentions; now Eleanor wanted to inform the young woman of hers.

She took a slow, steadying breath, and knocked.

'May I help you?' the butler, ponderous but with a kindly smile, looked down on her.

'My name is Eleanor McCardell. I'd like to speak with Isobel, please. She doesn't expect me, but I am a friend of hers.'

The butler glanced at her dress, slightly worn but respectable, and after a second's hesitation, nodded. 'Won't you come in, miss?'

'I'd rather not.' Eleanor smiled apologetically. 'No doubt you've heard of the typhoid sweeping the city. I'm nursing a sufferer myself, and I've no wish to spread the contagion.'

The butler took a step back, an expression of fearful distaste on his face. 'Could you please ask Miss Moore to meet me outside? Perhaps we can take a turn in the park, where the air is fresh.'

'I will speak with her, miss.' The butler left quickly.

A few minutes later, Isobel came outside, a cloak thrown over her shoulders, her expression one of alarm 'Eleanor!' She stretched out her hands, dropping them suddenly as she remembered the disease that threatened them all. 'We are all praying for dear Margaret. Have you any news from my brother's household?'

Eleanor shook her head. 'Only that Margaret remains the same. Her fever lessens, and then spikes again. The doctor says it must break in the next few days if we're to have hope.'

Isobel paled. 'Is it that close, then?'

'I pray not. The doctor still seems to think we have some hope, although how much, I could not tell you. Margaret has always been strong.' Eleanor paused. 'There is another matter of which I would like to speak to you. Perhaps we could walk?'

Isobel frowned in confusion, then nodded. 'Very well.'

A few minutes later they were walking through Boston Common, the wind buffeting their faces and pulling their cloaks more tightly around them.

'You know of Margaret's school,' Eleanor began tentatively, and Isobel nodded.

'For the immigrants?'

There was something in Isobel's tone that Eleanor didn't quite like, but she knew there was no point dwelling on it now. 'We've had to close the school since the typhoid epidemic started,' she told Isobel. 'There are no teachers, since I'm nursing Margaret, and with so many ill . . .'

'A pity, I'm sure.' Isobel's brow wrinkled in confusion, as if she could not understand why Eleanor was discussing this with her.

'It seems the worst of the epidemic has passed,' Eleanor continued. 'At least in the neighbourhoods we draw from for the school. It's time, I think, the school reopened.'

'After less than a fortnight?' Isobel raised her eyebrows. 'I suppose it must, if you can find the teachers.'

'Well . . .' Eleanor took a breath. 'I believe

I can.' She paused and then plunged ahead. 'You.'

Isobel was too ladylike to splutter, but she did a fair imitation, gaping at Eleanor in amazement. 'Me? But of course that is quite impossible!'

'Is it?' Eleanor asked softly. 'I know you might not seem an obvious choice . . .'

'Oh, you think not?' Isobel asked a bit sharply, and Eleanor smothered a smile.

'I only meant, considering your station in life, and, I'm sure, your many occupations . . .'

'There are not that many.' Isobel pulled her cloak tighter around her, staring off at the naked branches of an oak tree, stark against a slate-grey sky. 'I wouldn't know the first thing about . . . anything.'

'The pupils are able learners. They're hungry for knowledge, they merely need someone to feed it to them. The school has primers and slates, thanks to Henry, and the older children can tell you what we've already done.'

Isobel was silent. Finally, she looked at Eleanor, a strange glint of vulnerability in her eyes. 'Why did you ask me?'

'I thought it a good match,' Eleanor replied with a smile.

'And you could think of no one else!'

Isobel's lips twitched in a smile.

'Actually, I did think of someone else. Caroline Campbell.'

Isobel's expression darkened, and her fingers twisted the silk of her dress. 'He loves her, you know.'

Eleanor did not pretend to misunderstand. 'I don't know about that.'

'He's been gone for nearly a month,' Isobel said flatly. 'And he has not written me once, not even a note. It almost makes me feel . . . ashamed . . . for my hopes.'

'We all hope,' Eleanor told her gently. She would not pretend that Isobel's hopes had more foundation than she believed them to. Although she'd not spoken to Caroline in many weeks, and Ian the same, she'd seen the glances between them at the last party.

'Do you think Ian wants to marry Caroline?' Isobel asked. 'She seems such a fluttery, silly girl! I know I can't aspire to *much* better, but still . . .'

'I cannot predict the future. But Ian was never the right man for you, Isobel, as far as I could see.' She sighed, thinking briefly of Rupert. 'We cannot choose love sometimes. It chooses us.'

'I agree with that.' There was a note of bitterness in Isobel's voice, and when she spoke again, her voice was hard. 'Well, it is not over yet. I still have sufficient hope to think my cause not completely lost. He will tire of Caroline, I think; she amuses, but that is all.' Isobel's shoulders stiffened. 'We shall see what happens when Ian returns . . . which nest he flies to.' Her smile was slightly grim as she turned to Eleanor. 'Very well. I'll do it. I don't know what society will think, although charity has been the fashion. At this moment, I don't care what anyone thinks. I've spent enough time wasted on fruitless hopes and dreams. I want to *do* something with my life.' Her face suddenly looked childlike, the expression in her eyes lost, vulnerable once more. 'And perhaps some dreams . . . aren't so hopeless . . . in time?'

Eleanor smiled and, without any need for words, reached over and squeezed Isobel's hand.

Ian's heart was singing with anticipation as he left the stage coach and hurried back to his own home. He smothered the pang of guilt at being gone such a long time — once people learned of his discoveries, he was sure they would be understanding.

'Master Ian!' His butler and manservant, Davies, looked stunned at Ian's arrival home. 'I didn't expect you . . .' He faltered and then tried to draw himself up.

Ian waved him aside. 'I do apologize for my lack of contact, Davies. I was only planning to stay in Hartford for a few days — a week, at most, but events overtook me. I did write to Eleanor.'

'Yes, but it was so vague.'

'I'm sorry, as I said, events overtook me.' He smiled and began to rifle through the pile of post left on his desk. 'I don't suppose anything too important has happened while I've been away? Where's Eleanor?'

'She's been staying at the Moore household,' Davies replied. 'Mrs Margaret Moore came down with typhoid, and your sister has been nursing her.'

'What?' Ian dropped the letter he was holding, and it fluttered to the ground. 'Typhoid, in the city? I had no idea. . . .'

'It came upon suddenly, or so I heard, from a ship.'

'Will Margaret . . . will she be all right? Is she recovering?'

The manservant shrugged helplessly. 'I couldn't say. The only news I've heard is from your sister, when she came back for a change of clothes, and that was several days ago.'

'Dear heaven.' Ian's face was pale. 'I should go there immediately.' He glanced at the letter on the floor, then picked it up. The handwriting was loopy and girlish, and his heart skipped a beat. He tore open the envelope. 'Ian, I have spoken to my uncle and I'm afraid for the future — mine, and certainly ours, if anything is to pass between us! Please call on me at your earliest convenience. Caroline Campbell.'

The note was dated over four weeks ago. Ian stuffed it in his pocket, grabbed the coat he'd only just taken off, and hurried for the door. 'I'll be back . . . I'm not sure when . . . don't wait up for me, Davies!'

His mind seethed with questions as he hurried towards the Rydell residence. What could have happened to make Caroline so anxious? And what of Margaret, and Eleanor?

It seemed as if his entire world had tipped upside down during his absence, and he only hoped it was in his power to right it.

He felt the sudden weight of his own selfishness, pursuing his dreams and personal glory — for he knew that possibility had entered into his own thoughts — instead of his responsibilities at home. Caroline, the woman he loved; Isobel, the woman he'd thwarted; Eleanor, the woman currently in his care. He'd left them all with little more than a word, barely a thought.

Shame burned through him and roiled through his gut; his fists clenched as uncertainty and anger directed at himself seethed within him. Let it not be too late, he thought, for any of them. *This time, let me not run away like the boy I once was, shamed and angry. Let me stand up to my responsibilities.* Dear God, let me meet them full on!

He turned the corner, and soon came to the front of Rydell's rented house. He hesitated only briefly, not wanting a direct confrontation with Rydell. Yet, he acknowledged, perhaps it was time.

He lifted his hand and knocked.

The butler, Taylor, opened the door. 'May I help you?'

'I need to speak with Miss Campbell. I believe she expects me.'

There was a flash of something like regret in the butler's eyes, his impassive expression marred only by a long, thin scar down one weathered cheek. He shook his head. 'I'm sorry, sir. Miss Campbell is out.'

'Out? Where?'

Taylor hesitated, then shook his head again. 'Out.'

Ian clenched his fists in frustration, then forced himself to remain calm. 'Of course, I see,' he said. 'Do you know when she might be in to receive visitors?'

'I couldn't say.'

There was a movement behind the butler, and then Ian heard the voice he dreaded.

'Taylor, who's there?' Rydell came to the door, smiling in unpleasant satisfaction at the sight of Ian. 'Ah, Crombie. I thought you might come sniffing round here sooner or later.'

Ian refused to rise to the taunts. He wanted Caroline now, and no other. The burning need for revenge which had fuelled him for so long felt like ash. His eyes were cold, his voice steady, as he spoke. 'I need to speak to Caroline.'

'It's Miss Campbell to you, you arrogant little pup. And I'll have you know that you may not come to call on my niece again.' Rydell paused, his chest swelling with pride. 'She is, after all, engaged to be married.'

Ian felt a cold, plunging sensation within him. Surely Rydell lied. 'I beg your pardon?'

'My niece,' Rydell informed him clearly, 'is engaged to be married to Matthew Dearborn.'

Ian shook his head slowly. 'You lie.'

'I assure you, I do not.'

'I would speak with her, then.'

Rydell's face suffused with anger. 'And I tell you, you will not, not now, not ever! You have been a thorn in my side — nay, my finger — you weasely little mongrel, for far too long and I will close this door in your face now, sir, and bid you to not darken my door or annoy my household any longer!'

Rydell made to close the door, and without thinking, Ian shoved against it, blocking it open. 'I assure you, Rydell, I have no desire to annoy you any further. You are nothing to me; the mistakes I made in my boyhood, thanks to your trickery, are naught now. It is Caroline I seek, and I will find her. You cannot keep me — or trick me — again.'

'Get out of here,' Rydell choked, and Ian smiled grimly.

'With pleasure, sir.'

His hands shoved in his pockets to keep them from shaking, he strode down the street in the oncoming twilight.

It was but a few minutes' walk to the Moores' residence, and Ian went there with haste. A parlour maid admitted him, and he found Eleanor in the kitchen, weary and worn looking, drinking tea.

'Ian! Oh, thank Providence you've returned to us!' She flew to him, and Ian drew her close.

'I'm sorry, Eleanor, I didn't come sooner,' he said, his cheek pressed against her hair. 'I've been abominably selfish in regard to you . . . and others.'

'Never mind that. I'm pleased you're back, is all.'

'Still . . .' Ian took in a shuddering breath.

Eleanor pulled away to look at him, her eyes bright. 'Are you planning to change, then?'

'Oh, yes.' His tone was fervent and she smiled.

'That's all right, then. Sit down, you look exhausted.' She bustled around the comfortable room, fetching him tea. 'I'm sorry to greet you in the kitchen; I've been fixing Margaret's trays myself, though she doesn't touch them.'

'How does she fare?'

Eleanor pursed her lips, shaking her head slightly. 'The fever has not broken.'

'Does the doctor think it will?' Ian asked, and she met his anxious gaze with bleak eyes.

'He makes no promises. It's been a fortnight, but still, there's hope. There is always hope. You could see her yourself, Ian. I'm sure Henry would appreciate the gesture.'

Ian nodded his assent, and they sat in silence for a moment, their thoughts on Margaret. 'How is Henry?' he asked finally. 'And Rupert?'

'They are both anxious for her, Henry

most of all. He is like a ghost, wandering through the rooms of the house; he neither eats nor sleeps. Rupert has taken the brunt of managing the shipping business. He looks worn out though thoroughly enjoying his responsibilities, I am sure!' She smiled slightly, still thinking of the shocked look on Rupert's face yesterday when she had not given him an answer. He loved her. It was still a new, wondrous, trembling thought. 'He is concerned for Margaret, of course,' she added hastily. 'As we all are.'

'I shall look on her at once.'

'Have you spoken to Isobel?' Eleanor asked, then could have bitten her tongue. Ian still wore his travelling clothes; he'd obviously come directly to the Moores'.

'Not yet, but I will, Eleanor.' For once he did not rise irritably to her questioning. 'I will not fail her either.'

Chapter Fourteen

Henry closed his eyes, fighting against a wave of fatigue that threatened to consume him. He'd been sitting by Margaret's bedside for nearly three days, since her fever had broken.

At first, it had seemed the happiest of news, the beginning of recovery. But Margaret had not awakened. She remained asleep, her eyes closed, lashes feathering on her pale, waxen cheeks.

The doctor had shaken his head wearily. 'If she wakes, we can anticipate a full recovery.'

'If?' Henry demanded in a choked whisper. 'What do you mean, if?'

'A sustained, high fever can lead to problems in the brain,' the doctor explained. 'Irreversible damage.' He paused, regret etched in every weary line in his face. 'I'm sorry, Henry.'

Sorry, Henry thought now. Everyone was

sorry. Everyone looked on him with wretched expressions of compassion. Pity. It availed little for Margaret.

He took her limp hand in his, wishing he could transfer his energy, his sheer will, to her fragile form.

'Margaret . . . please . . . please wake up. There's so much for us to live for.'

The door clicked open, and Eleanor stood there uncertainly. Henry smiled in tired greeting.

At least Eleanor did not ask the obvious, if there had been any change. She simply bustled in and took the tray of uneaten food left for Henry earlier. 'You do need to keep your strength up, Henry,' she reminded him gently and he shrugged.

'Do you think . . . Eleanor, do you honestly think she'll recover? Or have her wits been addled by the fever?' Henry looked at her almost desperately, as if she could actually have an answer to that question.

'If I know Margaret,' Eleanor said quietly, 'I know she's not ready to quit living just yet. She had plenty of plans, and I warrant she still wants to see them put into action.' She gave a fleeting smile, and Henry returned it.

'That much is true, at any rate.'

Eleanor left quietly, and Henry turned

back to his wife. Her fingers, usually limp in his, seemed to flutter. He glanced down, hope lurching to life within him.

'Henry?' Margaret's voice came out in a scratchy whisper, and Henry had to blink the tears from his own eyes to see his wife, awake, alert, *alive.*

'Margaret, oh thank Providence. I was afraid . . .'

'It'll take . . .' Margaret paused, struggling for breath. 'It'll take more than that to . . .' She closed her eyes briefly, opened them, and smiled. 'To finish me off.'

Henry chuckled, his fingers tracing the dear lines of her face. Margaret was back, and still so wonderfully herself.

Later that day, Henry stood in his study, feeling more cheerful than he had in weeks. Margaret had spoken with both Eleanor and the doctor, as well as taken a little broth.

'It'll be a while yet before she's up on her feet,' the doctor warned, although he was smiling, as relieved as any of them at Margaret's progress. 'She needs to stay in bed and not tire herself. The last thing she wants is a relapse!'

'Rest assured, I will take every precaution,' Henry said with fervour.

'You know how Margaret is,' Eleanor told Henry after the doctor had departed. 'She'll think she's strong enough to wade right back in, and she'll be cross with us if we don't let her.'

'Perhaps,' Henry admitted ruefully. 'But it's for her own good.'

Eleanor nodded. 'Hardly what Margaret wants to hear! I'll go and see if there's anything she needs.'

Margaret was leaning against her bolster, looking pale and tired, and yet with a brightness in her eyes as she looked out the window, at the bare branches of the oak trees. 'The leaves are all gone,' she said as Eleanor entered. 'How long have I been abed?'

'Over a fortnight. We feared for the worst, you know.' Eleanor smoothed the counterpane and perched on the end of the bed. 'You can't know how wonderful it is to see you like this, awake and well.'

'And as weak as a kitten!' Margaret closed her eyes briefly. 'I couldn't even manage a spoonful of broth to my own lips.'

'You were very ill.'

'I know.' Margaret glanced at Eleanor again, her head still resting against the bolster. 'I suppose the school has closed?'

'Actually, it hasn't.' Eleanor smiled at the look of surprise on Margaret's face. 'To be fair, it closed for a week, but then I enlisted the aid of another teacher.'

'Another! But who was willing to take it on?'

'Isobel Moore,' Eleanor said quietly. 'And she's doing quite well.'

'Isobel! I never would've thought . . .'

'She might seem to care only for parties and gowns, but once she was in the school, it was quite different. She loves the small children, the way they clamber for a place on her lap.' The affection, Eleanor had wondered silently, that Ian had not been able to give her. 'And she can be stern when she needs to be.'

'Does she plan to continue?' Margaret's tone was both curious and guarded. Eleanor knew how dearly she held the school to her heart.

'I certainly hope so. The number of children coming to our door is overwhelming without another teacher. Since the typhoid epidemic, many more have come, wanting help. A way out, perhaps.'

'I thought she'd only a head for marriage and children,' Margaret admitted in a low voice. 'She'll be labelled a bluestocking after this.'

'I don't think that matters.' Eleanor glanced out the window at the bare branches, the grey sky. 'Sometimes our hopes and dreams change.'

Margaret nodded, a new bleakness in her eyes. 'Sometimes they have to.'

When Eleanor returned downstairs, Henry was speaking with one of his clerks in the foyer. 'Pardon me, Eleanor, but I must speak with Aubrey here. A matter of business, most pressing.'

Eleanor nodded her understanding, but her brow furrowed as she saw Henry's strained expression, the worry clouding his eyes as he ushered his clerk into the study.

What with Margaret being ill, she hadn't thought a moment of Henry's business . . . or even Rupert's involvement.

Had something gone wrong?

'You wanted to speak to me of Rupert?' Henry asked as Aubrey, his office manager, closed the door of the study.

'He's not come into work for nearly a week, sir. I did not wish to disturb you, with your wife being so ill, but I've become worried.'

Henry didn't think Aubrey sounded worried. Smug, more likely, and relieved to have a rival knocked out of the way. He couldn't blame him; it was hard enough to get ahead in this city.

'Rupert has been doing some business for

me,' Henry said. 'A private matter. I expect he is detained in resolving it.'

Aubrey looked as if he wanted to object — to what, Henry wasn't certain. Perhaps the very fact that Rupert had business he'd not been aware of. Henry felt a twinge of sympathy, equally mixed with irritation.

'Have you not seen him either, sir?'

Henry paused. It was true, he realized, with a lurch of guilt and fear. Rupert hadn't shown his face for several days, nearly a week, as Aubrey said. It had been the longest he'd been away since he'd arrived. And he'd been calling here every day since Margaret's illness. 'I haven't,' he admitted uncomfortably. He knew Rupert was looking into the forgery. Was it possible something had happened?

Something dangerous? 'What do you think has happened, Aubrey?' Henry asked abruptly.

'I couldn't say, sir. I went to his rooms, and spoke to the char woman. She hasn't seen him in a week, and his rooms were empty. It looked as if no one had slept there for several days, at the least.'

Henry felt a fluttering of panic, and forced it down. 'There was no message from him?'

'None at all.' Aubrey paused. 'It seems as if he's left, whether on his own volition or not . . .' He broke off delicately, and Henry frowned.

'I hardly think he'd leave, with his sister so ill! He's not that kind of man, Aubrey.'

'No, indeed not.' Aubrey's impassive face and hard eyes told Henry clearly that he wished Rupert to be that kind of man.

Yet Henry knew he wasn't. So where was he? Henry knew he had to find out himself. He was ashamed that he hadn't turned his attention to Rupert and his forgery investigation earlier. He turned to Aubrey. 'Thank you for bringing it to my attention, at any rate. I shall look into it directly.'

'And if he returns to the office?'

'You may send him to me.'

Henry showed Aubrey out, then stood in the foyer, his sense of unease deepening with every moment. If he hadn't been so consumed with Margaret's health, he would have noticed Rupert's absence days ago.

Crucial days? Henry experienced another stab of fear. He'd sent Rupert on a mission he knew was dangerous, and hadn't given it much of a thought since. What kind of employer did that? What kind of man?

'Henry, is everything well?' Eleanor stood in the doorway, her face troubled. 'I heard raised voices.'

'A business matter . . .' Henry glanced at

Eleanor, remembering the affection Margaret was certain existed between her and his brother-in-law. Perhaps she knew something. 'Eleanor, have you seen Rupert this past week?'

'Rupert?' Eleanor's eyebrows raised. 'No . . . that is, I haven't . . .' She blushed, and then, as if realizing the seriousness of the matter, took a step forward. 'Why do you ask me? Haven't you seen him? He's been in the office, hasn't he?'

Henry shook his head grimly. 'Actually, he hasn't. Aubrey just came and told me.'

'But if he hasn't been here . . .'

Henry hunched his shoulders. 'He was on a bit of business for me, a sort of investigation.'

'An investigation? What do you mean? He's a clerk!'

Henry was reluctant to tell Eleanor the details, yet his own guilt forced it out of him. 'There was a forgery, money passed to me that was false. I asked Rupert to find the source.'

'Find the source!' Eleanor repeated incredulously. 'But counterfeiters are considered to be some of the most dangerous criminals. The papers are full of the stories . . . horrible ones.'

'Rupert felt capable of the task, I assure

you,' Henry said. 'I wouldn't have asked him otherwise.'

'Of course he did! He thinks he can do anything!' Eleanor shook her head in despair.

'He's not a child, Eleanor.'

'But he's missing, isn't he? He's in danger.' Eleanor gazed at him bleakly. 'It's not like Rupert to disappear, not with Margaret so poorly. I myself wondered why he hadn't come recently . . .' She twisted her hands in her apron, her face now shadowed with anxiety and even fear. 'We shall have to look for him! What if he's been waylaid? Or ill himself? I can go to the hospital.'

'Eleanor, I won't have you troubling yourself over this,' Henry broke in. 'I told you, it's dangerous, and the typhoid is still rampant in parts of the city.'

'Which part?' Eleanor's eyes flashed. 'Because I assure you there's no part of this city I haven't been or wouldn't go to see Rupert safe!'

Henry looked at her in surprise. 'You care for him, then?'

'Very much,' Eleanor whispered. 'And I never got the chance to tell him.'

Henry's heart lurched as regret and guilt swamped him once more. 'We'll find him, Eleanor. I'll hire a private investigator. We can look in the hospitals and charity houses.'

'I'll go.'

'It's not fitting . . .'

'Don't tell me what to do, Henry!' Eleanor lifted her chin. 'I've been working in an immigrant school, after all. I shall take Ian.'

'Wait, at least, to see what the investigator might discover!' Henry pleaded. 'I won't have you tramping the streets to no purpose. There is more danger than you think.'

'Apparently so.' Eleanor's eyes sparkled with tears, and Henry didn't blame her for her waspish tone. It was his fault Rupert had gone missing, *his* error of omission. Perhaps others could help more than he could. 'We'll find him,' he said again, but whether it was to convince himself or Eleanor he wasn't certain.

Eleanor glanced at him, her eyes now hard and bright with determination. 'Yes. We will.'

Maggie laid her hand against her mother's bump, her face filled with delight when she felt a foot kick hard against her palm. 'I felt it! She's a wee, strong thing, isn't she?'

Harriet, one hand on her back, chuckled. 'It might be a boy, Maggie.'

'No, it can't be,' her daughter replied with conviction. 'We need another girl.'

Harriet nodded. 'I see.' Maggie and

George had been scrapping and fighting like wolf cubs lately, cooped indoors as they were. She had heard Maggie expressing her dislike of her brother and boys in general more than once.

It had been a difficult few weeks, as the cold weather closed in, the days grew dark and the ground hard with frost.

With news of the bairn, Betty had cheered, and in the last few weeks had roused herself to help with simple chores and dandle Anna on her knee.

Harriet was grateful for the help, but her heart was ever more glad to see the bloom in Betty's cheeks, the brightness in her eyes. She'd feared the older woman would fade away to nothing after Sandy died.

Now, Harriet thought, feeling the child within her kick again, there was hope for the future. She thought of her own silent, secret hopes . . . ones she hoped to voice this evening, when the children were abed.

'Mamma, you think it's a girl, don't you?'

Harriet smiled down at her daughter. 'I'll be happy with a healthy bairn, Maggie, boy or girl.'

'We'll know in the spring,' Maggie said philosophically, and Harriet nodded.

'Yes. In the spring.'

That evening, with a pile of mending in

her lap, Harriet broached the subject she'd long been waiting for. 'We're well enough here for the winter, aren't we?' she remarked, nodding in satisfaction at the blazing fire, the twisted ropes of dried onions and peppers that hung from the rafters. There was a salted ham in the loft, and plenty of venison in the smokehouse.

'We'll do all right,' Allan agreed, but his eyes twinkled as if he could guess her thoughts.

'Aye, it's a comfortable house.' Harriet nodded again. Betty watched her speculatively, her hands busy with a piece of needlework. She took a breath. 'But we've two homes now, haven't we, and we've only need of one.' She leaned forward to gaze earnestly at her mother-in-law. 'You know your place will always be with us, Mother, and we're glad to have you.'

Betty nodded, a strange smile on her face. 'I've been grateful for a daughter such as you.'

'Thank you.' Harriet bit her lip, and Allan chuckled.

'Out with it, lass. You've a bee in your bonnet for sure, now what is it?'

Surely he knows, Harriet thought. Allan always seemed to know what she was thinking. What her dreams were. 'I want to go back to our farm,' she said quietly, her eyes on the dancing flames of the fire. 'We've room enough for Mother, and it's home there.' She turned quickly, apprehensively, to Betty. 'Not that this isn't comfortable, and bigger than our place to be sure! But it's . . .'

'Not home. I know.' Betty sat back, her smile gentle. 'I remember how it was. When we arrived on that ship all those years ago — nearly thirteen now — I was dreadfully homesick. I wanted nothing more than to return to the old country, the old ways. Even draughty Mingarry Castle, and goodness knows that wasn't comfortable! I hated the trees here, the darkness of the forests. The roughness of it all.' Betty looked up, her eyes bright. 'And yet, with time, this became home to me, perhaps more than ever before, because Sandy and I built it together, with our own hands. And our sons.' She paused, her expression distant. 'It will be hard to leave it.'

Harriet felt a fluttering of hope in her breast, even though she ached for Betty's loss and sadness. 'Then you'll . . .?'

'I'll go,' Betty agreed, her voice firm with purpose now. 'In the spring, after the bairn is born. You need to be in your own house, on your own land. Goodness knows it was important to Sandy all those years ago, and to Allan. Everyone needs to find their own place.'

'We'll always be glad to have you with us,' Allan said gently. 'Your home is with us now.'

'So it could be,' Betty agreed. 'But I won't be coming with you. Not this time.'

'What do you mean? You won't stay here on your own?'

'No, I think not.' Betty paused, carefully drawing her needle through the cloth. 'I have two other children still living, and I would like to see them before I'm laid to rest.'

Harriet dropped her mending in shock, the pile sliding from her nerveless fingers. 'You can't mean . . . ?'

'Yes.' Betty looked up and smiled. 'Come spring, I'm going to go to Boston.'

Eleanor gazed bleakly out of the drawing-room window. Grey sky met grey buildings, the black branches of leafless trees pointing defiantly towards an unforgiving sky.

The whole world seemed to have turned grey, caught in the death throes of autumn. Eleanor felt as if she were grey, as well. Lifeless and yet churning with fear since she'd discovered Rupert was missing.

She turned away from the window, fingers plucking restlessly at her dress. Henry had hired a private investigator to look into the matter, and the man was due to arrive any moment with a report on his initial findings . . . if there were any.

Where was Rupert? The question tormented Eleanor with the unanswerable possibilities. Henry had told her the bare outline of Rupert's mission; the very idea of him tangling with criminal counterfeiters was enough to make Eleanor feel ill. She forced her mind away from dire imaginings of Rupert attacked, helpless and hurt . . . or worse, dead.

'Please God,' Eleanor whispered. 'Keep him safe.' It had taken this threat of danger to make her realize how much she truly loved Rupert. Now she would do anything — go anywhere — to find him and keep him from harm.

If only it were not too late.

'Eleanor.' Henry came in the room, followed by a balding, pink-cheeked man who wouldn't have looked tough enough to do what he was alleged to do, if not for his rather grim smile, and two missing teeth.

Eleanor nodded her greeting, her insides twisting as if filled with live snakes. 'Have you heard anything?' she burst out, and the man shook his head regretfully.

'There's no sign of him, and no one's talking.' The man glanced at Henry. 'I visited the merchant you thought he'd gone to see, and the man insisted MacDougall left his offices as safe as could be, but the trail goes dead after that, so . . .' He spread his hands.

'The merchant must be lying,' Eleanor couldn't help but say. 'Have you questioned him further?'

'As much as I'm allowed,' the man replied drily. 'If there were more evidence . . .'

'What about investigating this merchant?' Henry asked. 'His background? Any record or sign of criminal involvement?'

'Plenty,' the man assured him. 'Although I couldn't prove it. He's been associated with counterfeiting, but not enough to pin it on him. If he's involved, he's on the bottom of the pile and there's someone he's terrified of. That much is clear.'

'So what can you do?'

The man shrugged. 'Frankly, nothing. It's more than my job is worth to nose into a counterfeiting ring. The small men, like this weasel, well, I can deal with him. But if the higher-ups receive word that I'm getting curious . . .'

'You'll end up the same as Rupert?' Eleanor finished sharply. 'I wouldn't pay this man a penny, Henry. The limits to his job are the same as ours!'

'Eleanor, you are overwrought.'

'Of course I am! What would you expect? But I could've questioned a merchant the same as he did . . .'

'And discovered his links to the criminal world?' Henry looked at her sternly, although it was softened by a flicker of compassion.

'Very well.' Eleanor drew herself up. 'I shall go to the hospitals and charity houses, see if someone has found him. If he's been attacked — hurt . . .'

'I wish you well, madam,' the investigator told her stiffly. 'Although I fear that to be a thankless errand.'

'If I find Rupert, that is all the thanks I need!'

'I meant,' the man said quietly, 'that the criminals Mr MacDougall was involving himself with would hardly escort him to a hospital, or even leave him on the street.'

'That is quite enough.' Henry looked sharply at the man, shaking his head. 'I will not have any ladies in my house distressed by information they could hardly need or want to know. We'll talk elsewhere.'

The investigator sketched a small bow,

and Henry escorted him from the room, silencing Eleanor with one sharp look.

Eleanor sank on to a chair, exhausted and, as Henry had said, overwrought. What point was there in flying at the private investigator? No, her energies were better employed elsewhere.

Looking for Rupert. *Finding* him.

She thought of the detective's words, the kind of men Rupert had tangled with. He was more likely to be in a back alley of the Murder District, or at the bottom of Boston Bay, than in the hospital. She closed her eyes. The torment of the last day, realizing Rupert was in danger or worse, lay heavily upon her. She wanted Ian, to have his comforting presence, his advice. Unfortunately, he was working, and had been since she'd discovered Rupert was missing.

Yet the hospital was the most sensible place for her to go. Her hands clenched into fists, she rose from the chair and hurried to fetch her bonnet and shawl.

'Miss, where are you going?' One of the parlour maids, her face anxious and pinched, looked at Eleanor curiously.

'Out. Tell Mr Moore that I'll be back for supper.'

'By yourself, Miss? I don't think —'

'I shall have my brother with me.' Eleanor

snapped, and with that she hurried into the oncoming darkness.

It was a short walk to the Massachusetts General Hospital, although Eleanor was conscious of the curious and often disapproving stares of people unused to seeing a well-dressed young woman out alone.

She hurried through the common, keeping her head down. Although the public gardens were frequented mostly by gentlefolk, there could be unsavoury characters lurking in the shadows, ready to pounce on an unsuspecting pedestrian.

I don't care if my reputation is in shreds by the evening, she thought recklessly. *All that matters is Rupert.*

If only she'd had the chance to tell him!

You did have the chance, Eleanor reminded herself mercilessly. *You just were too frightened to take it.*

She closed her eyes briefly, pictured his face, the usually harsh lines softened by affections . . . tenderness. Why hadn't she spoken, admitted her feelings? She'd barely been able to admit them to herself, and now . . .

'It's not too late,' she whispered aloud. 'It can't be.'

If she found him now, she promised herself, she would tell him she cared and more besides. She would confess all that was in her heart.

She found the hospital, the impressive Bulfinch Building pointing its domed roof to a now darkened sky, the first stars flickering like needlepoints in black cloth.

'Miss? Are you in need of help?' A gentleman in a frock coat, a pile of fusty books under one arm, looked at her in concern.

Eleanor glanced at him, and decided she could trust him. 'I'm looking for a doctor, Ian Crombie.'

'Ian! I know him well. I believe he's just finishing his round of patients. May I take you to him? Although . . .' the man hesitated, fidgeting with his neck cloth uncertainly. 'A hospital is no place for a lady.'

'He's my brother, and it's quite urgent,' Eleanor said firmly. 'Take me to him.'

Nodding, the man took her arm and led her into the hospital. Her heart thudding, Eleanor was barely aware of her surroundings, fatigue and anxiety once more threatening to overwhelm her.

She stopped suddenly when Ian's face swam in front of her, and he grabbed her shoulders to steady her. 'Eleanor! Why are you here? What's happened?'

Eleanor blinked back sudden tears, forcing herself to be calm. 'It's Rupert, Ian. I'm looking for him. I have to find him.'

'Find him? Where has he gone?'

She bit her lip. 'Henry hired him to investigate counterfeits — he's been missing a week, and we've only just found out!' Tears spilled as the emotion overcame her. 'I thought he was staying away for my sake, to give me time . . . I'd hoped . . . but he's in danger, Ian! Or dead. The detective thinks it's a lost cause.'

Ian's expression sharpened. 'Henry has hired a detective?'

'Yes — he fears the worst as well! He's so consumed with Margaret, he won't *do* anything and . . .' Eleanor gulped back a sob. 'I can't sit back and wait! I won't!'

Ian put his arm around her shoulders. 'Then we shall do something. Do you think he might be hurt? At the hospital?'

'It's possible, isn't it?' Eleanor scrubbed her eyes with her fists like a child.

'Unlikely,' Ian replied soberly. 'But we can try. I can look through the wards.'

'I want to come with you.'

'A hospital is no place for a lady,' Ian began, and Eleanor let out a sharp laugh.

'That's what he said.' She jerked an arm towards the retreating back of the man who had led her to Ian. 'Ian, do you really believe, with all your modern innovations, that I shouldn't be here? What of the women patients on the wards? Besides, I've been in a sick room for the last fortnight. I think I can walk through a hospital ward.'

'A ward is very different from a sick room,' Ian told her quietly. 'I think you'll find Margaret's surroundings were a good deal more comfortable than the poor unfortunates who reside here.'

'I've no doubt of it, and all the more reason to find Rupert . . . if he's here.'

'So be it.' Ian turned on his heel, then seeing Eleanor's pallor, took her arm. 'Take care,' he whispered softly. 'We can't have you ill, as well.'

'I'm fine.' Eleanor tried to shake off his arm, though she realized she was secretly glad for its comforting weight. Since Rupert's disappearance, she'd felt so alone. So afraid.

Despite Ian's warning, Eleanor was not prepared for the stench of illness and unwashed bodies that assailed her when she entered the first ward. She knew hospitals were widely regarded as places to die, rather than to be made well. People with any money at all hired doctors in their home, as Henry had done for Margaret. Hospitals were for the poor, the desperate, the near dead. And now Eleanor saw it with her own eyes.

She scanned the faces in the beds with a desperate hope, trying not to flinch at the naked suffering, the open sores and moans of pain or pleading. There was nothing she could do.

'I told you, Eleanor,' Ian said in a low voice as a woman reached sightlessly for Eleanor's hand, moaning for someone to help her. 'Have you had quite enough?'

'If Rupert is here, I will find him.' Eleanor moved along the rows, wishing she could take pity on the unfortunates before her, yet knowing there was little she could do, even if she had the time or resources. It was hard enough to resist the urge to press her handkerchief to her nose. 'Why are the hospitals like this?' she whispered. 'You're a doctor, Ian. You're meant to make people *well!*'

'I know it,' Ian replied tersely. 'And I am working towards that end. But there is much even the wisest doctor does not yet know, and we fight superstition and fear. Besides . . .' he shrugged helplessly. 'There are so many ill, and only a fraction of them make their way here. I fear your task is hopeless, Eleanor. If Rupert was hurt, the best we can hope for is that he was brought to someone's house. We could do a search.'

'Then why not start here, for heaven's sake?' Eleanor moved on determinedly.

Ian did not attempt to sway her again, even when she faltered at the sight of a man lying in his bed, his eyes staring lifelessly ahead.

'I'll notify the doctor on duty,' Ian whispered as he closed the man's eyes with gentle fingers. Eleanor could only nod.

She wasn't willing to admit defeat, even when the last ward had been walked. 'Perhaps someone knows . . .'

'Knows what? There are so many patients.' Ian shook his head.

'This is *Rupert,* Ian!' Eleanor rounded on him fiercely. 'Rupert! The boy you played with when you were but a child! Your friend! How can you be so callous?'

'I am trying,' Ian said between his teeth, 'to be practical.'

Eleanor's shoulders slumped as defeat, and all its implications, threatened to engulf her. Ian once more put his arm around her shoulders. 'I'm sorry, dear. I know you care for him.'

'I do.' Tears threatened to fall once more, and Eleanor kept them back only by sheer force of will. She could not sob like a child in the middle of the hospital. She would not.

'I can ask the doctor on duty,' Ian said quietly. 'Let him know what kind of man we're looking for. At least if someone comes in now, we could be notified.'

'Thank you, Ian.'

Eleanor watched as Ian found the doctor on duty, a harassed young man in a blood-stained coat.

'Lord knows, Crombie, there's a hundred men in here who fit that description!'

'Someone who's been attacked,' Ian said in a low voice. Eleanor knew he didn't want her to hear, but she strained to listen anyway. 'Likely to have been brought by someone who didn't want any part of it, or that would be my guess. He would have been beaten . . . or worse.'

'You sound like you know quite a bit about this man,' the doctor said gruffly. 'For not being involved, that is.'

'He's my friend, and I fear for his life,' Ian snapped. 'Can you keep an eye out, then?'

'As much as I can for anyone,' the doctor replied irritably. 'I've been on duty for twelve hours as it is.'

'Very well, I understand. Whatever you can do.'

Ian turned back to Eleanor, and any hopes

she'd been secretly harbouring crumbled to dust. Rupert wasn't here, and even if he did arrive at some point, she wasn't likely to find him unless she walked the wards every day. And what of the other possibilities? Charity houses, or perhaps even in someone's home . . . or worse. She pictured him alone, on the pavement or dockside, hurt and friendless, or worse, dead, and a wave of panic roiled within her.

No. She would find him. Somehow.

'But how?' Eleanor whispered aloud.

'Eleanor, I demand you return home,' Ian said as he took her elbow and led her to the front doors. 'You look ready to drop, and you can be of no use to anyone — Rupert included — if you aren't well and rested.'

'Don't speak to me as a child, Ian!'

'I'm speaking to you as a patient, and a doctor,' Ian said gently. 'I mean what I say.'

Eleanor sagged against him. 'How can I rest, or sleep, when I don't know where he is?' she whispered.

Ian turned so they were facing each other. 'Eleanor,' he asked softly, 'do you care for him truly?'

The emotions tumbling within her were too difficult to explain, or even sort out. Too much had happened too quickly. Eleanor felt tears making cold tracks on her cheeks, and she didn't even have the energy to wipe them away. Gazing at Ian, she could only nod.

'Oh, my dear.' Ian enfolded her in a hug. 'We'll find him, I promise. I'm off duty, I'll go to the docks and look there. We'll find him, Eleanor.'

Eleanor choked back a sob, her cheek pressed against Ian's wool coat.

A carriage rolled up the curb, and Ian gently pulled her back to arms' length. 'Here's a hansom cab. Why don't you take it home? I'll alert you the moment there's news . . .' He opened the door, only to jerk back in surprise at the sight within. 'There's an injured man in here!'

'That's why I'm taking him to the hospital,' the driver said grimly. 'Before he bleeds all over my cushions. They had to pay double for me to take him like that, I can tell you.'

'I'll get a stretcher . . .' Ian hurried off, and Eleanor peered in the shadowy interior of the hansom. The man was lying prone on the cushions, his head covered by a blood-stained bandage. He moaned, turning slightly towards her.

'El . . .'

Eleanor gasped, and scrambled into the cab, heedless of her dress, of the dirt and blood. Tenderly she touched his hands, his cheek.

'Eleanor!' Ian called. 'What on earth . . . ?'

'Ian, stop, don't you see?' Eleanor turned to her brother, tears of happiness now blurring her eyes. 'It's Rupert.'

Chapter Fifteen

Sunlight streamed through the window at the end of the ward. Rupert lay propped up in bed, his face pale and drawn. A huge smile transformed his features when he saw Eleanor's slight figure standing hesitantly in the doorway. 'Eleanor. I'm glad to see you.'

'Not as glad as I am to see you,' Eleanor said tremulously. She moved to stand by his bed. Rupert wanted to take hold of her hand, but he didn't want to scare her. Eleanor, his brave Eleanor, looked as if she could be blown away by a mere whisper of wind.

'You needn't be afraid,' Rupert said softly.

'Afraid?' Eleanor looked at him incredulously, and Rupert didn't know whether to laugh or be nervous.

'I'm perfectly well . . .'

'Perfectly well?' Eleanor repeated. She took a step backwards, shaking her head. 'Rupert MacDougall, do you have any idea what you've been through? What you put your family through?'

'My family?' Rupert asked. 'Or you?'

'Both!' Eleanor snapped. She looked angry now, and Rupert had a feeling if he were not lying helpless in a hospital bed, she would hit him. 'You've been missing for a week. A week! And when Henry told me you'd gone after those forgers . . .' She pressed a fist to her mouth before lowering it to point a shaking finger at him. 'We thought you were dead!'

'But I'm safe,' Rupert reminded her as gently as he could.

'Safe?' Eleanor very nearly shrieked. 'Safe? When you've been knocked on your head so you didn't even know who you were?'

'I always knew who I was . . .'

'When we saw you last night, you were insensible. The doctor said he didn't know if you'd ever regain your senses.'

'I suppose that is still open to argument,' Rupert joked, but Eleanor just shook her head, tears in her eyes.

'We've all been beside ourselves with worry. We daren't even tell Margaret, in her weak state.'

'Margaret?' Rupert leaned forward, wincing slightly at the pain in his head. 'Is she better? Is she out of the worst?'

'She's weak as a kitten, but she'll make a full recovery. Her fever broke three days ago now.'

'Thank goodness.' Rupert leaned his head back against the wall, grimacing in pain.

'Your head,' Eleanor exclaimed. 'You mustn't move, Rupert, in case you injure yourself further.'

'Fortunately for me I have a hard head.' Rupert smiled up at her, but Eleanor only looked annoyed.

'A fine time to joke, when someone attempted to take your very life!' Her hands fluttered at her sides, as if she wanted to examine his head but was afraid to.

Rupert caught one of her hands in his. 'Are you truly angry with me, Eleanor, or dare I hope that your ire hides a feeling more dear?'

Eleanor half-heartedly attempted to pull her hand away, but Rupert held her fast. 'I told you how I felt about you, Eleanor. I love you. I want you to marry me.'

Eleanor looked down, blinking back tears. 'Do you know — can you imagine,' she whispered, 'how it felt to think you might be lost — dead — and I'd never told you how I felt, because I was too afraid?'

His eyes blazed as he looked at her steadily. 'Tell me now.'

She looked at him, smiling, yet with tears on her cheeks. 'I love you, Rupert. And if that was indeed a proposal, I'll marry you.'

Rupert kissed her palm. 'You've made me the happiest of men.'

'Ah, the patient is awake!' Ian cleared his throat, and Eleanor stepped quickly away. 'And apparently on the mend,' he added, shooting his sister a considering look.

Eleanor blushed and looked away.

'My head hurts something fierce,' Rupert admitted cheerfully. 'But I think I'll live.'

Ian sat on the edge of his bed. 'So, can you tell us what happened? Who attacked you?'

'That I don't know. Whoever it was, he came up behind me. I'd barely a chance to realize someone was there before I was out.'

'And then what happened?' Eleanor asked. 'How did you come to the hospital?'

Rupert shook his head slowly. 'Do you know, I couldn't say for certain. I lay on the pavement stones for I don't know how long — I was drifting in and out of my senses. Eventually I woke up in a bed. It looked to me a simple place, somewhere near the harbour. I could hear the sound of the sea, and the ships in port. A woman was tending me, and I heard voices in the other room, one of whom I took to be her grown son. I don't know how long I was there. Most of the time I was insensible. The woman gave me a bit of broth, and bandaged my head. I owe my life to her, I think.'

'You surely do,' Ian agreed sombrely. 'Why did she send you to the hospital, though? Most common people are afraid of the hospital. They see it only as a place of death.'

Silently Rupert agreed with this assessment. As much as he approved of Ian's ideas for reform, what he'd seen of the hospital thus far had been dirty and full of despair. People came in here, and they as likely did not come out. Rupert was thankful to be an exception.

'She became afraid,' he explained simply. 'I heard her talking to her son. He was shouting, saying someone was looking for me. I think he would've been happy to dump me back on the paving stones, but she had more of a conscience. She put me in a hansom and sent it to the hospital, or so I've come to believe. I wasn't aware all the time of what was happening.'

'Who was looking for you, I wonder?' Ian asked, frowning.

'The forgers, no doubt,' Eleanor whispered fiercely. 'To think how you put your life in danger! And Henry let you! Urged you, even!'

'You're not to blame Henry,' Rupert said firmly. 'It was my idea as much as his. He wouldn't have asked, and I wouldn't have offered, if danger were a concern.'

'And why wasn't it?' Eleanor demanded. 'If not for yourself, then think of those who care for you!'

Rupert linked his fingers with hers. 'Aye, I do now. But as you'll remember, I wasn't so certain who might care for me . . . or not.'

Eleanor blushed, and Ian looked speculatively at both of them. 'Have you discovered who the forgers are?' he asked.

Rupert shook his head regretfully. 'I never heard a name. My inquiries into the forgery had led me to a wine merchant by the docks. Phillips was his name. He mentioned another man named Summers. I suspect this Phillips was in the forgery ring, but kept mostly in the dark. He was a greasy little fellow, but scared.' He paused, smiling ruefully. 'More frightened of his betters in the forgery ring than of any threat I could make.'

'And rightly so,' Eleanor interjected with some heat. 'Rupert, those men could kill you.'

'They haven't managed so far,' Rupert replied, and Eleanor pursed her lips.

'Not for lack of trying.'

'Who do you think this Summers is?' Ian asked.

'A middleman, perhaps. I'm not sure. Perhaps just another underling like this Phillips, taking the dirty money and passing it on, bringing it into the market. Summers was meant to be buying twelve cases of port, although who knows, perhaps it was just a paper transaction to mask putting the money in action.'

'But who benefits from that?' Eleanor asked. 'The man at the top — or men — are putting the money into action, aren't they? Why would they just give it away?'

'A fair point,' Rupert replied musingly. 'But perhaps it was only a small amount.'

'Still . . . they're hardly making counterfeit money just for other people to use?'

'No, they surely are not,' Ian agreed. 'So why all this secrecy? What would a man like Summers — or Phillips — gain from taking the forged notes? Why wouldn't the counterfeiters just take it for themselves?'

'To distance themselves,' Rupert said suddenly. His eyes blazed. 'They must be testing it to see if it is able to pass through the market. And look, it was discovered at the first transaction!'

'So what now? They know not to put it into use. Won't they just stop?' Eleanor looked hopefully between the two.

Ian shook his head. 'It can't be that easy. If it were, they wouldn't have chased after Rupert, would they? I think there's too much invested in this scheme for them to abandon it so easily.'

Rupert and Ian exchanged darkly significant looks, and Eleanor clenched her fists. 'What are you suggesting you do? Stop them single-handedly?' She turned to Rupert. 'You were not appointed saviour of this city, or has no one made that apparent to you yet?'

Rupert chuckled. He wanted to snatch her up into his arms, but his head pounded abominably and he knew he was too weak to do much more than hold out a supplicating hand.

He hated being weak. He hated weakness in himself, and he despised those who took advantage of it in others. Perhaps that was what motivated him, he thought. He knew forgery rings exploited the weak, the common man who couldn't tell the difference between a real note and a bogus one. And, in the end, even if the forgers were caught, the common man was left with a fistful of useless dollars.

'Rupert . . .' Eleanor's voice was low. 'Are you actually considering, in your present state, to chase after this man Summers? Do you not think the person who tried to kill you before will try again, doubly so, the more you persist? And what can you hope to find? Henry won't get his money back, not at this stage, and neither will any poor soul who has been fooled. The best you can hope for is to break up this ring of forgers, and as like as not they'll start again, somewhere else.'

'Not if they're in prison.'

'Prison!' Eleanor shook her head. 'I know enough of this country — and this world — to know the men who go to prison will not be the scoundrels who are behind this crime. They'll be the dogsbodies who were pushed into it because their own lives were so hopeless.'

Rupert's eyes danced. 'Why, Eleanor, you sound like a positive crusader.'

'The only thing I'm crusading for is your safety,' Eleanor retorted. 'If not for yourself, then for me.'

Ian cleared his throat. 'Perhaps I should leave you two to sort this out . . .'

Eleanor turned on him fiercely. 'Don't leave! Perhaps you can talk some sense in him, if I can't.'

'I don't think there is anyone in the world who could sway Rupert more than you,

Eleanor,' Ian replied. 'But I fear I would not try, even if I could. It is for Rupert to decide his own fate.' He sketched a slight bow to Rupert. 'And if I can aid him in his search, I will do my best.'

'Thank you, Ian.' Rupert looked profoundly grateful, and Eleanor looked as if she'd suffered a personal betrayal.

Ian smiled faintly. 'I've been informed that you are to be released on the morrow, to recover more comfortably at home. The danger is passed. All you have to look forward to now, I'm afraid, is a rather sore head.'

'Amen to that,' Rupert replied with a grin. 'I look forward to more comfortable surroundings.'

'Indeed.' Ian left swiftly, and Rupert was left gazing in helpless affection at his intended.

'I'm not being this way to hurt you,' he said softly. 'You do know that, don't you?'

'I know you are an insufferably stubborn man.' Eleanor gave an unladylike sniff, only just holding her tears at bay. 'I don't want you in danger.'

'I don't want to be in danger, either.' Rupert leaned back and closed his eyes. His head throbbed terribly. He felt a heaviness, the burden of what he needed to discover.

Perhaps Eleanor was right, and there was little he could do. Even if he caught the forgers, someone would still go free, someone with power and influence who could escape the arm of law. Yet he couldn't just give up. And, he realized with a sudden pang, he couldn't go back to pushing paper. He felt more needed, more purposeful, tracking these criminals than sitting in the shipping office, dreaming of the time when his neatness with numbers would bring him recognition.

He felt more alive.

'Rupert,' Eleanor whispered. 'What are you thinking?'

'I'm thinking,' Rupert replied slowly, 'that I love you very much, and I hope you love me.'

'You know I love you!'

'Yes, but this is part of who I am, Eleanor. Who I want to be.'

Eleanor looked troubled and even a little afraid. 'What are you saying?'

'That this is what I want to do. And if we are to marry, you marry that part of me.' He spread his hands, helpless and yet certain. 'You marry *all* of me.'

Harriet leaned against the table, her eyes closed. The pain she was feeling receded, and she sighed in relief. Surely it was just a common twinge.

'Mamma?' Maggie looked at her in concern, her apron full of potatoes. 'I fetched the potatoes from the root cellar.'

'Thank you, lass.' Harriet smiled and straightened, trying for a brisk normality.

Then she felt another wave of pain, and nearly stumbled.

'Mamma?' Maggie dropped the corners of her apron, and potatoes rolled and scattered across the floor. Harriet clutched the rungs of the chair to steady herself. 'Mamma!'

'Maggie, *cridhe,* I'm all right,' Harriet said between ragged breaths. 'It's the bairn, that's all. The bairn is coming.'

'But . . .' Maggie shook her head. 'You said not till spring! And we haven't even started syruping yet!'

'I know. This wee boy seems to have made up his mind to come early.'

'It's a girl, remember?' Maggie's teasing smile disappeared quickly at the sight of her mother's obvious pain. 'What should I do?'

'Fetch your grandmother. She's gone to feed the chickens.' Harriet stumbled slightly as she made her way to the bedroom. 'Fetch her quickly, Maggie!'

She heard her daughter run out of the house. The slam of the door woke a sleeping Anna, but Harriet knew she could not fetch her daughter from the cradle, not in this state.

She eased herself on to the bed, closing her eyes. Today of all days, with Allan and George out trapping. It was barely March, far too early . . .

'Harriet?' Harriet heard Betty's anxious voice from the front door. 'Harriet!'

'In here, in the back.'

She heard Betty's quick footsteps, and Maggie crooning to Anna. A few seconds later, Betty was there, leaning over Harriet in concern. 'Is it the bairn?'

Harriet nodded. 'It's too early. Far too early.'

Betty pursed her lips. 'I've seen bairns come earlier and thrive. They know their own minds, they do.'

Harriet clutched her hand. 'But what if . . . ? I couldn't bear it, not again . . .'

'You never mind that,' Betty said briskly. 'What you need to do is think about that bairn in your arms, red-cheeked and wailing. Think on that, Harriet MacDougall.'

'I can't.' Tears leaked from under Harriet's closed lids. 'It wasn't meant to be like this. The pains are coming too quickly, too strong, I know it's not right.'

'It's just that little boy trying his best to

get out into this world. He wants to know what all the fuss is about.'

'Allan's not even here.'

'For the best, really.' Betty moved briskly to the linen chest and began to sift through the layers of cloth for old sheets. 'Of course, we haven't had time to prepare a layette for the poor creature, but I daresay he won't mind.'

'How do you know?'

Betty was concentrating on the sheets, tearing them into neat strips. 'How do I know what?'

Harriet opened her eyes and looked straight at her. 'How do you know it's going to be all right?'

The room was silent except for Harriet's laboured breathing.

'I know,' Betty finally said, her voice strong, 'because I've seen too much death and sadness to see it again. I know because between you and me, we will make this bairn live.' She reached forward and grabbed Harriet's hand. 'We can, you know. I know we can. Do you believe me?'

Harriet squeezed Betty's hand tightly as another pain assailed her. 'I do,' she finally gasped. 'I believe you.'

Margaret tossed her bit of embroidery away

in disgust. She'd been in bed for over a week, and was feeling restless. Henry insisted she stay in bed, and in her heart Margaret knew he was right. Even standing for a few moments had left her as a weak as a newborn kitten.

Still, this enforced bed rest was driving her to madness. She wasn't used to being still, to having nothing to do but think. She tended not to amuse herself with the usual ladylike pursuits, such as sewing or embroidery, and those activities were certainly not placating her now.

A quiet knock on the door had her leaning forward eagerly. 'Come in, come in.'

'You have a visitor, ma'am. Isobel Moore. I said you might not be strong enough —'

'I'm plenty strong enough,' Margaret retorted. 'Send her up, do, Hetty.'

A few minutes later Isobel stood in the doorway, as pale and elegant as always, yet also a bit careworn.

'Isobel, come sit down.' Margaret motioned to the chair next to her bed, and Isobel moved into the room.

'You're looking quite well, considering,' Isobel said with a flicker of a smile. 'We feared the worst, you know.'

'So everyone tells me. I assured Henry I'm not so easy to be got rid of.'

'As if anyone would be rid of you!' Isobel gave a little laugh, but Margaret could see she still looked anxious.

'And how are you faring? Eleanor told me how you stepped in as teacher during my illness. I can't thank you enough for such a service.'

Isobel waved her hand in dismissal. 'The children are all the thanks I need.'

'I must admit,' Margaret said candidly, 'I didn't think it a position to suit you.'

'Oh, I can well imagine.' Isobel's smile was brittle. 'I'm sure you thought I couldn't be bothered teaching ragged little children, some who don't know a word of English! I'm sure you thought I'd be afraid the poor little creatures would soil my gown, or give me lice, or some such.' Margaret could only stare at her in surprise. 'Didn't you?' Isobel continued. 'I daresay I once thought it myself.'

'Isobel, I didn't mean . . .' Margaret trailed off, unable to continue. It was what she meant, she realized, even if she had not intended to be mean-spirited.

'I know what you've always thought of me,' Isobel continued, a hard edge to her voice. 'You haven't had much time for me, have you? I can scarcely blame you. You were full of zeal and purpose, and I had my head high above you all, dreaming of the time Ian and I would marry.'

Margaret clutched the edge of the counterpane, kneading the silky cloth between her fingers. 'I had no idea . . .' she whispered.

'No idea that I knew? You needn't think I'm slow or stupid, just because I couldn't see the truth in front of me. It's plain to me now, of course, and I expect it was plain to everyone else. Ian doesn't love me. He never did. Any expectations I had — that Mother and Father had — were based on the affection a brother has for his sister, and nothing more. I know that now.'

'I'm sorry,' Margaret said after a long silence.

'So am I. It's hard to let go of your dreams.'

'I know how that feels.'

'But I didn't come here to speak of this, or to put harsh words between us,' Isobel continued. 'I came to tell you I want to teach at the school even after you return, if you'll have me. I imagine you'll need another teacher, especially if Eleanor doesn't return.'

'But won't Eleanor return?' Margaret asked in puzzlement.

Isobel smiled faintly. 'I suspect she might

have duties elsewhere, if her concern for Rupert is any measure.'

'Concern? Has something happened to Rupert?'

Isobel's face paled. 'Oh, I'm sorry! I shouldn't have spoken!'

Margaret leaned forward. 'I believe you should have. What are you keeping from me? Is Rupert ill?'

'He's all right now.' Henry stood in the doorway, his features softened with tenderness. 'Good morning, Isobel.' He nodded briefly to his sister. 'He's been in hospital, Margaret, but he's to be released to us tomorrow, and he'll make a full recovery.'

'Hospital? But why?'

'I'll tell you all about it, I promise you, but the doctor is here now to examine you.' He turned to Isobel. 'Would you mind asking the doctor to come up, please?'

Isobel excused herself, and Henry turned back to his wife. 'It is *your* recovery I am concerned about now, my dear.'

Margaret was not to be so easily placated. 'Why have you been keeping secrets from me?'

'Because you were ill to the point of death, and I didn't want to add one jot to your burden!' Henry spoke so fiercely Margaret shrank slightly against the pillows. 'Margaret, my love, do you have any idea how close I came to losing you? And in doing so, losing myself? I am nothing without you, Maggie. Nothing.'

Henry sat on the edge of her bed, and Margaret put her arms around him. For a moment there were no words that needed to be said.

Downstairs, Isobel sent the doctor up with a few, terse words. She felt strange and irritable, and she didn't know why. She'd accepted that Ian didn't love her; she'd resigned herself to being a spinster. Yet seeing her brother care so tenderly for his wife had sent a fierce stab of longing through her. She didn't want to grow old and shrivelled without love; she didn't want to have only causes and crusades to sustain her.

She was only nineteen, she could find a husband, or so her mother said when Isobel had informed her that the hopes for Ian had come to naught.

Isobel knew her mother believed this, but she had a more practical nature. She was leftover goods in Boston, discarded by someone who should have married her. Any suitors would be second rate.

She sighed, and was preparing to leave, when there was a knock on the door and the butler went smoothly to open it.

'Master Crombie . . .'

'Isobel.' Ian stared at her from the doorway, his face careworn and even a bit haggard.

Isobel's heart beat painfully as she gazed back at him, realizing afresh the full force of her feelings. 'Hello, Ian.'

The butler stepped aside, and Ian shed his coat and hat. 'I came to see how Margaret fares, but I am glad to see you as well. I've been meaning to call on you at home.'

'Have you?' Isobel had meant to sound diffident, but it came out cutting, sharp with hurt. She couldn't help it; Ian had been home for over a week.

A flush rose up his neck and face, and he looked down in obvious shame. Isobel felt a small prick of triumph. At least he understood that much, she thought. He should have called.

'Perhaps we can take tea in the drawing-room?' Ian asked quietly. 'If Henry wouldn't mind. I'd like to speak with you.'

'As you wish.' Isobel gestured to the butler, who went to make the arrangements. She led the way into the Moores' drawing-room, the bay windows overlooking the street.

'Isobel, I must beg your forgiveness. I should have called on you earlier, spoken with you . . . months ago. If I refrained from doing so, it was because I thought — hoped — there was no need.'

Isobel stood with her back to him, poker straight, tension turning her body into a long, poised column. 'No need?' she asked. 'How is that?'

'It became clear to me,' Ian said in a low voice, 'that your family had expectations of me. Of us. I wondered if you shared them. . . .'

'You never asked, though.' She still could not look at him.

'Indeed not, and that was to spare both of us an embarrassing scene.'

'It was a scene I have imagined many times,' Isobel replied in little more than a whisper. 'And I never thought it embarrassing.' There was an agonized moment of silence, and she forced herself to continue. 'But then, I thought you loved me.'

'Isobel . . . I'd hoped to love you! I wanted to love you. It seemed so sensible, so right in many ways, and I thought with time . . .' He trailed off, taking an uncertain step towards her. 'I have always regarded you with great affection.'

'Sisterly affection.'

Ian sighed heavily. 'Yes.'

There was a discreet knock at the door, and the maid entered with the tea. Isobel dismissed her and began to pour, grateful for the actions to mask her grief, her humiliation, which threatened to swamp her.

'I'm sorry,' Ian said quietly. 'I should have explained all this sooner. I've been a coward in many ways, and I don't use that word lightly.' He paused, his expression strangely remote. 'I don't believe I've ever told you the circumstances that brought me to Henry's ship, and then to Boston.'

Isobel shrugged. 'A family argument, Henry said.'

'Yes, but a bit more than that. I was young and rash, and I did something very foolish. I sold our farm — one that my family had owned for a hundred years — for a pitiful sum, and I did it because I couldn't be bothered to read the contract properly.' Isobel's eyes widened in surprise, and Ian nodded, realizing he felt no bitterness. 'Yes, it sounds quite unbelievable, doesn't it? Unbelievably foolish, but I was so intent on playing the man, I behaved like the worst kind of little boy. Even more so, after the deed was done, I fled. I signed on Henry's ship, and I have not seen my older sister — who bore the brunt of my burden — since then. My younger sister, Eleanor, I've only seen recently, and my father, I was told, died from the strain.' He smiled bleakly. 'Not the actions of a hero, are they? Or even of a gentleman. Perhaps the most odious thing of all is that I've blamed someone else for my own stupidity. He was not entirely innocent, of that I can assure you. But I've come to realize it was my fault. If I'd read the contract — if I hadn't been so vain . . .' He shrugged. 'Things might have been so very different.'

Isobel stared at her teacup, twisting it between pale fingers. 'Ian, why are you telling me this?'

'I suppose,' he replied after a moment, 'because I realize I've done it again. I've been so intent on playing the doctor, I've forgotten to be the man. I left Boston for nearly a month, to conduct what I deemed important experiments for medicine. I did it in the name of science and humanity, while ignoring the fact that I was neglecting the humans God deemed to put in my care.' He shook his head. 'I won't do that again.'

'You seem to blame yourself for rather a lot of things,' Isobel said with the ghost of a smile.

'Yes, and I intend to make reparation.' Ian leaned forward anxiously. 'Isobel, tell me what I can do. I know how the tongues wag in this city's society. Most people expected us to marry.' He took a breath. 'We still could.'

Isobel was temporarily robbed of speech. Her eyebrows rose, and her teacup returned to its saucer with an inelegant clatter. 'Ian, you don't want to marry me!'

'That's not true,' he returned stolidly. 'I care for you a great deal, and I imagine that in time we could come to love each other with the love of a husband and wife. Many marriages have been built on less.'

'This is a tempting offer?' Isobel couldn't help but sound a bit querulous.

'An honest one. I will do right by you, Isobel, if you'll have me.'

'Well, I won't.' She pushed herself up and paced restlessly to the window, shocked to realize just how tempting Ian's offer actually was. For shame! Was she so desperate, so pathetic? 'I admit,' she said after a moment, her voice shaking only slightly, 'that I would like a bit more out of my marriage, yes, even love as a husband and wife before the vows are spoken!'

'I understand.'

'But you think I won't get it?' She turned twitchily to him.

'Isobel, you are deserving of a man far greater than I am. I only want to do what is honourable.'

'You love Caroline Campbell,' she said after a moment, her tone now dispassionate.

Ian blinked in surprise. 'She is marrying someone else.'

'Is she? Who told you?'

'Her uncle himself.'

'Perhaps he was lying.'

'I thought so, but . . .' Ian shrugged. 'I have not been able to see Caroline, and she has not tried to see me.'

'She hasn't been in society this last week,' Isobel mused. 'Of course, things are quiet now, especially with the typhoid. And yet . . . I wonder. Her uncle, you know, is not late of this city, and he has been received in society simply because of his connections in England. But the company he keeps here! That awful businessman, so coarse and unrefined.' She shook her head. 'I wonder if he tells the truth, is all.'

Ian sat back appraisingly while Isobel turned her bleak gaze back on the street, wondering if it was pride or defeat which caused her to plead Caroline's case to her beloved.

Chapter Sixteen

The plaintive cry of a baby was the sweetest sound Harriet had ever heard. She opened her eyes, waves of fatigue rolling over her.

Betty stood beside the bed, smiling, although her eyes were clouded with anxiety.

'The bairn?' Harriet asked, her voice coming out in a rusty croak. 'Is it all right?'

'A fine little lad.' Betty bustled over to the cradle by the window and picked up a swaddled bundle. 'See for yourself.'

Harriet gazed at the tiny, perfect face with wonder. 'What a wee thing — Allan could hold him in one hand!'

'Aye, I can.' Allan stood in the doorway, grinning. 'He might be a wee thing right now, but I warrant he'll grow to be as strong as his brother here.' George peeked his head round Allan, looking both excited and afraid.

'Mamma? You're all right?'

'Aye, I am.' Harriet struggled to a sitting

position. 'Tired, though. I can't even remember . . .'

'You fainted,' Betty said quietly. 'Right at the end. But it didn't matter. Your son came into this world healthy, and I think he'll stay that way.'

'You don't think he's too small?'

Carefully Betty handed the baby to Harriet. 'Feel the weight of him. He's small, but solid. He'll do fine, I'm sure.'

Harriet nestled the baby close to her. He was tiny and wrinkled, wizened in the way of newborns, like a little, old man. But he was hers, and that made him beautiful.

Betty stepped back, taking George's hand in hers. 'Maggie's tending Anna by the fire. She's been an angel, that one — they both have.' She tugged gently on George's hand. 'Come now, my little lad. We'll leave your Mam and Pa alone for a bit.'

Harriet looked up at Allan as he closed the door, her face still shadowed with remembered worry and strain. 'Allan, I was so afraid.'

He came towards her swiftly, dropping a gentle kiss on her forehead. 'I know, my love. I'm sorry I wasn't there. If I'd any idea . . .'

'How could we?' She shook her head. 'I wasn't expecting to think of it even until after the syruping.' She paused, closing her eyes briefly. 'I know many women suffer greatly, the loss of not one child, but two, three, or even more. Mrs MacDonald has been expecting at least eight times, with only one living. But ever since we lost little Andrew, I've been afraid, so afraid . . .' she trailed off. 'Perhaps I'm just weak.'

'I could never think of you as that.' Allan softly caressed the tiny head of their son. 'I long to see a bloom in your cheeks again. We must all look after your health. It's a fearsome thing, bringing a new life into this great big world.'

'That it is.'

Allan perched on the edge of the bed. 'What shall we name him?'

'I hadn't even thought that far.' Harriet smiled. 'What do you think to naming him Archie, after your brother?'

Allan's face lit with hope. 'Would you mind that?'

'Of course not. It's good to remember our loved ones.' She thought briefly, as she often did, of the little wooden cross out in the copse, of the child and dreams she'd buried there. Then Harriet looked down at wee Archie, nuzzling against her, his mouth opened in plaintive demand, and she smiled.

She had much to be thankful for.

■ ■ ■ ■

Ian gazed out at the bare branches lining the common, the dirty snow piled underneath. A man, the collar of his coat turned up against the wind, hurried past.

Impatiently Ian turned away, sifting randomly through the papers on his desk. His mind seethed with questions, questions to which he could find no answers. Ever since Rydell's butler had told him that Caroline was engaged to be married, and then Isobel had given him another shred of hope, he'd tried to discover the truth.

He'd asked for her at shops and modistes, trawled the best streets of Boston for a glimpse of her face, but to no avail. His delicately worded queries had merely resulted in shaken heads.

Where was she? Something was wrong, Ian felt, and he vowed he would discover what it was.

A knock sounded at the front door, and Ian heard the low murmur of male voices. A moment later, his manservant entered his study. 'Master Crombie, Master Henry Moore and Rupert MacDougall are at the door, awaiting your pleasure.'

'Bring them in, Davies,' Ian said, his voice

brusque with hidden anxiety as he remembered the business with the forgeries. 'And fetch us some brandy, if you please.'

The two men entered, Rupert walking slowly, his face pale. The doctor in Ian immediately rose to the fore. 'Rupert, sit down. You still look unwell.'

'A bit tired, perhaps,' Rupert replied in a voice strained with effort, 'but well enough to find these criminals.'

'Are you quite certain you're able to pursue this?' Ian asked. He took the other man's arm to help him to a chair.

'I'm fine.' Rupert shrugged him off. 'Nothing that a few minutes' sitting down won't cure. The longer we delay, the colder the trail gets. Who knows if Summers is even at his offices now. He might have become scared, gone underground.'

'Perhaps,' Henry acknowledged. 'We could let the law handle this, you know, Rupert.'

Rupert scowled. 'I thought we'd already talked about this.'

'The money will be a loss anyway,' Henry persisted in a quiet voice. 'I can accept that. Lord knows, I'm grateful to have my family safe. I don't need to be chasing after criminals and dollar bills.'

'It's not about the money.' Rupert's eyes were hard. 'It's about justice. You know as well as I do that forgerers go free. It's impossible to find the men at the top, the men who matter. So the marshals end up arresting a bunch of petty criminals instead of the true masterminds, the true evil.'

'And how,' Henry replied, 'do you intend to find these masterminds, if the US marshals cannot?'

'By following the trail, one step at a time. And the first step is Summers.'

Henry shook his head wearily, and Rupert turned to Ian. 'Ian, you promised you'd help me. Does that stand true, or did I come here for naught?' Ian was gazing out the window, and Rupert made an impatient sound. 'Aren't you even listening?'

'I'm sorry.' Ian tore his gaze away from the passing pedestrians with reluctance. He'd caught a glimpse of a cloak, a loose tendril of curling, blonde hair, and he'd wondered if it was Caroline. Half of him wanted to run out of the room and chase the woman to find out. The other half knew it was hopeless.

'Ian?' Henry prompted, looking at him in concern.

'I'm sorry. I've a few things weighing heavily on my mind.'

'Something other than the matter at hand?' Rupert raised his eyebrows in polite disbelief, and Ian felt a prickle of irritation. 'As a matter of fact, yes. As dear as this cause may be to you, Rupert, I've no great desire to chase down criminals. My profession is to heal, not to hunt.'

'Don't come, then.' Rupert half rose out of his chair, and Ian held up a hand.

'I don't mean it like that. I promised to accompany you, and I do out of a brotherly concern for you as much as a desire to see justice served. If I appear out of sorts, forgive me. It's only because I received news this past week of Caroline Campbell's engagement, and it has tried me sorely.' He tried to smile, and failed. 'I know you have the anticipation of a happy home ahead of you, whereas I have not. So again, forgive me.'

Henry looked surprised. 'Caroline Campbell engaged? I'd no idea. To whom?'

'A man named Matthew Dearborn,' Ian replied bleakly. 'I've attempted to make inquiries about the man, but little is known about him. He's a businessman, wealthy, but hardly in Boston's society circles.' He thought of Isobel's description of him: coarse and unrefined. Yet obviously wealthy.

'And you know for certain she is engaged?' Henry persisted.

'No, not for certain. Rydell told me she

was, and I've no recourse but to believe him. Caroline hasn't attempted to contact me since.' He thought of the note she'd sent. *If there is to be any future for us. . . .*

Now it appeared there wouldn't be. Yet he'd gone over it in his mind many times. Surely she couldn't have been forced into an engagement, even by Rydell. She couldn't be held prisoner in her own house. The answer, it seemed, was that she'd found another. Or, more likely, he thought bitterly, she'd realized the simple life of a poor doctor's wife was not the kind she sought.

'He always takes what I want,' Ian said in a low, savage whisper. 'And derives pleasure from it, as well. And this time hurts the most.'

'You'll never get Achlic Farm back,' Rupert said quietly. He put a hand on Ian's shoulder. 'As much as you might strive for it. Rydell wouldn't sell it to you for sheer spite.'

'I know that. I've given up Achlic. I've realized my own blame in that transaction.' Ian spoke quietly, this time without bitterness. 'I'd hardly want to go back there now. My future is here, in Boston, in research. But . . .' He smiled painfully. 'This is still a bitter pill to swallow.'

'But don't you see, Ian?' Rupert exclaimed. 'It's because of men like Rydell, men who take advantage of the weak for their own selfish gain, that I want to stop these criminals! It's precisely men like Rydell who would stoop to this kind of activity, and the only way for it to be stopped is to find them ourselves.'

Ian gazed out the window. The woman in the street was long gone, and so was Caroline. Why couldn't he just let go? He'd had to give up his first dream, of regaining Achlic Farm. It wouldn't hurt him much more to relinquish another. And perhaps, this time, justice *could* be served.

'All right. Let us go, then, and find this Summers.'

The address Phillips had given Rupert was also by the docks, a small, shabby office near some disused warehouses. The wind from the harbour was chilly and unforgiving, and it took all of Rupert's strength to keep walking steadily, and betray no sign of his weakness to the others. He rapped on the door, but the empty, echoing sound within had the men exchanging uneasy glances.

Ian tried the knob, and the door swung open, revealing an office hastily cleared of furniture and papers. A scrap of paper blew across the dirty floor, and Henry picked it up.

'A receipt of some kind. Mostly scrawling.'

'Whoever was here, left quickly,' Ian mused. 'He must have been afraid.'

'Afraid of the law, or of the men who gave him the false money?' Rupert queried shrewdly.

There was a scrabbling sound in the back, and Rupert raised a finger to his lips.

As quietly as cats, the men moved forward.

The room in the back was dingy and small, and a man was cowering in the corner, rifling through a stack of old papers. He turned in terror at the sound of the men in the doorway, and cowered all the more.

'Who are you? What are you doing here? I've nothing to hide . . .' The man was gabbling in fear.

'Is that so? What are you doing here, Summers?' Rupert asked coldly.

'How do you know my name? Did — did *he* send you?'

'Maybe he did.' Rupert folded his arms. 'Tell me his name to be sure.'

Summers opened his mouth, then closed it again. 'I know you. You're the one who's been sniffing around. You're meant to be dead!'

'Are you the one who made a mess of that

job? Because if you're planning to kill someone, you should stick around to make sure the job's been finished.'

'Worthy advice,' Summers sneered, though his hands were shaking with fear. 'I'll remember it the next time.'

Ian strode forward and grabbed the man by the collar. 'Give us one good reason not to hand you to the law this moment.'

'Don't! Don't!' Summer shook his head frantically. 'I didn't try to kill you, I swear it. It was the other that did it — his man.'

'Whose man?' Rupert demanded.

'Do you think they tell me his name? I know he's important, and he's angry. He never intended for it to happen like this, and he doesn't care about the likes of us! We're a nuisance now, we are, and he's as like to get rid of us as he is you.'

'Is that why you've cleared out of here?'

Summers nodded.

'Why did you come back?'

'I had some papers. Letters. If they'd found them, they could have tracked me down. I'm nothing to you, I swear I'm not! It's him you want, the man who gives me the money.'

'And who is that?'

'I tell you, I don't know his name.'

Rupert gave him a little shake. 'Tell us

what he looks like, then.'

'Tall. Grey hair. A scar on one cheek. You'd think he's nice at first, but he's cold as ice . . . like a snake. He's killed before, and he'll do it again.'

'And that's all you know?'

Summers gulped and nodded.

Rupert stepped back, satisfied. 'Let's go from here. There's not much else we can learn.'

'Wait.' Ian held up a hand, his brow furrowed. 'A scar on one cheek, tall, you say?' Summers nodded, his eyes darting between each man. 'I think,' Ian said, 'I know a man like that.'

CHAPTER SEVENTEEN

Caroline gazed at her reflection in the looking glass. Her hair was swept up with ringlets about her temples *à la reine,* now considered to be the latest fashion; her evening dress of tulle, over a pink satin slip, was fresh from the modiste's. There were satin leaves embroidered on the bodice, and a deep hem trimmed in pink velvet, another satin leaf at each point.

She glanced at the bonnet on her dressing table, a creation of pink watered silk with crimson-dyed feathers, meant to be worn set back from her stylish curls.

She sighed, giving the bonnet an irritable little push. A few weeks ago these clothes would have sent her into spasms of delight. She would have eagerly paraded them at the latest musicale or dinner dance with silly, girlish pride. Now they seemed like a bribe, tainted by her uncle's belief that she would marry Matthew Dearborn.

The last few weeks had been a rude education, Caroline saw now. Her innocence had been torn from her, innocence which she now realized had in truth been blindness or even sheer stupidity. Nothing shielded her now from the stark reality of her uncle's expectations or feelings for her. Marry Dearborn or be reduced to a pauper, shamed in front of all society.

Caroline had considered her alternatives many times. She lay in bed at night, watching the moon sift shadows across the floor, and imagined what would happen if she thwarted her uncle and married Ian.

Would he even let her? Caroline thought she knew the limits of her uncle's power, but now she realized she hadn't the faintest inkling. Four nights ago he'd insisted she dine with Dearborn; if she refused, he would have her sent home to Lanymoor. When Caroline had replied that Lanymoor was preferable, he had smiled coldly and told her that an asylum might be a better choice.

She'd stared at him in disbelief, her insides suddenly coated in ice. 'You wouldn't do something so monstrous,' she whispered.

Uncle Edward regarded her with flat, expressionless eyes. 'Do not presume to know what I would or wouldn't do, Niece. Your tender feelings have no import.' His smile was flinty even though there was a certain bleakness to his face. 'Realize I am desperate.'

Caroline shivered in memory. Surely — *surely* — her uncle would not be so monstrous as to have her committed to such a place, no matter how desperate he might be?

The very thought turned her blood to ice once more, her mind numb and frozen, incapable of any plan of escape.

And then, of course, there was the fact that Ian had not called on her since his return several days ago. She knew he'd returned for Eleanor had sent a hastily written note, explaining her absence by her relative's illness with the typhoid.

Caroline shivered; she did not particularly want Eleanor visiting, carrying dreaded contagion.

And yet . . . what of Ian?

Caroline had begged Taylor to tell her if Ian called, and he'd promised he would. Despite the butler's loyalty to his employer, Caroline believed he had a certain softness for her. At any rate, she spent most of her time gazing out the windows, watching for Ian's dear, familiar figure.

He didn't come.

There was a knock on the door, and Caroline's maid peeked in nervously. 'Master Dearborn has arrived, miss. He's in the study with your uncle.' She gestured to the bonnet. 'Shall I help you with that, miss?'

Caroline shook her head. The feathered confection had been a delight to choose at the modiste's, but now she had no stomach for it. 'I'll go without, thank you. You're dismissed.'

She stared once again at her reflection, her eyes huge and blank with fear, her face pale and drawn. She wished desperately there was something — anything — she could do to change the horror of her circumstances.

If only Uncle Edward would tell her what scandal threatened them all. Had he been dishonest in business? Perhaps it could be remedied. Perhaps there was a way out he hadn't seen. Perhaps if they discussed it . . . Caroline shook her head. There was no way her uncle would discuss business with her, no matter how desperate he was. Any questions she asked he would no doubt view as impertinence, and she would incur his fury.

And yet what was there left to lose? Marriage to Dearborn made her skin crawl. She pictured his cadaverous face, his smile cold and unpleasant, and shivered.

There was nothing left to lose, she knew, and only her freedom — her happiness — to gain. Whatever slender hope there might be, Caroline knew she had to grasp at it. What else was there?

Dearborn was in the study with her uncle right now, most likely talking about business. Perhaps something would be mentioned that would enlighten her. Dearborn had some power over her uncle, that much Caroline understood. But what was it? And could it be broken?

Her heart lurching in her chest, her palms slick and sticking to her satin gloves, Caroline moved quietly down the stairs.

The servants, for once, were out of sight, no doubt at her uncle's request. She tiptoed to the study door and leaned her head against the wood panel.

'Things are getting close, Rydell,' Dearborn said, his voice slow and yet strangely menacing. 'Someone's been nosing about. It's taken care of, but I don't like it when the dogs start sniffing.'

'I've taken every precaution . . .' Rydell answered. Caroline was amazed at the plaintive, wheedling tone her uncle adopted.

'Apparently that's not enough. I wonder if I should cut you out of production completely.' Dearborn's voice was musing, and Caroline had the uncomfortable feeling he was toying with her uncle, coldly amused by the other's man obvious toadying.

'There's been nothing in the papers. . . .'

'If it gets that far, we're done for,' Dearborn replied brusquely. 'Have some sense, man.' A pause, and Caroline heard the clink of glasses. She imagined Dearborn standing there, smug and sleek in his frock coat, pouring her uncle's good brandy into a snifter without so much as a by-your-leave.

'I fear,' Dearborn said, sounding more amused than ever, 'that your usefulness has come to its end.'

'Never . . .'

'Of course, there is the matter of the debt you owe me.'

'But you said Caroline —'

'Ah, yes. Caroline. I might be willing to forgive much if the girl comes to me willingly. But remember, Rydell, you will always be in my employ.' He chuckled indulgently. 'My power. It would only take the mere whisper of something *criminal* to reduce your standing — and all this — to ashes.'

Caroline stood still, her heart beating so loudly she feared both men could hear it through the study door. Criminal? What was her uncle involved in? Her mouth dry with fear, she moved away from the door, only to have a hand come down hard on her shoulder. She whirled around to see Taylor, his expression grim.

'Eavesdropping is not the pastime of ladies, Miss Caroline.'

'I . . . I didn't hear anything . . .' Caroline stuttered, and Taylor shook his head, holding a finger to his lips warningly.

'Come with me.'

But it was too late. The door swung open and Dearborn stood there, a strangely complacent look on his face. Rydell stood in the background, his face pale, his features pinched.

Dearborn's cold gaze swept Caroline from head to foot before he nodded and stepped aside. 'Ah, Caroline. Why don't you join us?'

Caroline stood rooted to the floor, her face drained of colour, her heart hammering. She could not think of a single thing to say.

'Come in, do, Caroline,' Dearborn urged with an unpleasant smile. 'We were just talking about you.'

'She doesn't need to be involved . . .' Rydell began, and Dearborn chuckled.

'Developing a conscience now, Edward? A little late, I should think.' He grabbed Caroline by the elbow, pinching her as he pulled her into the study. 'What did you hear, my dear? You might as well tell me. We're almost family.'

Caroline swallowed. Her throat was dry, her heart beating wildly. Dearborn closed the door with an audible click. 'Well, Caroline?'

She shook her head. 'I didn't hear anything.'

'Oh, no? Why don't I ask Taylor?'

'He wouldn't . . .'

'Taylor!' Dearborn barked. 'Come in here.'

The butler entered, bowing slightly in front of Dearborn. 'Yes, sir?'

'What did this chit hear? You were outside the door, I know you were. Tell me what she knows.'

Taylor's face was implacable but his eyes slid briefly to Caroline before returning to rest on Dearborn. 'I couldn't say, sir.'

'Oh, couldn't you?' Dearborn snarled. 'You're here on my sufferance.'

'What?' Caroline glanced between the men, bewildered.

'Haven't you realized?' Dearborn barked with laughter. 'Taylor's mine. I put him here to keep an eye on your uncle, and you as well. He's done quite a good job of it too, I might add. Told me when your uncle was getting cold feet, your silly schoolgirl ideas about running away. Running away!' He laughed again, leaning closer to her, his eyes full of silent menace. 'Did you not think I would find you? I'll find you anywhere, my girl. You *and* your uncle.'

Caroline turned to Taylor. She had thought him her ally. 'You betrayed me, didn't you?' she whispered.

'There was nothing to betray,' Taylor said coolly, and Caroline's last remnant of hope disintegrated to dust. She had trusted Taylor to tell her if Ian came, if he had looked for her. She knew now the butler would have said nothing. 'He's come, hasn't he?' she said. 'And you sent him away.'

'I suppose you mean that fool doctor?' Dearborn interjected. 'I've kept my eye on him as well. You're well rid of him, my dear. What a shabby little fellow! He wouldn't have brought you anything.'

'And you would?' Caroline filled her voice with scorn. 'I can tell you, sir, I don't want anything *you* could give me!'

The slap Dearborn gave her made her eyes water and her ears ring. Caroline held one hand to her cheek in shock. No one had ever hit her before.

'That wasn't necessary, Dearborn,' her uncle said nervously, and even Taylor's face showed a flicker of unease.

'She needs to know her place. And I'm the one to show it to her.'

At that moment Caroline could feel the bars of her prison forming around her. If she gave in now, she would never be free. Her life would be one of utmost despair, married to a man she hated and could not even respect. A man who held no tender feeling for her at all. A man who clearly had no conscience about abusing her. She took a step towards the door, in the pretence of stumbling for balance. 'What do you want of me?' she asked in a low, trembling voice.

'Isn't it obvious? Your social connections. It is not,' Dearborn added with silky contempt, 'as if I hold any regard for your quaint charms, my dear.'

'Clearly. Well, sir, you see how badly I am placed.' Caroline raised her chin. 'There is little I can do, so I suppose it suits me to heed your words and agree to marry you.'

Dearborn's eyes narrowed, and even her uncle's obvious relief was tinged with suspicion.

'It's that easy, is it?'

'What do you expect?' She held her hands out in front of her. 'I am a woman in a strange land with few recourses. However . . .' Her own eyes narrowed, and Caroline hoped she was up to playing this role. 'If you want a willing wife, a pleasing one, then you would do well to please me.' She held her breath, hoping she'd guessed correctly that this brand of audacity would amuse Matthew Dearborn.

There was a tense pause, and then he chuckled drily. 'And how, you brazen chit, might I please you?'

'In all manner of things.' She smiled sweetly. 'There are dresses, of course, and I mean to be well outfitted with jewels. You hardly want your wife to look a peasant, do you? And I require my own carriage, of course.' She met his gaze coolly. 'For shopping, and the like. If you wish to enter society, sir, you must be prepared to pay for it.' For a moment, she was afraid she'd gone too far. She saw the latent rage in Dearborn's eyes, but then he shrugged expansively.

'As you wish.'

'I believe we were going to supper?' Caroline queried. 'I left my bonnet upstairs. It's a pretty confection, all the latest fashion. I daresay people will notice it.' She raised her eyebrows. 'May I fetch it?'

Dearborn had had enough, and he shrugged impatiently. 'As you like! I care not for such fripperies, I assure you.'

Caroline executed a quick curtsy before

hurrying out of the room. She knew Taylor was dogging her footsteps, and her heart was beating so fast she felt she might choke on it.

What to do now? This was her only chance, surely. She knew if she continued in the charade she'd constructed, she would never escape. She stood in the doorway of her bedroom, and turned impatiently to the butler. 'If you please, Taylor, I need a moment alone!'

'My master would not like me to leave you,' Taylor said with cold finality and Caroline felt a wave of dread ripple over her. This was not going to be as easy as she thought.

'I think your master understands me better than you do,' she snapped. 'Have we not reached an agreement? I'm not likely to go fleeing into the night, after all!' That was precisely her plan, yet she forced herself to look at the butler contemptuously.

'I think,' Taylor said quietly, 'that perhaps I understand madam better than Mr Dearborn does.'

'You have a nerve!' Caroline exclaimed, and slammed the door in his face. She paced her bedroom, wiping her palms on the side of her dress. Her mind raced. Taylor was waiting on the other side of the door; what could she do? There was nowhere to go, nowhere to hide.

'Miss Caroline?' her maid looked up from the dressing room in surprise. 'Have you changed your mind about the bonnet?'

Caroline glanced at the article on the dressing room table. 'Yes, I'll wear it.' She would have to, now. She was just reaching for it when she saw the servants' door. It led to the back hallway down to the kitchen, cleverly disguised as part of the wall. She'd never had cause to use it, or even care of its existence.

Now it might be her lifeline.

Taylor knocked on the door. 'Miss Campbell, you are wanted downstairs. Now.'

'Talk,' Caroline whispered to her maid. 'Talk now, as if I am in the room.'

'But you are in the room . . .'

Caroline shook her head, opening the servants' door quietly. 'A little faster, if you please!' she called out querulously. 'Mr Dearborn is waiting.'

The maid looked confused, but after a moment's hesitation, answered dutifully. 'Yes, miss. I'll hurry as much as I can.'

Caroline nodded encouragingly, then tiptoed down the steps. She'd just reached the bottom of the stairs when she heard her bedroom door burst open, and Taylor demand, 'Where is she?'

Caroline started to run. She flew past shocked skivvies and bootboys to the back-door, wrenching it open and stumbling across the slick cobbles in just her evening slippers. She had reached the street when the front door opened and she heard Dearborn shout furiously. 'After her!'

'You know a man like that?' Rupert glanced sharply at Ian. Dusk was falling outside the barren office, and Summers stood in front of them, shifting from foot to foot with distinct unease. 'Who would that be?'

Ian shook his head slowly. 'I think . . . I can't be sure of course . . .'

'Spit it out, man!' Rupert said impatiently, and Henry placed a restraining hand on his arm.

'Careful now. We can't be running helter-skelter around the city accusing people of forgeries!'

'We're hardly doing that!'

Summers was backing slowly out of the room. 'You don't need me then, gentlemen? I just came for a few papers. I'll be off . . .'

'Not quite so fast,' Rupert began, but Ian shook his head.

'Let him be. It's not him we're after.'

'Whom are we after, then?'

Ian took a deep breath. 'Rydell.'

'Rydell?' Henry repeated, his voice filled with surprise. Rupert's glance was equally incredulous.

'You doubt me?' Ian said. Colour flared in his cheeks. 'I told you, I know a man like that.'

'Rydell does not have a scar on one cheek!'

'No,' Ian returned with some heat. 'But his butler does.'

There was a moment of tense silence. Summers took the opportunity to scamper from the room, the front door of the office slamming with a hollow, echoing sound.

'Perhaps his butler bears a scar,' Henry began carefully, 'but that is hardly conclusive evidence.'

'It makes sense, doesn't it?' Ian demanded.

'Why would Rydell, a gentleman of good standing, be involved in a forgery?' Rupert shook his head. 'He has far too much to lose.'

'But what if he doesn't?' Ian persisted. 'What if he's in debt?'

'In debt? What with his holdings in Berwick and Mull, not to mention one of the nicer town houses here in Boston! If he's in debt, his creditors seem willing to overlook a good deal.'

'Who knows what the situation is?' Ian said. 'But the truth is, his butler is the man

Summers saw.'

'The butler *looks* like the man Summers saw,' Henry corrected. 'Ian, there is a difference.'

Ian shrugged in impatient frustration. 'You were willing to rush down here to the docks to pursue a slim lead, why all this pussyfooting about now? Especially you, Rupert!' He shot his friend a furious glance. 'You were the most eager of us all to pursue these criminals, yet now you shy away at the last gate!'

Both Henry and Rupert were silent. Rupert looked at Ian with a strange compassion that made him uneasy. The papers blew and rustled about their feet.

'Ian,' Rupert began quietly. 'No one knows more than I how deep your hatred of Rydell runs, and for good reason. I was there when he swindled you out of Achlic Farm. I remember your father, your sister, even Eleanor at the time. I know what you all went through.'

'No, you don't,' Ian returned in a voice so low Rupert and Henry barely could hear it.

'Perhaps not the same as experiencing it myself,' Rupert allowed. 'And Lord knows, it would fit together neatly for you if Rydell was guilty. Why, his lands might even be forfeit! But it isn't that simple, Ian. It can't be.'

'You think I'm in this for revenge? To finally best Rydell?' Ian looked at them both in disbelief. 'I'm not such a petty little man that I would create a scandalbroth out of nothing! That I would attempt to frame an innocent man!'

'No one is saying anything like that,' Henry interjected hastily. 'But surely you can see yourself how you might want it to be true?'

'Want it? Yes, I do. I want to prove he's a criminal, because he was one eleven years ago and no one could lift a finger against him! Now he's got in too deep, and the law will finally have him, I swear it!' Ian looked fiercely at the other men. 'This is not about revenge. It's about justice.'

'Ian, you cannot run after Rydell based on the report of a scar!' Henry's voice was urgent. 'It would create a horrible scandal that your career as a doctor might never recover from. Rydell may be new in this city, but he is titled and wealthy and has influence. He could ruin your prospects completely . . . ruin your life.'

'He did that already once. He won't do it again.' Ian lifted his chin. 'If you won't accompany me, so be it. But I intend to drive to Rydell's house tonight and confront him.'

'There are other ways!' Henry persisted. 'Discreet inquiries. I can have his butler followed. . . .'

'There isn't time. Don't you realize? There is Caroline to consider. If Rydell is involved in something criminal, it's only a matter of time before he drags her down with him.'

'Surely he wouldn't . . .' Henry began.

Rupert shook his head grimly. 'I know that man, and he cares nothing for his own niece. Ian is right. If Rydell is involved in something criminal — or dangerous — Caroline may be at risk.'

'Then you'll go with me?'

Rupert sighed heavily. 'On one condition — that you don't knock down any doors in your anger! We can't burst into Rydell's house as if we had a right to be there, Ian, and we can't bully him like a greasy little conman as this.' He jerked a thumb towards the door Summers had recently scampered out of. 'We need to conduct ourselves as gentlemen.'

Ian drew himself up. 'I intend to always conduct myself as a gentleman,' he said.

The street in front of Rydells' town house was deserted. A chilly wind blew dead leaves down the darkened street.

Ian marched resolutely up to the door and knocked. After a few moments, the butler answered.

All three men stared silently at the long, thin scar running delicately down one cheek. 'Lord Rydell is not at home,' Taylor said shortly, but Ian just shook his head.

'I know he is. I saw the lamp in his study. Let me in, Taylor. You won't keep me out this time.'

'Ian . . .' Henry said in a low voice of warning. He looked at Taylor uncomfortably.

'Oh, dash it, why should I bother with the niceties? I know he's in there, and I know what he is!' Ian shouldered past Taylor. Rupert and Henry, exchanging uneasy glances, followed.

'I must insist you stop at once! This is a breach —' Taylor broke off, for the three men were standing in the doorway of Rydell's study.

Rydell sat in a chair by the desk, his shoulders slumped, his expression haggard. 'I thought you might come,' he said, his eyes on Ian. 'When he told me someone was asking questions. . . .'

'Who told you?'

'Haven't you worked that bit out yet?' Rydell's smile was cold and mirthless, but there was a new weariness in his eyes, in the dejected set of his shoulders. 'Or do you think I'm working alone?'

'My lord,' Taylor said softly, 'think about what you are saying.'

'It doesn't matter anymore, Taylor,' Rydell said quietly. 'They know, and even if they haven't put all the pieces together, they soon will. And why should I bother to defend him? Cover up? He's ruined me. I'll have no place in society now.'

'You are getting ahead of yourself!' Taylor's voice was sharp, hardly the tone a servant would take.

'No, he isn't,' Ian said. 'He's right. We'd sussed him out already.' Ian turned to Rydell, the blaze of triumph in his eyes. 'So why did you do it? Debt, I suppose?'

Rydell's face twisted with bitterness. 'Yes, debt. And my creditor just happened to have a scheme to make us all rich. Or so he said.'

'I remember someone saying something like that to me,' Ian said softly. 'It turned out he was a liar and a cheat.'

'Still haven't forgotten the past, lad, have you?' Rydell shook his head. 'It's eaten you with rage your whole life . . . and all for a field.'

'A field?' Ian took a step closer, his fist raised. 'A *field?* My family's livelihood, you mean.' His voice shook. 'My family's life. We'd owned that farm for over a hundred years.'

'Then you should have read the contract a bit more closely,' Rydell sneered. 'You were so desperate to prove yourself then! I don't think much has changed.'

'Perhaps not. But I vow I won't stand aside and let innocents be hurt by your greed and cowardice. Not this time.' Ian started forward, but Rupert laid a steadying hand on his arm.

'This isn't about your revenge, Ian. No matter how much you want it to be.'

Ian started as if from a dream, and dropped his fists. 'Where is she, Rydell?'

'Gone.'

There was a tense silence in the room as the three men digested Rydell's cold words.

'Gone?' Henry repeated. 'Gone where?'

'He's got her. She tried to run, of course, in those foolish slippers she insisted I buy! Must keep up appearances, you know.' Rydell's lips curled into an ugly smile. 'He caught her at once, and took her to his carriage.' He spread his hands. 'And as far as I'm concerned, he can have her. She was nothing to me but a bargaining chip, and even as that she failed.'

'Who has her?' Rupert asked.

Ian shook his head. 'Of course. Dearborn. Her *fiancé*.' He sneered the words, but there was an icy fear creeping up on him, choking him. 'You forced her into that liaison, didn't you? It's Dearborn who's the mastermind behind all this, pulling your strings!'

'Didn't I say as much?' Rydell gave an elegant shrug, smiling slightly. His cold gaze rested briefly on Taylor. 'And this manservant, so thoughtfully provided to keep watch on me! Well, it's over now, Taylor. And you can tell your master I said so.'

Rupert glanced appraisingly on the cold, hard face of the butler. 'So you were Dearborn's agent?' he said softly.

Taylor's gaze jerked to Rupert, and then just as quickly moved away. 'I will say nothing,' he said coldly, his eyes on Rydell. 'And I advise you to do the same.'

'It's too late, Taylor!' Rydell laughed, then sagged against the cushions. 'It's too late.'

'How can you sit there?' Ian demanded in a furious whisper. 'When that criminal — that murderer — has your niece, one of your only relatives? Do you have any idea what he might do to her? Why just being in his carriage alone will ruin her reputation in this city.'

'Do you think, my dear boy,' Rydell said softly, 'I have any care for reputations now?'

He gestured to the room around him. 'All this is but a forgotten dream now. I'll be fortunate if I don't go to prison.'

'Indeed you will!' Rupert said, a faint pity mingling with his own sense of satisfaction. 'But just because your life might be in shambles doesn't mean you may throw your ward to the wolves. Have you no shame, sir? No compassion?'

Rydell was silent for a moment, his expression shuttered. 'No,' he said at last. 'No, I don't.'

Ian shook his head slowly. 'What sort of man are you?'

Rydell was silent again, looking down, almost as if his mind were elsewhere. 'What kind of man am I?' he repeated softly. 'But you know the answer to that question already.'

'I don't want to believe it of you.' Ian's voice was low. Could Rydell — his enemy — hold himself in as little regard as Ian did?

Rydell looked up at him, his eyes filled with misery, his face bleak. 'Believe it.'

And for the first time, Ian felt pity for the man who had cost him so much.

A quarter of an hour later, Rupert, Henry and Ian hailed a hansom cab outside Rydell's home and headed for Dearborn's offices by the docks. Rydell had given the address to them reluctantly while Taylor watched in impotent fury.

Rupert longed to arrest the man, but he could not do the deed himself and it would be impossible to find a US marshal at this hour, willing to arrest a gentleman's servant on what could be seen as a flimsy pretext. No doubt Taylor would be long gone before they'd even found Dearborn.

Ian was not certain whether fear of personal injury or a belated concern for his niece had made Rydell offer the information. Right now, he didn't care which it was. He just wanted to see Caroline safe.

'I'm sorry, Ian,' Rupert said quietly as they rode towards the harbour. 'I didn't believe Rydell could have . . . I didn't believe you, and I should have. It hardly seems possible, and yet . . .'

'Desperate men are capable of much,' Ian finished grimly. 'I almost feel sorry for the rogue — at least I might, if Caroline is safe.'

Henry closed his eyes briefly. 'Please God, let her be.'

'Why would Dearborn harm her?' Rupert asked in as reasonable a tone as he could muster. 'According to Rydell, she's his entrée into society. Harming her or her reputation is hardly likely to serve him well.'

'He's desperate, and cornered,' Ian replied. 'And men in those conditions attack.'

'Dearborn is cold-hearted. He'll look to his best interests first.'

'I hope so,' Ian said. 'Because for once, his best interests might be ours as well.'

The address Rydell had given them was a darkened warehouse in the North Bay district, much like the other buildings that lined the harbour. By day, they bustled with trade, sailors and merchants moving cargo and conducting business. Now, all was empty, silent. A discarded newspaper blew down the street, and Ian saw the shadow of a huddled figure in one of the darkened doorways. He suppressed a shiver. This was not a place he wanted to be on such a night, and yet . . .

Caroline was here.

They disembarked from the hansom and stood in front of the front entrance to the warehouse.

'Dearborn's most likely in there,' Rupert said in a low voice. 'The element of surprise might be —'

'Gentlemen, come in, come in.' The door had opened without them realizing it, and Matthew Dearborn stood there, smiling genially as if for all the world he was inviting them into his parlour.

'Where is she, Dearborn?' Ian demanded.

'By "she" I presume you mean the charming Miss Campbell,' Dearborn replied. 'My fiancée?'

'Your . . .' Henry shook his head a fraction, and Ian fell silent. There was more at stake here than arguing about words.

'Won't you come in?'

'Of course we will.' Rupert stepped across the threshold. 'You realize, of course, that the police know where we are? And that they are aware of who you are and your actions as of late?'

'I would not presume to know of what you speak.' Dearborn's manner was all civility, but there was a hard, flinty coldness in his eyes that left no room to mistake just what kind of man he was.

'You cannot continue to protest your innocence,' said Henry. 'We have evidence.'

Dearborn glanced at the three of them, standing shoulder to shoulder in the doorway, and laughed softly. 'I do feel as if I've been visited by the three Musketeers! I congratulate you on your show of bravery. It really is most impressive.' And still chuckling quietly, he turned and walked down the hall.

Rupert and Henry exchanged uneasy glances. The hallway was dark, draughty, and who knew what — or who else —

awaited them in the maze of offices and storerooms.

Ian, however, strode forward. 'Where's Caroline?' he demanded.

Dearborn glanced over his shoulder. 'I'll ask you to refer to my intended as Miss Campbell, sir. You are far too familiar.' Dearborn opened a door and disappeared inside. Ian followed, with Henry and Rupert behind him.

'You may choose to take this lightly, Dearborn,' Ian said through gritted teeth. 'But I'm not leaving here till you have surrendered her to me.'

Dearborn stood in the centre of his office, a messy, sparsely furnished room lit only by a handful of flickering tallow candles, dripping wax on to some old papers. He spread out his hands. 'Do you see her here?'

'Rydell told us you had her,' Rupert said quietly.

'Ah. I thought he might turn coward. Well, I'm finished with him at any rate.'

'Are you?' Rupert challenged with a mirthless laugh. 'Indeed you must be, since you are finished yourself.'

'You sound so certain, I wonder if I should be offended.'

'You are a forgerer,' Ian cut across Dearborn's words. 'A criminal, and we have evidence. I'm sure this warehouse is full of fake bills. This is where you keep them, isn't it? And we know the petty men you've roped into your scheme. No doubt they would testify against you.'

'Oh, no doubt,' Dearborn agreed drily, 'for they aren't easily frightened, are they?'

There was a tense silence, and then Rupert said slowly. 'Are you saying that you will intimidate them into silence?'

Dearborn smiled. 'My dear sir, if you choose to make that suggestion, then so be it.'

'You are a rogue!' Ian exclaimed. 'Don't you realize the game is up? You had aspirations to a gentleman's status — well, play the man now, and admit your guilt! It can only go against you if you don't.'

'Can it?' Dearborn smiled so slyly that Ian felt the first prickle of true unease. 'You say you have evidence,' he continued smoothly. 'Yet I do not see it. You say you have witnesses, yet somehow I think they've already scuttled back to their safe little holes, and cannot be found. It appears, my dear fellows, that you do not have a case.'

'At any rate,' Rupert said quietly, 'your money is useless. The marshals and every bank will know what the bills look like. They won't pass anywhere.'

'Perhaps,' Dearborn allowed, 'that might be a small problem, until, of course, we take them elsewhere.'

Ian's hands curled into fists and he suddenly launched himself at Dearborn. 'Where is she, you worthless thief, common criminal that you are? *Where is she?*'

'Ian.' Henry pulled him back even as Dearborn stumbled against the wall. 'You cannot — !'

'He's lying!'

Dearborn's lip was bloody and there was a bruise on his cheek. 'I told you, I don't have her,' he said, his voice ragged and yet still unruffled. 'If it's the girl you want, take her. She's useless to me as it is. Rydell's washed up and she'll be shunned by society. I hardly want a pariah for a wife!'

'And you think we'll see you sneak away with your counterfeit money?' Rupert demanded. 'We'll have justice —'

'Justice?' Dearborn laughed, a sharp, unpleasant sound. 'There is no justice in this country, haven't you realized that? I've bought half a dozen of your so-called police to look the other way already. If there's something to line their pockets, they don't care.' He shook his head. 'Do you actually think anyone is going to listen to your sad little story? Or care? Of course, it's very touching that you believe in this idea of justice, but I'm telling you now, boys, it doesn't exist. You leave this warehouse tonight, and stop troubling me, and take the girl if you want her. I'll go on my merry way and no one is the wiser for it.'

Rupert shook his head. 'If that's true, why did you try to kill me? You wouldn't have had your man take a rock to my head if you weren't scared.'

There was a tense silence, while all the men looked at each other. Then Dearborn's shoulders sagged.

'Very well,' he said quietly. 'You shall have it your way. I'll play the gentleman.' With slow, deliberate movements, he picked up a candle and walked towards the door. 'You want your evidence?' he asked, but no one answered.

Rupert looked worriedly at Henry and Ian, but they were focused on Dearborn.

Dearborn stepped across the threshold, then turned to them with a smile. 'Here is your evidence,' he said, a savage note entering his voice, and he threw the candle into the room. It landed on top of a pile of papers with a hiss, and while Henry and Ian jumped away from it, Dearborn began to shove the door closed.

Rupert threw his shoulder against the

door, his arm knocking into the jamb. There was a cracking of bone and he fell back with a grunt of pain.

Still, it was enough for Henry and Ian to throw the door open wider. Dearborn, seeing his plan failed, was running down the corridor.

The papers had taken light, and flames licked eagerly at the old timber frame of the warehouse.

Ian hoisted Rupert up. 'Help me, Henry. I think he's broken his arm.'

By the time they'd dragged Rupert to the corridor, thick, grey smoke was billowing everywhere. There was a loud crack as an old beam above them split and plunged to the floor below.

'Just a little bit longer,' Ian urged. Cradling his arm, Rupert staggered onwards.

There was no sign of Dearborn in the corridor, although with the smoke and flames it was nearly impossible to see anything. More beams were falling, scattering hot ash and embers in their wake.

'When the flames reach the money,' Rupert gasped, 'the building will go up in seconds.'

'What of Caroline?' Ian demanded. 'What if he was lying and she's here?'

'Ian . . .' Henry shook his head. 'We can't

take that risk. No one would get out alive if we went searching every room in this place!'

'I could —'

'No, you couldn't.' Henry pointed behind them. Bills had caught fire, and the building was nearly engulfed in flames. 'Now help me get Rupert out of here, before we all turn to cinders!'

Ian nodded, a new bleakness in his eyes, and grimly focused on the doorway ahead of them. His lungs burned, his eyes stung so that he could barely see, and he'd already brushed sparks from his coat with blistered hands.

Finally they stumbled into the street, choking and gasping for breath.

'Is he gone?' Rupert demanded, bent over, his broken arm cradled against him. 'Dearborn . . . he must have escaped . . . he's long gone by now.'

Ian shook his head, and closed his eyes briefly. 'I don't know.'

'Look.' Henry pointed to a window on the second storey. A man stood there, a dark shadow silhouetted against the flames. He was clutching packets of bills and screaming in terror.

'Save me!' Dearborn shouted. 'For pity's sake . . .'

Instinctively, they started forward, but it

was far too late. Even as they heard the echo of Dearborn's desperate plea, the supporting beams of the warehouse collapsed, and he fell backwards into the fire.

Ian, Henry, and Rupert stood there, silent and stunned, while the ash of thousands of counterfeit bills drifted down on them in a gentle rain.

Chapter Eighteen

It was well after midnight by the time the three men reached Ian's house. A light flickered in the front window, and as they approached the door Eleanor's pale, anxious face appeared by the curtains.

She threw open the door before any of them touched the handle, her shawl thrown carelessly over her nightdress, her hair tumbling about her shoulders. 'What has happened?' she demanded in a voice both querulous and near tears. 'Caroline Campbell arrived here a few hours ago, beside herself with fear, and her gown torn! And now you . . .'

'Caroline's here?' Ian demanded, his voice hoarse. 'Oh, thank heaven. I was afraid . . . afraid she'd . . .' He grabbed Eleanor by the shoulders. 'Where is she?'

Eleanor opened her mouth to answer, but then she saw Rupert, still holding his hurt arm, and gasped. 'Rupert! What has happened to you? You're hurt . . . again?' Quick as a flash she turned to Ian. 'You went with him, didn't you, to find the men? And look what has happened!'

'It's over, Eleanor,' Rupert said gently. 'We found them.'

'I can see that plainly,' Eleanor snapped. 'For how else would your arm get hurt?' She looked ready to rage, but then the life seemed to sag out of her and her shoulders slumped. 'You'd better all come in . . . there's a fire in the front parlour. I'll send your man to go for the doctor.' She ushered them in, issuing instructions with a brisk manner that belied the fear shadowing her eyes.

Ian stood in the doorway of his parlour, gazing at Caroline. She stood by the fire, her face pale, eyes wide, the lovely gown she wore torn at the shoulder. There was a bit of dirt on her cheek.

'Caroline,' he breathed. 'Oh, Caroline.' And without another word, he moved towards her, arms outstretched. As naturally as if she'd always intended to, Caroline fell into his arms.

Rupert, Henry, and Eleanor regarded the warm embrace, varying expressions of surprise, delight and bemusement on their faces.

'Well,' Eleanor said after a moment. 'That's quite a welcome!'

'I feared for your life,' Ian said quietly. 'I was afraid you were in the warehouse, with Dearborn. Rydell said . . .'

'I got away,' Caroline said quietly. 'I ran from the house when I realized. He took me in his carriage, but I jumped out and ran again. He didn't follow me.' Her eyes widened. 'Ian, he is a criminal!' She stopped suddenly and looked at him. 'But how do you know? And where have you been?'

As quickly as he could, Ian explained the circumstances leading to their confrontation with Dearborn at the warehouse. 'And he's gone, poor soul,' he finished quietly. 'I suppose he went back for the money. His greed proved the death of him, in the end.'

'Forgery,' Caroline said wonderingly. 'I knew it was something, but to think . . . ! And what shall happen to my uncle?'

'He most likely will escape the arm of the law,' Henry said. 'Since he is titled and wealthy, and what evidence we might have had was destroyed in the fire. I imagine he will make a quick and quiet retreat to Scotland, but I'm afraid, Caroline, that he is quite ruined. What little money he had was tied up with Dearborn. If he sells his assets, perhaps there might be a small stipend.'

Caroline shook her head. 'I don't care about that. Of course, I'm sorry for my uncle, but . . .' she bit her lip. 'All I really want is you, Ian.'

'I'm a poor doctor,' Ian warned her. 'With little wealth or property.'

'That matters naught to me.'

'Are you sure?'

Caroline expelled a shaky breath. 'When my uncle was forcing me to marry Matthew Dearborn, I realized he was bargaining my life away, and for his own gain. If I'd made the agreement with Dearborn, to be his wife, his trinket, then I would have sold my very soul for what wealth he might give me. That was not a bargain I was prepared to make.' She smiled at him, her eyes shining with both tears and happiness. '*You* are what I want, Ian. Not what wealth or property you bring.'

Ian drew her to him, and Eleanor looked away. She found her eyes meeting Rupert's speculative gaze. Even with his arm broken, his face burned and his eyebrows singed, he looked wonderful to her. She wondered if their own love could survive the trials as simply as Ian and Caroline's seemed to.

A knock sounded on the door, and Eleanor took the opportunity to bustle away.

'That will be the doctor. Rupert must be seen — get him in bed, Henry!'

The rest of the night passed in a flurry of seeing to the men's burns. The doctor set Rupert's arm, telling him cheerfully that it was a clean break and should, God willing, mend quickly. It was only in the morning, with pale sunlight streaming on to the faded carpet of her bedroom, that Eleanor decided to speak to Rupert.

'He's asked you to marry him,' she told her reflection. 'Hold on to that.' Yet his words about accepting — marrying — *all* of him echoed in her mind. What did he mean by that? What future could they have?

A few moments later, she pushed open the door to Rupert's room. He lay in bed, his hair dark against the pillow. Eleanor hesitated in the doorway, not wanting to wake him. Just as she was about to leave, Rupert's eyes flickered open. 'Don't go.'

Eleanor smiled, but did not move forward. 'You need your rest.'

'I'm fine.'

Tears crowded her eyes and stung her throat. She blinked them away. 'For now, perhaps.'

'Eleanor?' Rupert looked at her cautiously.

'How often are you going to put yourself in danger?' Eleanor asked. She felt a deep misery at even having to ask the question, yet the answer tormented her.

'Not very often, I hope.' Rupert smiled wryly.

'Rupert, don't joke, please. Not now. I . . . I need to know.'

'Come here.' He beckoned to the side of the bed, and Eleanor came forward slowly. 'You know I love you?' he asked when she had perched on the edge of the bed, her fingers kneading the counterpane.

'Yes. . . .'

'And you love me?'

'Yes, of course I do, but —'

'I want to be a marshal,' Rupert said quietly. Eleanor's eyes widened. 'I saw how Dearborn used the law for his own gain. If he hadn't died, we might have got him in the end, but most likely he would have escaped with a slapped wrist. That's not right, Eleanor. That's not justice.'

'You're one man . . .'

'Oh, I'm not expecting to change the whole system,' Rupert said with a smile. 'I'm not a crusader. But someone has to start to make changes, one person at a time. I want to make a difference, and I suppose I'm vain enough to think I can.' He took a deep breath. 'But last night, when we were in that old warehouse, surrounded by flames, death seemed only a few footsteps away, and I realized something.' He paused, his voice hoarse. 'I realized that pursuing that dangerous dream doesn't matter nearly as much to me as you do. So, say the word, and I won't.'

'What do you mean?' Eleanor whispered.

'I won't become a marshal if you do not wish it,' Rupert said. 'I could keep working for Henry. We could settle in Boston. You matter more to me, Eleanor.'

Eleanor swiped at the tear that slid helplessly down her cheek. 'You would give that up . . . for me?'

'There is no question of it.'

In that moment, Eleanor knew she loved Rupert more deeply that she'd even imagined . . . loved all of him. And she could not — would not want to — deny him the dream, the gift, he'd been given. 'I think,' she said slowly, a tremulous smile on her lips, 'that we might start making changes *two* people at a time. I want to be with you, Rupert. All of you.'

Silently, gratitude shining in his eyes, Rupert lifted her fingers to his lips.

The Boston commons were bursting with flowers and birdsong as the two families gathered by Christ Church.

A little over fifty years ago, the church sexton had hung two lanterns in the bell tower to signal the military's movements for Paul Revere. Now, however, the church was full of laughter and chatter as it emptied out of wedding guests.

Caroline and Ian, newly married, clasped hands on the steps of the church. Harriet, holding baby Archie in her arms, Maggie, Anna and George clustered around her, blinked back tears. She hadn't seen her brother for over ten years, and the sight of him as a man, and married at that, was near to overwhelming. Allan put his arm around her. 'Did you ever think we would be gathered like this, and in Boston?' he marvelled.

'I'd always hoped,' Harriet said softly. 'When Ian left all those years ago, as a ship's boy of all things! I'd feared we'd never see each other again. If Father could have . . .' She trailed off, a shadow of sadness in her eyes.

'I think that way of Archie as well,' Allan said quietly. 'And my father. We've lost so many, and yet . . .' he glanced down at little Archie, a smile tugging at the corner of his mouth. 'I'm thankful,' he finished simply. 'I'm surely thankful.'

Ian approached them, Caroline at his side. 'Harriet . . . it's so good to see you here, to have you with us on this day. I've dreamed of us being together again.'

'So have I.' Harriet smiled warmly.

'And this little fellow!' Ian glanced down at baby Archie. 'A handsome lad.'

Harriet turned to smile at Caroline. 'You've changed greatly since I last saw you, drumming your heels on the pianoforte stool,' she said with a little laugh.

Caroline grimaced, but her eyes danced with happiness. 'I should hope so! I was a spoilt brat then, I know it.'

'You weren't so terrible,' Harriet said, but Caroline only shook her head.

'If anything, I was worse.' She tucked her hand firmly in Ian's arm. 'Thank goodness someone brought me to my senses.'

'And me to mine,' Ian returned with a gallant little bow, and they all laughed.

On the other side of the steps, Rupert put his arm around his mother, his other hand clasped tightly with his wife's. 'Shall we adjourn to the wedding breakfast?' he said with a smile, for the two families — Crombies and MacDougalls — had planned a celebration at Henry and Margaret's residence.

Betty nodded, still in awe of this new son of hers, self-possessed and very much in love. The last time she'd seen Eleanor, her daughter-in-law had been a slip of a girl. Now she was a woman, and a wife.

The Moores' dining-room rang with laughter and happy chatter as the families gathered there a short while later.

'A toast, for the bride and groom!' Henry announced, raising his glass of champagne.

'The brides and grooms,' Allan corrected with a grin, for there had been a double wedding that day.

'Indeed,' Henry agreed. 'To Rupert and Eleanor, and to Ian and Caroline!'

After everyone had toasted the new couples, Henry cleared his throat for a further announcement. 'It is my distinct pleasure to tell you all that we have happy news of our own.' He glanced tenderly at Margaret, who, in an action very unlike her, blushed and looked down. 'My dear wife is expecting,' Henry said in a voice ringing with pride.

Betty clapped her hands over her mouth, a look of delight stealing over her face. Cheers broke out across the room.

Later, after the festivities had died down, Harriet and Allan, Margaret and Henry, and Betty gathered in the parlour. The newly wedded couples had retired to their private quarters.

Outside a soft, purple twilight descended

on the square, and a whisper of a breeze blew at the curtains by the open window.

'So much has changed,' Harriet said softly. 'To think of Rupert becoming a marshal in the Ohio Territory! I'd no idea he had it in him.'

'He was always one for adventure,' Betty said reminiscently, and Allan smiled.

'That he was. And now Ian, a doctor, with all these fancy experiments with the ether! Do you suppose anything will come of it?'

'If I know Ian, something surely will,' Harriet said. 'There's no one like him for sheer determination.'

'And you,' Allan said with a smiling nod towards his mother. 'Will you be happy here, living in a city?'

'Oh, yes,' Betty said firmly. There was colour in her cheeks, and a sparkle in her eyes that had not been seen since Sandy had died. 'I'm needed here. Why, I can hardly wait for that bairn to be born!' She glanced warmly at Margaret, who smiled in return.

'Nor can I,' she said softly.

'You know,' Henry said to Allan and Harriet, 'you can stay here as long as you like. You're family, you are always welcome.'

Allan and Harriet exchanged a silent, understanding look. 'We thank you kindly,' Allan said after a moment, 'for this has certainly been a homecoming, and a wonderful one at that. But we belong up on the island. That's our home. It always has been.'

Henry nodded his acceptance. 'I thought as much, to tell you the truth.'

Later, after they had retired to their bedroom, Harriet stood in front of the window, watching the moonlight shift in silver patterns across the cobblestones. Allan stood behind her, his arms around her shoulders. 'It's turned out all right, hasn't it?' Harriet asked softly. 'I feel God has given me far more than I'd ever dreamed of asking for.'

'Aye, He has.' Allan dropped a kiss on her shoulder. 'In the end, we came through. We all came through.' He paused, and she could feel his smile against her hair. 'Happy, my love?' he asked.

Harriet gazed outside. The night was dark and soft, a warm breeze like a whisper against her cheek. 'Aye,' she replied quietly. 'I'm happy.'

ABOUT THE AUTHOR

Katharine Swartz wrote her first story at the age of five, 'The Christmas Rose', which had a print run of one. Since then she has written many stories and serials for magazines. After living for six years in England, she now resides in Connecticut, USA, with her husband and three young children. *Another Country* is her second novel.

We hope you have enjoyed this Large Print book. Other Thorndike, Wheeler, and Chivers Press Large Print books are available at your library or directly from the publishers.

For information about current and upcoming titles, please call or write, without obligation, to:

Publisher
Thorndike Press
295 Kennedy Memorial Drive
Waterville, ME 04901
Tel. (800) 223-1244

or visit our Web site at:

http://gale.cengage.com/thorndike

OR

Chivers Large Print
published by BBC Audiobooks Ltd
St James House, The Square
Lower Bristol Road
Bath BA2 3SB
England
Tel. +44(0) 800 136919
email: bbcaudiobooks@bbc.co.uk
www.bbcaudiobooks.co.uk

All our Large Print titles are designed for easy reading, and all our books are made to last.